THE BUSINESS OF LOVE

CHERIS F. HODGES

Genesis Press, Inc.

Indigo Love Stories

An imprint of Genesis Press, Inc.
Publishing Company

Genesis Press, Inc.
P.O. Box 101
Columbus, MS 39703

All characters in this book have no existence outside the imagination of the author and have no relation whatsoever to anyone bearing the same name or names. They are not even distantly inspired by any individual known or unknown to the author and all incidents are pure invention.

ISBN: 13 DIGIT: 978-158571-373-8
ISBN: 10 DIGIT: 1-58571-373-2
Manufactured in the United States of America

First Edition Cheris F. Hodges
Second Edition 2010

Visit us at www.genesis-press.com or call at 1-888-Indigo-1

DEDICATION

I would like to dedicate this novel to all of the readers who kept asking me whatever became of Malik and Shari from Revelations. *This book is also dedicated to every hard working woman who has chosen work over herself time and time again. Yes, you can and should have it all.*

–CFH

ACKNOWLEDGMENTS

This book was especially fun to write. Thank you, Sidney Rickman my editor on this project. You made this story flow even better than I thought it could.

To my agent, Sha-Shanna Crichton, thank you for all your advice and for fighting for me. Special thanks to Darren 'Jaz' Vincent, owner of RealEyes Bookstore in the Charlotte, North Carolina arts district NoDa. Thanks for being so supportive.

CHAPTER ONE

Anticipation of New Year's hung in the air like the huge diamonds around Jill Atkinson's neck. The ballroom at the Hilton was decked out in pink, white, and silver decorations, and balloons hung in the air ready to drop as the clock struck twelve. In the happy din, Jill glanced around the room as the countdown began. She wasn't looking forward to another year, because she was expecting much of the same, success in the boardroom and nothing but exercise equipment in her bedroom.

"Ten," the elegant crowd yelled in unison.

Jill wrapped her arms around herself, wishing that she was half of one of those lucky couples that filled the ballroom. When was the last time that she'd had a date? Two years ago? Unfortunately, she couldn't hit the clubs on the weekend and troll for men. She had a reputation to uphold. She was, after all, the CEO of a Fortune 500 company. Everything she did, every decision she made, was under a microscope.

"Nine."

Jill looked up at the mirrored ceiling, which reflected a lonely woman dressed in a strapless powder blue Roberto Cavalli gown. Sure she looked good, but she didn't feel celebratory. Tonight she was lonely. She wanted to be holding someone's hand other than her own and waiting for the new year to roll in, be with a man who would hold her and kiss her at midnight. She wanted to be celebrating something more personal than her company's bottom line. She wanted to be celebrating love.

"Eight."

Focusing on her reflection, Jill ran her fingers through her auburn tresses. The woman who had everything wanted to be like everyone else in the room, in love or falling in love. But it didn't seem as if that was ever going to happen. Men wanted things from her, business advice, investment capital or a piece of her company but they never wanted just the woman. They never wanted her heart. Jill didn't want to be alone all of her life, ending up a bitter old woman with no family to pass her legacy on to. What was the purpose of building an empire if it died the moment she left the Earth? But the desire to pass along what she'd built wasn't the total story. Jill actually *hungered* for a family.

She peered out at the crowd from her vantage point on the round stage, and then pasted a fake smile on her face. As the boss, she had to put on a front of happiness, make it look as if she had it together and nothing got to her. No one needed to know how lonely and sad she was at that moment.

"Seven, six, five, four, three, two, one! Happy New Year!" the crowd boomed.

As silver balloons with the DVA logo began to drop from the ceiling, pooling around her feet like water and the band played a jazzy rendition of "Auld Lang Syne," Jill enviously watched couples share their first kiss of the new year. It was her party and she wanted to cry because once again she was alone on New Year's Eve, just like last year and the year before and the year before that one. She'd never shared a midnight kiss as the new year rolled in. For some reason, this New Year's Eve tugged at her heartstrings more than the others did. Could it be that getting older and watching other people her age settling down and starting families was actually getting to her? Or maybe that old Billy Dee Williams line from *Mahogany* was true: Success without someone to share it with was nothing. Jill took a deep breath and fought back her tears. Because she had no one to share her mega success with, she truly felt that she had absolutely nothing. For years, she'd explained that trying to build her company into one of Atlanta's most successful computer consulting firms left no time for relationships. But now Jill was making money hand over fist. She had transformed her company from an unknown to a nationwide power-house. When she went home at night, however, all she had was an empty bed and a stair climber.

Stop feeling sorry for yourself, she chided. Jill Atkinson, CEO and owner of DVA Inc., didn't have time to lament her nonexistent love life. Forcing another smile to her face, she took the mike from the stand and began to deliver her traditional New Year's speech.

"Happy New Year," she exclaimed with forced gaiety. "I can't tell you how happy and blessed I am to be spending this night with you all. As you know, last year was a banner year for DVA, and it wouldn't have been without your hard work and loyalty. I'm forever in your debt."

"We love you, Jill," someone shouted from the floor.

Blowing a kiss like a rock star, Jill returned the love before continuing with her speech. "Tonight's about partying and having fun but come Monday, it's back to business so that we can make the coming year even bigger and better than any year in company history. Happy New Year!"

Thunderous applause erupted from the crowd as Jill walked off the stage into a sea of adoring employees and friends. She shook hands with her executives and hugged other employees, like the ones who worked in the mailroom that she saw only during parties like this one. From the bottom to the top, employees respected her because she was fair and treated them with respect. She didn't play favorites and people liked that.

Whenever anyone needed something Jill gave, whether it was a gift for a retiring employee or contributing to a fundraiser for someone's child.

"Good speech, boss lady," said Malik Greene, DVA's marketing president, when he caught her alone for a moment.

Jill smiled at Malik and his wife, Shari Walker-Greene. Seeing the happy couple made her heart lurch, though. Jill loved Malik and Shari and cheered for their union because of what they'd overcome to be together, but watching them tonight—holding each other and exchanging looks of longing desire—was nothing short of torture.

"Don't you two look lovely," she said as she hugged Shari. "I love that dress."

"Thank you, but you're the belle of the ball. Blue's definitely your color," Shari replied.

Malik made a gagging noise. "Women. You could turn a trip to the grocery store into an episode of *America's Next Top Model*."

Shari playful smacked him on the shoulder. "You should be glad you're surrounded by beauty."

Taking Shari's hand in his, Malik kissed it gently, and Jill cringed inwardly. She wished she knew such a love. Her last relationship had ended because her boyfriend felt intimidated by her power, money and prestige. Not that Jill was the type of woman to lord her status over anyone in her personal life. Unfortunately, her name was so well known in her circles that when she introduced herself, men tended to shrink away from her. Besides, most of the single businessmen she knew were more interested in winning her company than her heart.

Jill watched Malik wrap his arms around Shari's waist and kiss her on the neck. Why couldn't she have someone in her life to hold her tightly and kiss her when he thought no one was looking? *Stop being jealous of their happiness. One of these days the right man will walk into your life,* she thought. But those words echoed in her head, not her heart. Jill knew she was going to spend the rest of her life alone.

"All right, you two, I'm going to take off," Jill announced, unable to take another moment of watching them express their love.

"Why? The party's just getting started," Malik said. "And it's your party. How are you going to leave your own party before things get exciting?"

Jill scoffed at him. "You know I'm going into the office in the morning, but you two enjoy your night."

After exchanging kisses with Malik and Shari and grabbing her mink wrap, Jill stepped out into the crisp night air, happy to be out of the ballroom. But as she looked around the streets of Buckhead, she saw just as many couples cavorting there as were in attendance at the party. Young, old, black, white—everybody had somebody except her. Instead of waiting for a cab or calling her car service, she decided to walk the three blocks to her empty penthouse, fifteen floors above the nightclubs, traffic, and crowds. Like most things in her life, she owned it and the highrise it was in. Even though it was filled with tenants and people, Jill couldn't have been more alone—a fact that saddened her tonight. Wrapping her shawl around her bare shoulders, Jill turned and headed in that direction.

Inhaling sharply, she tried to shake off the New Year's Eve blues. It was just another New Year's. It wasn't as if she hadn't spent New Year's alone before. She decided that she was going to go inside, put on her favorite terrycloth robe, play some John Coltrane and get a jump on the ton of work she had to do. She was going to streamline her files, look at a few companies to bring under the DVA umbrella and organize some sort of charitable event for the coming year. Yes, she'd spend this night just like she spent most others, up to her ears in work.

Walking into her place, she kicked off her shoes in the foyer. As they thudded against the marble floor, the echo seemed to accent the emptiness of her personal life. Reaching down to massage her aching feet, Jill decided that she was definitely going to take advantage of the New Year's Day offer at Thelma's, a new spa on the edge of Alpharetta, maybe even invite Shari along. She and Malik's wife had become fast friends, and Jill had witnessed how Shari's love transformed her protégé from a wannabe player into a devoted husband. Honestly, Jill hadn't expected their marriage to last a year, but four had passed.

Good for them but I wish it was me, she thought as she headed for the kitchen.

It wasn't often that Jill allowed herself to wallow in self-pity, but tonight was a good night to do it. Jill made her way to the kitchen to brew a pot of coffee for her night of work. Standing in the middle of the kitchen, she could have sworn she smelled smoke, but she shrugged it off and began to brew a pot of Colombian coffee. While the coffee perked, Jill headed to her home office to boot up the computer. The minute she walked in, she saw curls of black smoke seeping from the vents. Without a second thought, she grabbed her laptop and rushed out the door and down the emergency staircase, running down twelve flights of stairs, clad in her stocked feet and designer dress, only to run into a wall of flames on the third floor. Blinded by the black smoke, her lungs burning as she tried to breathe, she clutched her laptop to her chest as if were the one thing that could save her life.

"Oh God, don't let me die tonight!" she exclaimed before collapsing.

❧❧

Atlanta fire captain Darren Alexander had seen a lot of things in his fifteen-year career as a firefighter, but never had he seen a woman cling to a laptop computer with such zeal, as if her life depended on saving the machine. Darren scooped her up into his arms.

"I have a victim in the stairwell," he said into the radio on his shoulder. "Ready an EMT. It looks as if she's inhaled a lot of smoke."

Rushing down the stairs, Darren took the woman outside to the waiting emergency medical technicians.

"Is everybody out of the building?" he yelled as he came out.

"Yes, sir. The fire's under control as well," another fireman answered.

Nodding, Darren then turned his attention to the unconscious woman in his arms. He could tell she was someone who was well kept. Her café au lait skin looked as smooth as Norman Brown's latest jam, her plump lips looked ripe for kissing and despite the fact that it was disheveled, he could tell her hair was soft and silky.

He wondered what her story was. What was her name? Where was her man? Why was she home alone on New Year's Eve? And what was so damned important about that laptop?

Handing her over to an EMT, he watched as the technician placed an oxygen mask over her mouth and her eyes fluttered open, revealing a set of brown eyes that would melt an iceman's heart. Knowing that he should go and investigate the cause of the fire, Darren tried to walk away but his feet remained rooted in place.

"My files," he heard her say as she pulled the oxygen mask from her face.

"Ma'am, don't do that," Darren said, grabbing her hand. Her skin was just as soft as it looked. "You inhaled a lot of smoke."

She turned her eyes upward at him, causing a chill to run up and down his spine. What was it about this woman that heightened his awareness? He didn't know, but he was intrigued and he wanted to make sure she was all right, see her to the hospital and protect that laptop.

"But I have to get my . . ." She began to cough uncontrollably.

Darren placed the mask back on her face. "Breathe slowly."

She rolled her eyes, but did as she was told. Darren smiled, lighting up his grey eyes.

"You don't take orders well, do you?"

She shook her head.

Wiping his smudge-covered face with the back of his hand, he leaned down closer to her. "Relax and let someone take care of you for a change." Placing his hand on top of hers, he attempted to pull the laptop from her grip. "And that means letting this go. I'll hold on to it for you."

She was slow to let it go, but Darren gently pried it away. As the woman was loaded into the ambulance, Darren walked to his car and locked the computer inside. Now he was guaranteed to see her again.

❧❧

Jill tried to wrap her mind around what was going on. She was in the hospital, her building was on fire and her laptop—where was it? She sat up in the bed and frantically pressed the call button.

A nurse rushed into the room. "Yes, Miss Atkinson?" she asked breathlessly.

"I had a computer with me, where is it?" Her voice was hoarse because of the smoke she'd inhaled, and her throat burned with every word she spoke.

"Right here," a rich male voice said from the doorway.

Jill looked into the eyes of her sexy angel. "You saved me." Her eyes roamed his tight body, drinking in the man before her. His body was clad in black pants and a white, long sleeved tee-shirt, and she could see the outline of his muscular frame. He held her computer out to her. "And I saved this, too. I don't think I've ever seen anyone hold on to a computer so tightly."

"Well, I just—uh, I've never been in a situation like this before. I just grabbed what was in front of me and held on. By the way, what's your name?"

"Darren Alexander," he said, then sat on the edge of Jill's bed.

It was not often that she thought of a man as beautiful, but that was an accurate description of Darren Alexander. He had piercing grey eyes, smooth caramel skin and the biggest hands she'd ever seen.

She wondered what they would feel like stroking her in the middle of the night, spreading her thighs and…

"Are you all right?" he asked, breaking into Jill's thoughts.

"I guess I'm still in shock. Thank you for everything, saving me and my computer."

A smile tugged at Darren's lips. "Just what's so important about that computer? Vital government secrets? Are you a spy?"

"No," she said through laughter. "It's just work. I was about to sit down and go over some things before the smoke started coming though my vents."

"What do you do?"

"Marketing research," she said.

"Don't tell me you're one of those career first, everything else second, women?" he asked. "It was New Year's Eve. Why weren't you out partying with your husband or boyfriend?"

She smiled but didn't reply. Darren reached out and gently stroked her left hand.

"You're not married?" he asked.

Jill shook her head.

"Seeing someone?"

"No."

"Are you serious? A beautiful woman like you is single in this city? This is a joke, right?"

"Why do you find that so shocking?" she asked, then coughed again.

Darren shrugged his shoulders. "Because as Prince said, the beautiful ones are always taken."

Jill blushed. "Thank you for bringing me my computer."

"I still can't believe you were working on a holiday. When was the last time you had some good old-fashioned fun?"

"I went to a New Year's Eve party tonight and…" Jill stopped talking because the truth was she hadn't had fun in a long time. Not since she was a carefree college freshman at Spelman College many years ago.

From the moment she started DVA, her life had revolved around work, work and more work.

Raising his eyebrow at her silence, Darren replied, "That's just what I thought. I don't usually do this, but you should let me show you a good—no, a great time—when you get out of here."

Sitting up in the bed, wishing she was dressed in something more alluring than a puke green and white hospital gown, she asked, "Can you do that?"

Darren ran his hand over his smooth head. "Unless you have husband that's about to burst through the door, there's nothing stopping me from asking a beautiful woman out on a date."

Had she been a few shades lighter, Darren would have seen her cheeks turn rose red. He handed her his business card with his cell phone number scribbled on the back.

"When you're up to it, give me a call." Darren stood up and headed for the door, leaving Jill sitting in the middle of the bed with a wide smile on her face. "Take care, beautiful," he said before closing the door behind him.

Maybe it was going to be a happy new year after all.

CHAPTER TWO

The next morning, Jill was released from the hospital with a clean bill of health. She'd only suffered minor smoke inhalation. Though it had only been overnight, she was more excited about going home than a child anticipating opening Christmas gifts. Jill hated being confined and not being able to control the situation. Now that the unpleasantness of the fire was over, she could return home and relax.

And it was a good thing that she didn't have to deal with a messy clean-up in her penthouse. The fire and water damage was contained to the lower three floors and from her hospital bed she'd already got a restoration company on the job of cleaning up the lower floors.

As it turned out, the fire had been started by an electrical short in a first floor laundry room. No one was seriously hurt, which was a good thing, but Jill was going to make sure the maintenance company was fired.

Sighing, because this wasn't the way that she wanted to start her new year, she walked into her penthouse and checked her voice mail. There were three messages from Malik and Shari. They'd seen the fire on the news and were worried about her.

Pressing the speaker button on the phone, she dialed Malik and Shari.

"Hello?" Shari said.

"Shari, it's Jill, and I'm fine."

"Great, Malik and I were worried about you. Did your place get damaged?"

"Luckily no, but I had to spend the night in the hospital. Everything is fine, though, and I even got a date out of the whole ordeal."

"Really? Tell me about it?"

Jill absentmindedly twirled a strand of hair around her finger. "Why don't we talk about it at Thelma's? The spa is having a "new you," New Year's Day special. I was going to go there after leaving the office anyway. Now, I'm just going to go straight there. The work will hold until the office officially opens tomorrow."

"All right, that sounds like a plan," Shari said. "Jill, Malik wants to speak with you."

Jill could imagine Malik standing next to the phone bouncing up and down like an impatient child waiting to ride a pony at the state fair. She valued the friendship she and Malik had, even though his love of sex and women had almost gotten the company in a world of trouble a few years back.

Malik had had an affair with Greta DeVine, a former employee at the company. She had wanted Malik to be her man and when she saw the commitment he'd made to Shari, she'd lashed out at him with a bogus sexual harassment lawsuit. Because the company was owned by a woman, the lawsuit made national headlines. Jill had tried to protect her company and at the same time support Malik. However, she would have fired him if it had been necessary. The only time she ever wanted DVA in the news was for something positive. That was one of the reasons the company did so much charity work in the city of Atlanta. Jill wanted DVA's name linked to everything positive it could be.

No one was happier than she was when the allegations against Malik were proven false. Not only did her company keep its stellar reputation, but she hadn't been forced to fire one of her best employees and closest associates.

"Boss, why didn't you call me? Is everything all right?" he asked.

"Malik, I'm fine, nothing was damaged in my place and no one was hurt on the lower floors that took the brunt of the fire, smoke and water damage. Besides, I didn't want to disturb you and Shari. Married people celebrate New Year's in bed, you know."

"Jill, we're friends," he said. "I would've been glad to do whatever you needed. I'm glad you're all right, though. Please tell me that you're not going into the office today."

Laughing, she said, "No, I think I need some pampering and so does your wife. I can only imagine what being married to you is like."

"Funny," Malik replied. "But seriously, you deserve some R&R. Is there anything pressing you need me to do at the office?"

Sighing, Jill knew she needed more than rest and relaxation. She needed a little romance and renewal. Maybe she would get some of that with Darren. She pulled his card from her pocket and looked at it for a moment. Should she call him? And what would she say if she did call?

"Jill, you there?" Malik broke into her thoughts. "Did you hear me?"

"Yeah, yeah, tell Shari I'll meet her at the spa in about an hour," she said. "And there's no need for you to go into the office. Enjoy your weekend."

After hanging up with Malik, Jill poured herself a glass of water, still pondering whether she should call the fire captain. Though she took business risks routinely, when it came to matters of the heart, she wasn't as bold. The last thing she wanted was to end up broken and lonely, like the last time she'd given her heart away.

Jill had to wonder if those people who said it was better to have loved and lost than to never have loved at all had ever had their hearts trampled on.

Her heart crusher, David Branton, was an up-and-coming businessman in his own right. He had been making strides at Concurrent Computer

Corporation, one of Atlanta's fastest growing companies. DVA, at the time, was on the cusp of its mega success and many on the outside looking in saw it as wide open for a takeover. At the time, no one knew just how brilliant Jill Atkinson was when it came to business.

Jill met David at a technology mixer in Buckhead when she received her Business Person of the Year award. David was every woman's dream, six feet of pure satisfaction. He was the color of ebony wood and looked as if he belonged on the cover of *Esquire* Magazine with his sharp Armani suits and polished alligator shoes. His smile lit up a room and made women swoon as if he were the second coming of Morris Chestnut or Denzel Washington.

He immediately took Jill's breath away when he walked over to her and congratulated her. When he took her hand in his to shake it, neither of them wanted to let go. She had hoped that he would kiss her hand like an English gentleman just so she could feel the softness of his lips on her skin.

Though Jill didn't set out to make David her man, he definitely had her in his sights to be his woman. At least that's the way it had seemed as he wooed her with flowers, poetry and late night dinners at the office. David was in and out of her office so much that her assistant, Madison, joked that he should be on the payroll.

But Jill soon found that David had a hidden agenda.

He was trying to gather as much information as he could about the company so that Concurrent could bring DVA under its vast umbrella. One night when David brought her dinner, Jill went to the bathroom and he seized the opportunity to try to hack into her computer.

Jill had planned to emerge from the bathroom dressed in sexy black lingerie and five inch spiked heels, but she had left her bag with her clothes in it at her desk. When she walked into her office, she found him hunched over her computer, looking like Quasimodo's evil twin brother, with a floppy disk in his hand.

"What the hell are you doing?" she demanded.

"Uh-uh," he stammered. "I was just…"

Jill closed the space between them and slapped him with all of the fury inside her. "How could you do this to me? Was this all our relationship was about? You wanted to get your foot in the door so you could find out my company secrets? Son of a bitch!"

David stood up, dropping the disk on the floor. "Jill, I was just doing my job."

She shook with anger. "Your job? Was sleeping with me and professing your love to me part of your job? If you don't get out of here, you're going to be leaving in a body bag." Jill snatched the floppy disk from the floor and crushed it in her hands. "You tell your bosses at Concurrent you deserve a raise because you did a good job of fooling me. But those bastards will not get their hands on my company, no matter how many Uncle Tom assholes they send my way."

Heartbroken and disillusioned by David's betrayal, Jill vowed to make him pay.

She turned the tables on him by raising enough capital to initiate a hostile takeover of Concurrent. To raise capital, Concurrent had released shares to the public, hoping to increase the revenues before buying the outstanding shares back.

As an avid stock market watcher, Jill knew what she needed to do. Putting up some of her personal money, she bought the outstanding shares.

Once DVA owned 51 percent of the stocks, Jill fired all of Concurrent's top executives, including David, earning her a reputation as someone not to be messed with.

Concurrent proved to be a good buy. DVA's client base doubled, their reach expanded to firms in Canada, and unlocked doors that might have taken years for DVA alone to open.

Ironically, the biggest business deal of Jill's life had been motivated by a broken heart. She resolved not to mix business and pleasure again, because the next time, she might be left with a broken heart and no company. So she didn't swim with the sharks, or even dive into the deep end of the ocean.

Usually every man she met seemed to have some sort of issue with her status. If he didn't give her the "I'm so not on your level speech," then he was hitting her up for a loan to fund a business venture that Jill knew didn't have a chance in hell of being profitable. She wasn't a woman to these men, at least in her mind. She was just a means to an end.

God, please let this be different this time. Let Darren at least be a good friend, she thought as she poured herself another glass of water. Hopefully, he wasn't a big business page reader. Maybe this is was what she needed to do, date someone outside of her circle. If she were lucky, her business and everything else that normally got in the way of her relationships wouldn't matter with Darren.

Jill promised herself if things got serious with Darren, she would tell him the truth and maybe by that time it wouldn't even matter. Deciding that she was getting ahead of herself, Jill shook off the thoughts of Darren and ran upstairs to change into her spa attire—black yoga pants, a fitted tank top and matching track jacket.

About thirty minutes later, Jill and Shari were sitting in Corinthian leather spa chairs, soaking their feet in tangerine oil and sea salt with avocado masks covering their faces.

Reaching for her protein shake, Jill released a satisfied sigh. "I really needed this."

Shari nodded. "I know that's right. What a way to start the new year."

Jill took a sip of the shake. "Yeah, nearly burning in a fire and spending the night in the hospital."

"Uh, didn't you say met an incredibly sexy man?" She turned on her side and faced Jill. The blue mask on her face gave her a comical look. "For you to be excited about the brother, he has to be something special."

"I don't think anything is going to come from it. We meet people every day that we aren't meant to see again." She silently prayed that this wasn't the case with Darren because Shari had hit the nail on the head; she was excited about the possibility of seeing him again.

"You know what, sista; it's a new year and you need to stop hiding behind your career and take a chance on love," Shari said.

Jill scoffed. "I don't hide behind my business." But the words were hollow because Jill knew that she did hide behind DVA. She just didn't know it was that obvious.

"Really? When was the last time you went out on a date? A real date and not a business dinner? I know you haven't even accepted a date since I've known you. Do I need to tell you how many years that's been?"

Rolling her eyes back in her head, Jill didn't answer.

"That's just what I thought. Call that man," Shari said.

Jill smiled. "I don't think I'm going to call him. I've got too much work to do."

Placing her hand over Jill's, Shari said, "Last time I checked, you owned the company. Delegate some work to someone else. If you don't call him, you're going to be wondering what could have been. But I know how you feel, though. When you get off the dating train, it's hard to get back on it. I told Malik 'no' more times than I can count before I relented and went out with him. Look at us now. I can blow some of my marriage dust on you if you want me to and see what happens."

Jill smiled. "Maybe I should throw caution to the wind and call him. What do I have to lose?"

Before Shari could respond, a massage therapist came in and whisked her away, leaving Jill alone with her thoughts and her cell phone. Part of her wanted to call Darren; she had already saved his cell phone number in her electronic phone book. But would she come off as desperate? What happened to the days of men making the first move, she wondered as she slipped her feet into a pair of terry cloth slippers. Jill walked over to huge bay window overlooking the quiet garden and its lush greenery. Some of the ever-greens still had Christmas decorations on them. Christmas, like most holidays, had just been another workday for Jill and she was tired of it. She wanted a chance to have someone that she could relax with on holidays, someone to whisk off to Jamaica with, and someone to share that all-important New Year's kiss with.

Maybe Darren could give her some toe-curling sex that would end her self-imposed love drought. Shaking her head, Jill decided to take things slow. As she listened to the phone ringing, she almost hoped that Darren wouldn't answer.

But he did. His sexy baritone sent a chill down her spine when he said hello.

"Hi, Darren, it's Jill Atkinson, the lady from the fire."

"Oh yeah, as if I would forget. How are you?"

"Great. I got a clean bill of health, thanks to you," she said. Listening intently, Jill waited to see if he would recognize her name. But the conversation continued without a hitch.

"That's good to hear and I'm really glad that you called."

Closing her eyes and holding back a school girl squeal, Jill replied, "Really?"

"Yes, I have tickets to a concert at the Fox tonight. Wayman Tisdale is playing with some other local jazz artist. You do like jazz, don't you?"

"I love it. What time does the show start?" She fanned herself excitedly with her free hand. She had a bona fide date. Looked like clouds were starting to gather; maybe there was an end in sight to her love drought.

"Eight, but I was thinking we could meet for drinks first," he said. "Maybe we can go to the Shark Bar?"

"Maybe not," Jill said, knowing that she would be instantly recognized by the patrons who worked in her world. "Why don't we go to Mick's?"

"That works for me because I was just trying to impress you. The Shark Bar isn't my scene. Too many stuffy business types passing out cards and dangling

BMW key chains trying to pretend that they're the most important person in the world."

She laughed at his honesty because she definitely knew those types. "You saved my life. I think it's time for me to impress you."

"What time do you want me to pick you up?"

"Uh, why don't we meet at the Buckhead Marta station? You know how crazy traffic is and how much it costs to park downtown when there's an event going on."

"All right, that's fine with me. Why don't we link up around five-thirty, have an early dinner and a few drinks?"

"Sure, that sounds like a plan," she replied. Once Jill hung up, she took her first real breath since Darren answered his phone

She had a date.

❧☙

Hanging up the phone, Darren was all smiles. Jill's call had surprised him because he hadn't thought the beautiful woman was going call him.

"Who put that smile on your face?" his brother Cleveland asked.

"My date for the concert, so that means you give me my ticket back."

Cleveland pretended to stumble backward as he handed Darren the concert ticket. "You have a date, Mr. I'm-Through-with-Women?"

Darren pushed his brother. "She seems different. Remember the fire in Buckhead on New Year's Eve? She was in the fire, and I saved her."

Cleveland shook his head, causing his shoulder length Nubian locks to swing. "This is a sympathy date. Don't get too caught up. Once the whole hero thing wears off, she'll go her merry little way."

Darren looked at his brother, who was the spitting image of their father, except for the hair. His little brother had inherited his father's honey brown complexion, grey eyes and suspicious nature. Who knew what the future held for him and Jill? Regardless, he was looking forward to finding out.

When it came to risking his life to save another, Darren was gung-ho. He didn't mind running through flames to carry a trapped person to safety, but when it came to giving a woman his heart, well, that was another story.

He'd always believed that everyone has one great love of their life and he thought he'd found his in Rita Williams, who was the Atlanta Police Department's DARE officer. Many times, Darren and Rita had run into each other at events at local schools.

He had been taken with her beauty and her gentle way with the children. While he was working up the nerve to ask her out on a date, she beat him to the punch, inviting him to dinner and a movie on the next Friday night that he didn't have to work.

After three months of dating, Darren knew he'd found his soul mate. Rita had moved into his house and they'd begun planning their future. The next step had been to ask her to marry him.

Cleveland had warned Darren not to marry her. There was just something about Rita that he didn't trust. But Darren was in love and he even ignored his own internal warnings, telling him that he was moving too fast in this relationship.

They had been married less than three months when Rita told him that she was pregnant and Darren was overjoyed. Being a father was one of Darren's biggest dreams. He wanted a son who he could teach to be a firefighter like his father had done with him and Cleveland.

But it wasn't going to happen. Rita told him that she didn't want a child because she wanted to further her career at the police department. She was due to take the sergeant's exam and she had a good chance of moving up in rank. When she told Darren that she wanted to have an abortion, his heart had dropped to his stomach. How could she not want to start a family? Wasn't that what married people did?

Darren told her there was no way he would consent to her having an abortion. He wanted the child whether she did or not. After weeks of arguing, Rita took off for a few days. Darren had assumed she went to her mother's house in Savannah, but that wasn't the case.

When she returned home, Rita announced that she'd had a miscarriage. Darren was devastated but tried to be strong for his wife. It wasn't long before he found out that his wife had lied to him. Rita had not had a miscarriage. She'd gone to Savannah for an abortion. Even though she had told the people at the clinic that she was single, she had given them her Atlanta address. When the notice from the clinic came, Darren opened it and fury ran through his system like the rushing waters of a river in flood. She'd lied to him!

"Rita!" he yelled, slamming into the kitchen where she was cooking dinner.

"Darren, why are you yelling?"

He shoved the letter under her nose. "Care to explain your miscarriage? Looks like you had an abortion while you were in Savannah!"

Rita turned the stove off. "Darren, please let me…"

"Being a father meant the world to me and you knew that. I told you I wanted this baby."

"It wasn't your body! I was going to have to carry this baby for nine months."

Darren ran upstairs and began packing her things to throw her out of his house.

Rita was hot on his heels. "We can work this out. That baby wasn't right for us. We have time to have children, we're young."

He whirled around. "How can you say our child wasn't right for us? We're not teenagers; we made that child in our marital bed."

Tears streamed down Rita's cheeks. "It wasn't yours," she said in a voice barely above a whisper.

Darren gripped her shoulders. "What did you say?"

"The baby wasn't yours. I-I made a stupid mistake a few months ago while you were away training and…"

Darren threw his hands up. He didn't need to hear any more. Once her bags were packed, he tossed them and Rita out of his house.

After his divorce was finalized, Darren vowed never to let another woman into his heart. Sure, he'd had a few flings, but nothing serious, nothing that lasted more than a week. However, there was something about Jill that told him things would be different. The only kind of person that Darren couldn't deal with was a liar.

She's different, he thought as he headed to his closet to find something to wear for his date. *At least I hope she is.*

CHAPTER THREE

Jill and Shari walked out of Thelma's looking and feeling like supermodels. Jill's hair was deep chestnut brown, her eyebrows were waxed and her nails buffed and shaped. She felt as if the residue from the fire had been peeled away in the spa and she was more than ready for her date with Darren.

"Thanks for coming with me," Jill said as they walked to their cars.

"No problem and you have a good time tonight."

The two women embraced and said their goodbyes. As Jill drove home, chills ran up and down her spine as she thought about her date with Darren.

Still, she didn't know what she would say to Darren when the questions about what she did, where she lived and all of those get-to-know-you things came up. The last thing she wanted was to have yet another man either run away because she made too much money or a man who would look at her with dollar signs in his eyes. Which one was Darren, she wondered?

Hopefully neither, she thought to herself as she pulled into the parking deck of her building.

Rushing into her penthouse, Jill tried to figure out what to wear on her date. She decided to be elegantly simple, choosing a slinky black dress and matching duster. The dress highlighted the healthy glow of her skin. She would take her leather coat in case it grew colder during the evening.

Instead of wearing her favorite three-carat diamond earrings, Jill picked a pair of silver hoops and a teardrop necklace. It was modest jewelry for someone known for wearing big baubles.

Taking a deep breath, she took a seat on the edge of the bed and rubbed her hands together.

"It's just a date, not a corporate takeover," she told herself before standing and walking into the bathroom.

❧❧

At the MARTA station Jill saw Darren walking toward her just as the clock struck five-thirty. Breathing became an afterthought.

Wow, that man's gorgeous, she thought as she drank in his appearance. Darren was dressed in a pair of black wool slacks, a cream turtleneck and a black blazer. His skin seemed to glow in the cool winter air, giving his creamy caramel complexion a rosy tint. Watching him walk over to her was like viewing poetry in motion. He moved with the sensuality of Coltrane's sax, the coolness of Miles' horn and style of Duke Ellington's ivory tickling.

Jill held her leather trench together as a cold wind blew over her or maybe that chill came from the anticipation of being with Darren.

"Hey there," he said, giving her a friendly but tight hug. "What time is the train getting here?"

Jill glanced at the schedule. "In about five minutes."

Darren released her from his embrace, but draped his arm around her shoulders as he led her to a bench. "You look great," he said once they were seated and she loosened her grip on the coat.

"So do you."

Jill felt more nervous than when applying for credit at a bank. *Say something*, she thought. "How long have you been a firefighter?"

"About 15 years. It's a tradition in the Alexander family to be firemen. My father was a firefighter and so is my younger brother. You do marketing research, right?"

"Yeah, but it's nothing too fabulous. I get to work with those Shark Bar types you were talking about."

"I feel sorry for you. Not only do you have to deal with traffic every morning, but you've got to deal with those posers. What company do you work for?"

"DVA," she said.

"Do you enjoy what you do?"

Nervously she ran her hand through her hair. "I can't complain."

"That's not a ringing endorsement. If you don't love what you do, why do it?"

Jill patted his arm. "You know, I don't want to talk about business. My New Year's resolution was to stop focusing on work so much."

Before Darren could reply, the train arrived. He stood and held his hand out to Jill. Closing her fingers around his, she toyed with telling him the truth about what she really did, but decided against it because she wanted to have a good time tonight and not worry if he was with her for all the wrong reasons.

"Is this a sympathy date?" he asked before Jill could say anything. "I mean, I save lives for a living so that's not why I asked you out."

"No, not at all," Jill replied as they stepped on the train. "I wouldn't have accepted a date from you if I didn't want to. It doesn't hurt that you're cute."

Darren smiled and gently squeezed her hand. "You think I'm cute?"

"Actually, gorgeous, but I wouldn't want to inflate your ego," she said.

The train was nearly empty as they took their seats, giving Jill a chance to commit Darren's image to memory. Catching her gaze, Darren flashed her a brilliant smile.

"Tell me about yourself, Jill," he said.

She shrugged her shoulders. "There's not really much to tell."

"I don't believe that. What are you, a former model or something? Are you from Atlanta? And why aren't you married?"

"I'm not a model, never have been and Atlanta might as well be my home. I went to school here and just couldn't leave. As for the marriage part, I just haven't met the right man yet. So many people get married for all the wrong reasons and end up in divorce court. If it's not about love then there is no reason for me to waste my time. I don't feel that I have to get married just to keep up appearances. I want to be loved and I refuse to settle."

Nodding, he exhaled loudly. "I know the feeling."

Jill was glad he didn't ask her to explain what she was saying. *So far, so good*, she thought as the train came to a stop.

"We're here," Darren said as he stood and held his arm out for Jill.

A warm feeling rushed over her as she took his arm. This was the start of something good, or at least the potential was there.

❧❧

Sitting across from Jill, Darren was lost in her eyes. She was what people would call a brick house. He felt, though, that she was holding something back from him. There was something behind those brown eyes that tried to hide hurt. He hoped Jill wasn't one of those women who had been treated poorly by other men and put up this façade of bravado. He didn't want to have to break down walls, but Jill seemed worth it if that's what it took to get close to her. He could show her that real men still walked the streets of Atlanta.

Reaching across the table, he stroked her hand and looked into her eyes.

"What?" she asked, slipping her hand from underneath his.

"Nothing. Why don't we talk about something safe, since you don't want to let me in yet? Are you into sports?"

"Yes. I love football. I have season tickets to the Falcons. Michael Vick is amazing. We're going to the Super Bowl this year, watch. We're this season's Carolina Panthers."

"Season tickets? I've been trying to get over to the dome and catch a game."

"There's nothing like seeing Vick live. You should really get over there."

Darren leaned back in his seat. "Now I'm really curious. Why is a football-loving woman like yourself single? Do you know how many men want a woman that will watch football with him on a Sunday without asking 50 questions?"

She smiled and drummed her fingers on the table. "I also know men who can't stand to be around a woman who knows more about football than they do."

Chuckling softly, Darren said, "That wouldn't be a problem for me because I know everything about the sport. They call me ESPN at the station house."

Jill folded her arms across her chest and moved forward in her seat as if she were ready to battle for the ESPN title. "Who led the league in sacks last year?"

"That's easy, Patrick Kerney from the Atlanta Falcons," he said confidently.

"Wrong," Jill replied. "It was Dwight Freeney from the Indianapolis Colts."

"Who won the Super Bowl in 1971?" he asked, hoping to trip her up with a historic fact.

"The Dallas Cowboys beat Miami 24 to 3 in New Orleans."

"I'm impressed," he said, doing a mock bow to her.

Jill nodded like the queen of England. "Just call me the NFL Network."

"Maybe we can catch the game on Sunday, that is, if you don't mind hot wings and beer."

"Sure."

"But you have your season tickets. Are you sure you want to give that up to hang out with me?"

"Why not? I'm sure I can sell them to one of my co-workers. Malik Greene has been pressing me to go to a game all season."

Darren clasped his hands together, happy to have another chance to see Jill. "Then tell Malik Greene I said thank you."

Jill smiled and Darren's heart fluttered. She had a smile that reminded him of sunshine and warmth. Her face was angelic, ethereal. He was content just to look at her. Darren knew he was going to have to get to know Jill, learn everything about her—what she liked, loved, and disliked. His interest was piqued.

"Why are you staring at me?" she asked.

"Because I think we're going to have a lot of fun together."

They raised their water glasses and clinked them as if they were toasting with champagne.

"Here's to a beautiful friendship," she said, then took a long sip of water.

Though Darren toasted to friendship, he hoped for more and prayed Jill was the real thing—a lover he could claim as his own.

After dinner, Darren and Jill walked hand and hand over to the Fox Theatre. The venue had an ambiance that was meant to breed romance. The lights were soft and low, and candles burned on a few tables that were set up close to the stage. Their seats were in the balcony, where the lights were even lower. In the dimness, Darren thought Jill looked exotic.

It took every ounce of self control in him not to kiss her full lips as she watched the first act on the stage, moving her body in rhythm with the sensual saxophonist.

"They sound great," she said, turning to him.

"Yeah, the Southern Jazz Band has always been one of my favorites. I love going to Piedmont Park in the summer and listening to them."

Wayman Tinsdale took the stage and the crowd went wild, but Darren was cheering for a different reason. He cheered because he was sitting next to the most beautiful woman in the crowd.

As Tinsdale played his smooth grooves, Darren and Jill danced along with the other people in the crowd. He wrapped his arms around her waist, pulling her close to him as the music slowed. Their faces were inches apart and more than anything else, he wanted to kiss her. Jill turned away as if she felt a kiss was on its way to her lips.

By the time the concert was over, Darren's hormones were in overdrive. Holding Jill against him, dancing with her and feeling her rhythm made him long for her, ache for her and not want the night to end.

Jill had a smile on her face that spread from ear to ear. "This was a wonderful concert," she said. "Thank you for inviting me."

"I'm glad you came with me. I don't think I would have had as much fun dancing with my brother Cleveland."

"Nightcap? We can go to one of these bars and have a martini."

Darren looked at his watch. "Are you sure it's not too late?"

"Okay just admit it, I bored you to death and you want to get away from me as fast as you can."

"No, not at all, but I don't want you on the train too late all by yourself. Honestly, I really don't want this night to end."

The smile on Jill's face told him that she felt the same way.

"And you're going to take a cab home," Darren said. "That way, I'll feel better about letting you leave so late."

"Thanks," she said. "It's nice to know that gentlemen still exist."

Darren brought her hand to his lips and kissed it gently. "If you want me to, I'll ride back with you and make sure you make it in safely."

"No, no, that's okay. Thanks for the offer."

Darren and Jill headed for one of Atlanta's newest bars, Red. As the name suggested, everything was decorated in red from the floor to the ceiling. The bar was a deep red; the stools were covered in a blood red suede material. Tea candles burned in red holders, bathing the place in red glow.

"This is different," Darren said as they took a seat at the bar.

While Jill looked around the place, Darren studied the nuances of her face. Her eyes were shaped like almonds and in the candle light, they sparkled like stars. When her full lips curved into a smile, her mouth looked good enough to eat. She had smooth skin that he wanted to touch, to find out if she was as soft as she appeared.

"What can I get for you two?" the bartender asked. Of course she was dressed in all red.

Jill picked up a drink menu and gave it the once-over. "I'll have a strawberry martini," she said.

The bartender turned to Darren, "And you, sir?"

"I'll have the same."

Before too long, a DJ began playing R&B and hip hop. The bass reverberated throughout the bar and only someone without a pulse wouldn't want to dance. As the bartender set the drinks in front of them, Darren asked Jill if she wanted to dance.

She took a nervous sip of her drink. "All right."

Darren and Jill moved to the floor, easily pushing past the other couples. John Legend's "She Don't Have to Know" blared from the speakers. Darren moved rhythmically against Jill's body and she mirrored his moves. Darren felt himself getting aroused. Jill smelled like roses and womanhood. Her skin was silky soft and when her hair brushed against his cheek, he had to take a step back so that she wouldn't feel what she had done to him. It had been six months since he touched a woman, held a soft body against his hard one. He'd entered into a state of self imposed celibacy. But smelling and touching Jill made him want to break that vow. He wanted her long brown legs wrapped around him while he buried himself inside her. What kind of lover would she be? He wondered. Darren pulled her against his body again. From the way she moved, twisting her hips and wrapping her arms around his neck, he knew she would be a masterful lover. Darren was actually jealous of any man who'd had the pleasure of being with Jill, kissing her, tasting her and making love to her.

As the song ended and a loud southern hip hop song began to play, Jill and Darren returned to the bar to cool themselves with their drinks.

"You have some smooth moves," Jill said after downing her drink. "I haven't danced like that in a long time."

"I find that hard to believe. I would think that you would be out every weekend with a different paramour," he said. He was fishing to find out if there was someone in her life that he would have to push out of the way.

Jill laughed throatily. "Work keeps me really busy. I don't have a lot of time to date."

"I hope I can change that. You're too pretty not to have a life outside of an old office building."

She cast her eyes down shyly. "It's getting pretty late," she said.

"You know what they say about time flying when you're having fun," he said as he rose to his feet, holding his hand out to help Jill to her feet.

Electric currents of unspoken desire passed though them as their hands touched.

When Jill stood, her breasts brushed against Darren's chest, sending a ripple of lust down his spine. He was tempted to ask her if he could take her home, but Jill wasn't the kind of woman that he could see hopping into bed with a man she barely knew. Besides, he wanted more than something physical with Jill. She was a woman who deserved love, commitment and respect. If she would allow him, he'd give her all of that and more.

CHAPTER FOUR

Jill waved to Darren as the taxi took off from the curb. She wished he were sitting beside her, going home with her. But it was way too soon for that and if a one-night stand was all Darren wanted from her, she would be sorely disappointed. She couldn't deny that she'd had a great time with him, though. Darren was funny, sexy and made her smile with just a touch. Jill used to look at couples and wonder why they smiled at each other all the time, whether it was possible to be that interested in one person and what they had to say. She now knew the answer was yes.

Jill closed her eyes and relived the memory of their dance at Red. The way he moved his body against hers had ignited a fire inside her that had been dormant for so long. Jill was surprised by how boldly she'd danced with him, bumping and grinding against him, wanting to feel his erection pressed against her. She loved knowing that he wanted her. That fact sent her body into overdrive. Maybe that was why she'd pretended not to notice his longing as she danced like she was twenty years old again. She hummed the John Legend song as the driver took her home. The only thing that could have made the evening more spectacular would've been a kiss from Darren.

When he was checking her out in Red, she'd noticed that his stare lingered a little longer on her lips. All he had to do was lean over, because she wanted to taste him so badly she ached for it. And when he wrapped his arms around her waist, pulling her into his hips, she'd waited for the kiss, wanting the pleasure of tasting him, feeling his lips pressed against hers.

"Miss, this is your stop," the driver said.

Jill opened her wallet and handed him a $50 bill. "Goodnight," she sang as she exited the car. She didn't walk into the building; she danced inside, feeling happy from the inside out. And for the night, it didn't matter that she was playing a game of charades with Darren.

❧❧

The next morning as she was getting ready to catch up on her financial reports from the office and the work that she'd planned to do on New Year's Eve, her cell phone rang. Anyone who knew Jill knew Sunday morning was not the time to disturb her. She reserved Sunday for twenty-four hours of solitude. Since she didn't golf, no one ever bothered her for a Sunday meeting, but Jill knew on those golf courses, men were planning, plotting and scheming. So in the quietness of her penthouse, she did the same.

"Hello?"

"I hope I'm not disturbing you," Darren said. "I was just making sure my dance partner made it home safely."

She smiled and removed her reading glasses. "Yes, I did. I was going to call you later to see where we're watching the game." She also made a mental note to call Malik. She knew he would jump at the chance to have her 50-yard line seats in the Georgia Dome. She just hoped Shari would forgive her for taking Malik away from anything they had going on that day.

"Where else, the ESPN Zone?"

"That works for me. I'll meet you there at two. The Falcons play at four, right?"

Darren laughed. "As if you didn't know. You're probably in your living room watching ESPN."

She looked up at the TV. He was right. She always worked with the NFL Countdown show on mute. "You got me."

"I'll see you later. And by the way, I had a great time last night."

"So did I."

"Well, I don't want to keep you from whatever you're doing."

After saying goodbye to Darren, the last thing Jill wanted to do work. She picked up the phone and called Malik.

"Hello," Shari said.

"Shari, it's Jill, how are you?"

"Good. Is everything all right? I know you don't usually come up for air on a Sunday."

Jill laughed. "I know. Do you guys have any plans for today?"

"No, what's up?"

"I'm not going to use my Falcons tickets today and I was wondering if Malik wanted them."

"You know the answer to that. Hold on."

Jill smiled as she heard Shari call out for her "honey."

"Falcons tickets!" Malik said excitedly. "I would love to go."

"Great, if you can stop by my place around," Jill leaned back and looked at the clock, "eleven-thirty, I'll give you the tickets."

"What's the deal, Jill? You never give up your tickets. Are you all right?"

"I'm fine and if you must know, I have a date."

"What? Why don't you take him to the game? Show him a good time in your executive suite."

"I'd rather not. Darren and I are going to the ESPN Zone for football, wings, and beer."

"Hello, is this Jill Atkinson, Ms. Caviar, and Cristal? The woman who has almost as much money as God? And you're going on a date to the ESPN Zone."

Jill heard Shari ask, "She has a date? With the fireman?"

"Malik, we're just having a normal date, and he should be the one impressing me."

"And all it takes is ESPN Zone and chicken wings? Wish I had known that when I was single. Ouch! Shari, I was just kidding."

The next voice Jill heard was Shari's. "So you have a date?"

"Second date," Jill said excitedly. "We went out last night. He had tickets to the jazz concert at the Fox. Then we went out for drinks and he called this morning to make sure I made it home safely."

"He sounds like a keeper."

"I wouldn't go that far, we've just met and I haven't exactly been forthcoming with him."

"What do you mean?"

"Girl, I haven't told him who I really am. He asked what I did and I blurted out marketing research."

"Jill, this isn't something you can hide. Cameras follow you."

"Last night he suggested going to the Shark Bar and you know I had to say no. I just don't want this to be like every other relationship where he leaves me because I own my own business and make more money than he does or where he becomes a male gold-digger."

"What is lying to him going to solve?" Shari probed. "Tread lightly. You know you can't build a relationship on a lie."

"I know, I know," Jill lamented. "I'll tell him the truth."

"And when you do, you'll see that you were worrying for no reason."

Even though she said she'd tell him the truth, Jill knew she wasn't going to do it today. Today she was going to be a marketing researcher and have a regular date with beer and chicken wings.

Jill was going to have to get to know Darren to find out what kind of man he really was. And that was just impossible to do after two dates. It wasn't time for true confessions yet.

$$\text{\small{❧❧}}$$

A few hours later, Jill has pulled into the last free parking spot in the ESPN Zone parking lot. She emerged from her car dressed in a pair of jeans and a fitted Michael Vick jersey. She'd never worn her jersey before, it wasn't something that a CEO was supposed to wear, but today she was going to be a football fan with a date.

When she walked in, Darren was sitting at the bar watching the door. She waved to him and he crossed over to her, giving her a kiss on the cheek.

"Look at you. A true Falcons fan."

Jill did a twist like a runway fashion model.

"We can try to get a table, but everything looks pretty crowded," Darren said, holding his hand out to illustrate how crowded it was. "The Falcons draw a crowd when they're winning."

They headed for the bar. Darren tapped on the lacquered top. "Excuse me, are there any tables?"

"I think there's a booth over there." The bartender pointed to a spot underneath a TV screen.

Darren and Jill rushed through the crowd to get the booth. Once they were seated, she made note of his outfit, a pair of well worn black jeans and a Falcons turtleneck.

"I see you're quite the fan too," she said.

Darren winked and handed her one of the menus. "My brother may be stopping by. Number one, he doesn't believe I'm on a date and number two, he can't believe I found a woman who loves football."

Jill prayed that his brother didn't know who she was.

"You don't have a problem with that, do you?" Darren asked, misreading her silence.

"Oh, no. But why would your brother need to see proof of you being on a date?"

"Quiet as it's kept; I don't go on a lot of dates. Not that I don't have the opportunity, but I'm cautious about who I let into my life."

"I hear that," Jill said.

A waiter dressed in a referee's uniform walked over to the table and took their orders. Darren ordered a pitcher of light beer and a platter of chicken wings with both hot and mild ones.

Normally, Jill hated it when a man she was dating ordered for her. Maybe it was because she knew at the end of the date that somehow she'd end up paying for the rock lobster and caviar that he'd ordered to impress her.

Today she decided to go with the flow. Darren wasn't trying to be flashy by ordering for both of them. She liked him because he lived like a man who wasn't trying to prove anything to anyone. He wasn't a poser. So, how would he react when he found out that she was one?

When the waiter left, Jill had every intention of telling Darren she was the CEO of DVA, but as she opened her mouth, she changed her mind and asked, "So, why aren't you married, Darren?"

"Well, I was. But she committed the ultimate sin."

"What was that?"

"She lied to me. I can forgive a lot of things, except lying. When a person lies to you, they've made a conscious effort to deceive you. You tell one lie and you have to tell many more to cover it up."

His words were like jabs from Mike Tyson in his prime. She needed a beer and fast as Darren continued his litany.

"There is no excuse for lying. For some reason people today don't want to take responsibility for their actions, so they lie. I think Bill Clinton was a great president, but when he lied about the intern, I lost respect for him. And don't get me started on Bush. His lies have cost thousands of soldiers their lives and still we don't have any weapons of Mass Destruction and Bin Laden is still on the loose."

"Yeah," was all Jill could say.

"I'm sorry," Darren said. "I hopped on my soapbox when today was supposed to be about football."

"It's refreshing to hear your thoughts…"

"Big brother, what's up," a tall man with dreadlocks said.

Assuming he was Darren's skeptical brother, Jill smiled at him.

"Jill, this is Cleveland, Cleveland, Jill."

Cleveland and Jill shook hands. "Miss Jill, you are too fine to be hanging with the likes of my brother. Now, if you want to join me, I'm going to be sitting with a rowdy bunch of brothers over there." He pointed to a table a few feet away from where they were seated.

Darren playful punched Cleveland on the arm. "Don't make me put you back in your cage."

"Whatever." Cleveland turned to Jill. "So, my brother kept telling me about this woman he met who loves football so much she has season tickets to the Falcons."

"I don't know why people find it so odd that women like football. I mean, really, what's not to like? Brothers in tight pants, muscles rippling, and grown men crying when they don't make the playoffs."

Cleveland nudged his brother. "See, women always have an ulterior motive when it comes to liking sports." He smiled. "I'm going to get out of your hair. I've got to meet the guys. Jill, it was nice meeting you."

"Nice meeting you too." Inwardly, she released a sigh of relief. He didn't know her; at least he didn't seem to.

"That's my brother, got to love him because you can't shoot him."

"You guys are close?" she asked.

Darren nodded at her while he thanked the waiter for the beer. "Do you have any brothers or sisters?" he asked.

"I was an only child. So it was a little lonely growing up. But my mom put me in every after-school program there was so that I would realize the world didn't revolve around me."

"Cleveland and I made up our own after-school fun. We worried our poor momma to death, I believe. She keeps telling us when we have children they are going repay us for everything we did to her. A vision I hope she's wrong about, because we were a couple of hellions."

"Your mom is still living?"

He nodded. "Down in Marietta. Maybe you'll get to meet her one day."

She smiled. Not since high school had someone talked to her about meeting their parents. Jill had lost her parents in consecutive years. Her mother first, from congestive heart failure. That was one of the reasons why Jill worked out and ate right, no matter how busy she was.

A year later, her father died of a broken heart. After his wife's death he was overwhelmed with sorrow. He barely ate, didn't talk much and wouldn't leave their Macon, Georgia, home unless he was prodded, pushed and thoroughly convinced that he needed to do so.

Jill didn't like talking about her parents' death. She envied adults who still had their parents. She wished her mother and father could have seen her success. Joel and Clara Atkinson would have been proud of their "baby girl."

Darren and everyone in the restaurant erupted in cheers as the Falcons took the field. Jill cheered too, all the while watching Darren's big hands as he clapped. It felt very warm in there as she let her imagination run riot about those hands touching her in secret places, making her scream in delight. She couldn't remember the last time she had been so sexually charged. But that's what looking at Darren did to her. Maybe it was the fantasy of being rescued and knowing that Darren could do that—and had done it—that turned her on. A man hadn't taken care of Jill since her father. Most of the time, when someone met Jill Atkinson, romance, love, and femininity weren't things they thought about. It was always a job interview, an investment opportunity, a corporate partnership. But she was ready for more than that. She wanted a personal partnership, a love story where she played the central part. If the universe smiled on her and made Darren that man, she would be happy. But she knew that if she didn't hurry and tell him the truth, the universe would make her pay for her lie.

"You're kind of quiet over there," Darren said, glancing at her.

"I was just thinking about something."

"Care to share?"

Jill took her bottom lip between her teeth. "It was work related. Sometimes I have a one track mind."

"I do too," he said. Without warning, but much to Jill's delight, Darren leaned over the table, lifted her chin and planted the softest of kisses on her lips.

"I've wanted to do that since I met you," he said, not letting her chin go.

Heat rose to Jill's cheeks because she had wanted him to do it from the first time she looked into his eyes. "Can we do it again?" she said. "Just to make sure we really liked it."

This time, Jill took the lead in the kiss, pressing her lips against his and opening her mouth slightly as if inviting his tongue to visit and explore. Darren took the invitation, slipping his tongue inside, tracing the inside of her mouth as if he were Christopher Columbus exploring the new world.

When the crowd erupted into another round of boisterous cheers, they broke off their kiss and watched Michael Vick run 20 yards for a touchdown. Jill stood up and cheered, but her happiness had less to do with Vick and more to do with the kiss she and Darren had shared.

By the time the Falcons won the game, 34 to 13, Jill and Darren were stuffed with wings. They decided to take a walk downtown while they waited for traffic to clear out. In the slight breeze, which blew across them as they headed down Peachtree Street, Jill shivered and wishing she'd dressed a little warmer.

Darren draped his leather bomber jacket over her shoulders. "Better?"

"Much. Thank you."

"I like you, Jill. You're a breath of fresh air, you know."

"I like you too, Darren." She felt like a school girl flirting with her high school crush.

Darren reached out and took her hand. "Man, I wish I could get my hands on some playoff tickets. The Dome is going to rock."

"I know. Atlanta hasn't had home field advantage in the playoffs in a long time. The fans are really going to come in big time when the other team is on third down, especially if it's a passing situation," she said. "Maybe I can score us some tickets."

"Really? Are you connected or something? Those tickets are going to be hard to come by."

Since she knew someone in the Falcons front office, Jill could get the tickets just as easily as taking her next breath. But they couldn't be her normal luxury suite tickets. However, they damned sure couldn't be some nosebleed tickets either because she needed to be up close and personal with the Falcons en route to the Super Bowl.

"My company did some work with the Falcons and we did such a good job they are indebted to us,"

Jill said, then quickly covered with. "If I ask my boss nicely, I'm sure he'll get me a set of tickets."

"Either you're one of DVA's best employees or your boss doesn't like the Falcons."

Jill smiled nervously. "He's not a big football fan. He's into the Braves."

"I can't get with baseball. The games are too long and the beer is too high," he said with a hardy laugh.

"Well," she said as they reached Spring Street, "I guess we should head back. Unfortunately, I have some reports to go over before Monday morning. The holidays are truly over."

"Yeah, but meeting you was definitely a belated Christmas present," he said, and then kissed her hand.

Jill's face flushed. "Yes, it was for me too."

Once they made it back to their cars, Darren invited her out for lunch on Friday since he would be downtown. Jill accepted, but she knew she there was no way he could enter DVA's building. For the first time since she started the company, she regretted placing a huge portrait of herself in the lobby. There would be no way to explain that away. It was coming down first thing Monday morning.

"Why don't I meet you at the restaurant? The Three Dollar Café has a wonderful lunch menu."

"That works for me, but is there a reason you don't want me to come by your office?" he asked. "Your man works there, doesn't he?"

"Uh, I'm a very private person and the last thing I want is to be fodder for office gossip. That's all," she said. "And I think I already told you that I wasn't seeing anyone."

Darren's words about lies were ringing in her ears. This was her lie to cover the initial one. Pretty soon things were going to snowball, but she was having so much fun with Darren that she didn't want things to change just yet. Maybe they won't, she hoped.

If I tell him the truth now things shouldn't be that bad. I just don't want to mess this up before we even have a chance to get started.

During the drive home, Jill fought with herself about telling Darren the truth.

CHAPTER FIVE

The next day, Darren headed to the fire station where he would spend the next four days. He hoped for peace and quiet, but he didn't dare say that out loud. The fireman's credo was to hope for the best but expect the worse.

As he pulled a breakfast pizza from the microwave, Cleveland walked into the kitchenette area.

"Smells like breakfast is done," he said as he swiped a piece of his brother's pie.

"Help yourself," Darren said sarcastically.

"So, how did your date go? And don't think I didn't see y'all kissing like teenagers. I ought to call Ma and tell her you were acting like you didn't have any home training."

"I like Jill. She's a nice woman. And leave Ma out of this."

"But what do you really know about Jill, other than the fact that you like to kiss her?"

"We just met and I haven't proposed yet. I'm going to get to know everything about her."

Cleveland took a big bite of the pizza slice. "I know I'm the little brother, but I don't want you to be hurt."

"Didn't Momma tell you not to talk with your mouth full?"

Cleveland swallowed. "I said, I don't want to see you hurt again. If Rita wasn't a cop I would have…Never mind. She screwed with your mind and I don't want to see that happen again."

"It won't. Marrying her was a mistake, but I'm not going to let what happened in the past continue to wreck my future. I'm finally ready to let someone in again. And Jill and I are having fun together, not trying to rush off to the justice of the peace like I did with Rita."

"Jill better be on the up and up," Cleveland said as he snatched another slice of Darren's pizza.

"Touch my food again and…" Before he could finish his threat, the alarm sounded. The dispatcher's voice sounded through the PA system, alerting them of a three alarm house fire on Lenox Road. Cleveland and Darren hopped into action, forgetting their argument about the pizza.

Dressing with lighting speed in their turnout clothes, they dashed to the truck. Since they were shorthanded on the morning shift, Darren rode on the truck rather than in his battalion chief car. Riding with his men also gave him a chance to connect with them and view how city budget cuts were affecting them. When he sent his report to the fire chief, he prayed the city council and mayor would do something about it.

The house was fully engulfed when they arrived. Orange flames reached for the heavens and black smoke unfurled from the roof. Two companies were already on the scene, dousing the burning house with water.

Darren pointed his men in the direction of hot spots.

"There's somebody in there!" an elderly woman across the street exclaimed.

Pressing the button on his radio, Darren alerted the firefighters that someone might be inside. He pushed his oxygen apparatus in his mouth and rushed down to the scene.

Before he made it to the house, the air was shattered with the thudding of an explosion from the rear of the house. Lugging his oxygen tank and screaming into the radio, Darren ran to the spot where he heard the explosion.

"Is everyone all right? What was that?"

"Captain, Alexander is down," the firefighter relayed.

Darren ran like a gazelle to his brother's side. He spit his apparatus out of his mouth. "What happened?"

"The pressure inside the house caused an explosion and he was hit with some flying debris," one of the firefighters said.

Darren watched as the EMTs removed Cleveland's helmet. Fear flowed through his veins like blood. He couldn't lose his brother. Darren was taken back to the day his father died. It was the one time he'd let him and Cleveland ride along. An old plant near downtown had caught fire and no one knew that there were combustible chemicals left inside. As soon as Walter Alexander walked into the building, it exploded, the force blowing out the windows. No one survived. Seeing his father's lifeless body was an image Darren had never forgotten.

Looking at his motionless brother brought back those memories. Moisture pooled in his eyes. Cleveland couldn't die, not in front of him like this, not when they'd been arguing just minutes earlier. This wasn't right. Cleveland was too young. Darren kneeled over his brother.

"Captain," one of the firefighters said. "You all right?"

"How is he?" Darren asked once he found his voice.

Cleveland began to cough and try to get up, but the EMT forced him to lie still.

"Cleveland, be still." Darren turned to the technician. "Is he all right?"

"We're going to have to get him to the hospital and make sure there was no damage to his spine."

Darren nodded. "I'm going to ride with him." Before helping the EMTs load his brother on the ambulance, Darren turned control of the scene over to his second in command. As the technicians stabilized Cleveland, Darren held and squeezed his hand. He was relieved that he didn't have to call his mother and tell her that she'd lost another Alexander man to fire service. It was her worst nightmare.

When they got to the hospital, Cleveland was rushed into the emergency room and Darren had to wait. He hated hospital waiting rooms. The smell of sickness hung in the air and death seemed to be waiting around every corner.

Exhaling loudly, Darren sat down and waited for news. *Dear God, please don't let my brother die.*

Two hours later, a doctor walked in the waiting room. "Is anyone from the Alexander family here?"

Darren stood up. "Yeah, that's me."

"Cleveland is going to be fine. There was some swelling to his spine, but that should go down with medication and time."

"So where is he now?"

"We're going to move him to the intensive care unit on the fourth floor. You can see him in a little bit."

Darren reached out and shook the doctor's hand. "Thank you, thank you so much."

"He's a fighter. He didn't want to go."

Darren smiled. He knew his father had had a hand in that. Heaven wasn't ready for two Alexanders.

❧❧

Across town, Jill sat in her office doing something no one had ever seen her do. She was staring out of her wide window overlooking the city. Her mind wasn't on selling computer systems or investments in smaller companies that would increase her profit margins tenfold. Darren filled her thoughts. She licked her lips, hoping to taste him again even though their kiss was twenty-four hours old.

"Jill, Malik said he has an appointment with you," her assistant, Madison, said over her phone system.

"All right, send him in." Jill straightened her jacket and sat up in the chair.

Malik bounded through the door and placed a thick file on her desk. "Here are the new marketing plans for every department. Thank you for the tickets yesterday, too. I still can't understand why you did it."

Jill smiled. "Because."

Malik shrugged his shoulders. "You women kill me."

"Meaning what? I met a guy that I like, and we had a great time. I didn't want to come off as a being all high and mighty, trying to show him my entire hand at one time."

Malik sat down in the chair across from Jill's mahogany desk. "Ready for some real irony? I'm about to give you some love advice. You have to be honest with this brother. If you like him and want this thing to go somewhere, then you can't hide this from him. You are CEO of one of Atlanta's most successful companies. Your face has been on the cover of national magazines. How are you going to explain that away?"

"I have a twin sister?"

"Be serious," Malik said. "Jill, you beat me over the head about being honest. I really can't believe you're doing this."

"When the time is right, I'm going to tell him. Malik, you don't have a clue how hard it is to meet someone and connect with them. Men see me in two ways, either as a meal ticket or a business opportunity. But when Darren looks at me, he sees a woman."

Malik stroked Jill's hand as a brother would a sister. "Welcome to my life. I know you thought I was a dog for no reason, but the women I dated before Shari thought I was their one way ticket to Easy Street. That's one of the things that turned me on about my wife. She didn't want anything but my love. She didn't ask me how much money I had in the bank or what my credit score was."

Jill stood up and leaned against the window. "But my salary and net worth are printed in all of those magazines. Even if it only lasts for a few weeks, I want Darren to keep looking at me like a woman meant to be desired and loved."

"I hear what you're saying, but if I learned one thing from Greta DeVine, it's that it doesn't pay to lie."

Jill pursed her lips as if she had sipped rancid milk. "Please don't compare me to that psychopath. I'm not trying to ruin…" The chirp of her cell phone interrupted their conversation.

"This is Jill," she said.

"I'm sorry to bother you in the middle of the day," Darren said. "I just wanted to tell you that my brother is in the hospital."

"Oh my God, what happened?" Jill asked.

"We were on a fire, and there was an explosion. They're getting him set up in a room."

"What hospital is he in? Do you want me to come over and sit with you?"

"No, no, you're at work and I can't ask you to do that. I need to call my mother and let her know what's going on but I just can't talk to her right now. I don't want to ruin your day with my problems, but I felt like if I told someone what happened it would make it easier to tell my mom."

"No, it's okay. I'm glad you called. How can I help?"

"Talking to me right now is enough. Did I tell you I hate hospitals? You can just feel death waiting for people."

Jill leaned back in her seat, tears forming in her eyes as she listened to Darren talk.

"My mother really tried to talk us out of going into the fire department, but we felt like it was the best way to honor our father."

"Did the doctors say how Cleveland is doing?" Jill asked.

"He has some swelling on his spinal cord, but the doctors said with time and medication, he'll be fine."

"That's a blessing," she said. "I will definitely keep your brother in my prayers."

"Thank you and thanks for listening to me. You'd better get back to work."

"Darren, if you need to talk, call me."

"Thanks. I'll probably be at Piedmont all night or at least until my mom gets here. Then I have to go back to the station house."

"Have you eaten? I can bring you something to eat. You're not that far from me. You're going to need your strength for your brother and your mother."

"You're starting to sound too good to be true," he said.

Her desk phone buzzed. "Jill, Mr. Covington is on line one."

Jill gritted her teeth. She didn't want to hang up on Darren, but she had been waiting on this call all day. "I-I have to go," she said. "But I'll call you later."

"All right," he said. "Thanks for listening."

Jill hated hanging up on Darren. She was glad he thought enough of her to call but it was definitely making lying to him harder.

She reached down and picked up the phone. "This is Jill."

She half-heartedly listened to Mr. Covington talk to her about what a great investment DVA would be making if she bought 45 percent of his company's stock. He droned on and on about Bluetooth technology and hand-held computers changing the way Americans work. Jill sighed. His company would be a big risk, but if DVA didn't get in on the ground floor of this new trend, who knew what would happen in the future?

"Mr. Covington, I'm not saying yes and I'm not saying no. I need a comprehensive study on the growth of the technology and independent verification that checks out. I want more than 45 percent, too. If this is the next wave of computer technology, I want it to be a part of DVA."

"Jill, that sounds like a takeover to me," he said.

"No, not at all. It's more of a branding thing. DVA is known globally. You're not. I'm willing to brand your product and still let you have creative control. The only difference will be your marketing muscle, distribution capabilities and production qualities. Tell me, how many people can you reach now?"

"Well, uh, maybe a few thousand, but a capital invest…"

"Would be very risky. Look, I haven't even agreed to invest, but if I do, those are my terms. Take it or leave it."

Silence greeted her. Jill continued. "If we move forward, you'd be a subsidiary of DVA. And if it makes you feel better, you can keep your CEO title."

"I'll get the company statements to you in the morning."

When Jill hung up, she buzzed Madison, informing her that she'd be taking the rest of the day off. Something inside her told her she should go to Darren.

"Is everything okay?"

"Yes," Jill said. She was sure it was shocking for her employees to see her leave early. Usually the last person to leave the office, she didn't just burn the midnight oil; she drank it like nectar.

Her first stop was a florist shop on Peachtree Street, where she picked up a get well basket filled with daisies, sunflowers and tulips, along with two Mylar balloons, one with a fire truck and a Dalmatian on it and a silver one that read Get Well Soon. Next she stopped by Twist Restaurant, a new spot in downtown that featured soul food and vegetarian cuisine, where she ordered fried chicken, collard greens, macaroni and cheese and a slice of red velvet cake. She hoped Darren was hungry.

Instead of driving to the hospital, which was about a mile or so up the road from her office, Jill opted to take a cab. As the driver fought though lunch hour traffic, she reached into her purse and pulled out a pair of Jackie O type sunglasses and put them on. The last thing she need was to be spotted by a reporter walking into the hospital. She hated the media with a passion. Reporters seemed to relish publishing rumors and innuendo rather than searching for the truth. DVA matters could make a year long series for a serious journalist, but these days the big story seemed to be Jill's lack of a love life. Was she gay? Married in secret? Having an affair with one of her employees, particularly Malik Greene? Jill hadn't granted an interview since the *Essence* story that Shari had written and planned to do no more unless Shari was the interviewer.

Jill paid the driver and hopped out of the cab when it stopped in front of the hospital. As she strode inside, she felt nervous. This wasn't like walking into a business meeting. What if Darren didn't want her there? What if his brother had taken a turn for the worse? What if she were intruding? She'd only known him a few days.

Calm down, Jill, she chided silently as she approached the information desk.

She placed her hand on the edge of the desk, then told the attendant that she was looking for Cleveland Alexander's room.

"He's on the fourth floor in 423," the clerk said after typing his name in the computer.

Jill smiled and clutched her basket a little tighter as she went to the elevator. She closed her eyes as she boarded with a group of visitors. Everyone was carrying flowers, food or something else to make their loved one's stay in the hospital better.

The doors slid open when she reached the fourth floor. In the waiting room she spotted Darren sprawled out in a chair underneath an overhead TV. Slowly, with hesitant steps, she walked over to him. She hoped she would be welcomed.

When he heard the tap-tap of her heels, Darren sat up and smiled at her. "Jill, what are you doing here?" Rising to his feet, he took the basket from her hands.

"I didn't like the sound of your voice on the phone," she said. "So, I decided to see if you were all right."

Darren set the basket on an empty chair near him, and then turned to Jill. She held out the bag from Twist.

"The basket is for Cleveland but the food is for you. How is he?" she asked as she sat down.

"I just saw him a little while ago. Still heavily medicated, going in and out of consciousness." Darren opened the bag of food. "This is on time, Jill. I had already made the decision not to eat in the hospital cafeteria."

Jill watched him as he dug into the food. Obviously the man liked fried chicken, and she liked watching him work on the chicken leg. She was mesmerized by him; it was as if his eating hypnotized her, making her wonder how those lips would feel on her most tender spot, his tongue teasing her throbbing feminine desire. She inhaled sharply at the thought of it, his head between her thighs, and the roughness of his hair rubbing against her smooth skin.

"Jill," Darren said, his voice filled with concern. "Are you all right?"

"Wh-what?" she said, flustered by her thoughts.

"You were breathing kind of funny, like you were having an asthma attack."

She stood up to hide her embarrassment. She was having an attack of lust. "I'm fine," she replied, unable to face him.

He placed his hand on her shoulder. "If hospitals affect you this much, you can leave, and I won't feel bad. I appreciate you coming."

She spun around, her forehead brushing against his lips. The slight touch sent a tingling sensation down her spine. "I'm okay."

Darren took her hand and helped her into a chair. "This was really nice of you," he said.

"I try to do nice things, especially if I like someone." *Did those corny words just come out of my mouth? I sound like a desperate troll!*

"I like you too, Jill. I can tell already that you're special," he said. "It's hard to find honest and considerate people to deal with these days."

The smart thing to do right then would have been to tell him the truth. She should have told him that she wasn't exactly honest with him about what she did at DVA, that she wasn't in marketing, that she was the CEO. But Jill was silent. Words, which had never failed her before, weren't her friend. She opened her mouth but nothing came out. And to make matters worse, Darren gently kissed her bottom lip, making her nearly swoon.

"Thank you for lunch and for being here."

"You're welcome," she replied with a smile on her face. "I think I'd better head back to the office."

"Not just yet. I can't eat that hunk of red velvet cake by myself."

Darren and Jill shared the moist cake and she crumbled inside as she thought about how she was fooling him.

When Jill left the hospital, she headed to Lenox Square for some retail therapy. As she shopped, looking at the latest in *haute couture*, she wondered how Darren would react to her if she told him that she wasn't a marketing researcher. Maybe he would understand. After all, it wasn't a huge lie. It wasn't as if she were hiding a husband and three children or the fact that she was a transvestite. But that didn't matter. A lie was a lie and Darren had said that was the one thing he couldn't handle. But Jill wasn't ready to risk her budding relationship. Not just yet.

CHAPTER SIX

Cleveland Alexander was the talk of Piedmont Hospital. Not only was he in the hospital for a mere three days, but he walked out when he was released, despite the fact that the nurse wanted to wheel him out.

"I don't care about hospital policy, I'm walking," he'd told the short brunette before kissing her on the cheek flirtatiously.

Darren and his mother, Margaret, watched him with tears in their eyes.

"He looks so much like your father," she whispered in Darren's ear.

"Tell me about it. Acts like Pops too."

"Y'all gonna talk about me or help me in the car?" Cleveland asked jovially.

Darren took his brother's arm and helped him into the car. "Remember, the doctor said you have to take it easy. No running and jumping."

"That's right," Margaret said as she slid in the back of Darren's SUV. "That's why I'm staying with you until your rehabilitation is over."

"Ma, no, I'll be fine."

Darren playfully slapped his brother's cheek. "Shut up, baby boy. Ma is staying and there isn't anything you can do about it."

Cleveland glared at his brother, and then blurted out, "Ma, Darren has a girlfriend. She even sent me flowers."

Margaret kicked the back of Darren's seat. "You've been holding out on me, Son? Why haven't I heard about this or met her?"

"First of all, she isn't my girlfriend, but I am rather fond of Jill. She's a nice lady and we're just getting to know each other."

"The other one was nice too, at first anyway. Look how that turned out. Women nowadays want to act like men, so focused on a career and don't care nothing about starting a family or anything like that. You'd better make sure this one is nothing like that other one you married. I'm not going to take too kindly to another woman trying to play you for a fool. If I could have gotten my hands on that other heffa…"

"Ma, we just met."

"He saved her." Cleveland ribbed. "She was in a fire New Year's Eve and since then, he's been sniffing around her like she's just hot potatoes."

"Well, she'd better not break your heart, or she's going to have to answer to me."

Darren drove off and turned his music up to drown out the same tired conversation he and his family had been having since Rita's abortion. His mother was never going forgive Rita for what she did. Darren wouldn't exactly say that he had forgiven her, but it was time to move on. He couldn't be bitter, distrust every woman he came across because of what one had done.

And though he loved his mother dearly, Darren was happy to drop her off at Cleveland's townhouse in Lithonia. He was glad that his mother was there for Cleveland and ecstatic that she wasn't staying with him.

"Don't let that woman trick you," Margaret warned as she got out of the car.

"Ma, I love you, but I think I'm old enough to take care of myself." He kissed her on the forehead and got back into his truck.

Darren had to force himself not to peel out of the driveway. After all, he did have a date to prepare for, and he wasn't going to let his mother's notions put a damper on his evening with Jill.

❧❧

"Shari, thank you for coming here with me," Jill said as she and her friend walked into Neiman Marcus.

"I don't know why you need me to help you get ready for tonight. You have impeccable style."

Jill lifted her eyebrow. "Yeah, if I'm going to a business meeting. I want tonight to be special."

"I hate to beat a dead horse, but have you told him that you are DVA and not just an employee?" Shari asked as she flipped through the latest Carmen Marc Valvo dresses.

"With everything that happened with his brother, the time was just never right."

"And every day that you spend with him is going to make it harder and harder to tell him the truth." Shari placed her hand on her hip. "I want you to be happy, Jill, I really do. But you can't get happiness from a lie, no matter how hard you try."

Jill picked up a black and white Marc Jacobs dress with a flirty hemline, quarter-length sleeves and a red stripe running down the center. She had the perfect shoes to match it.

"Jill, you're going to show up for a date with this man in a $500 dress and expect him to buy that you are a marketing researcher?" Shari said, shaking her head as Jill picked up the dress.

"Men don't notice stuff like that."

"But they read the business section of the *Atlanta Journal-Constitution*."

Jill sighed heavily. The paper had just written a feature on DVA. Though she hadn't seen it, she was sure there was a photo of her included with the article. "One more date, Shari, and I will tell him the truth. But tonight, I want to feel like a real woman, a woman a man is attracted to because she's beautiful and fun. Not because he wants to make a business deal or wants me to further his career."

"I understand, but if you feel like Darren is going to be a leach, why even deal with him?"

That was a question she didn't have an answer for. Honestly, she didn't feel that way about him, but it was impossible to know what someone was going to do before getting to know them. Jill just wanted to get to know Darren without the trappings that went along with being Jill Atkinson. She'd had men romance her and slip her a business plan all at the same time. She didn't think Darren was like that, but before she told him the truth, she had to be sure. In a way, she was approaching the romance the same way she approached a business deal. Before she invested her total emotions, she was going to get all of the information she needed. There was nothing wrong with that, at least that's what she thought.

After shopping with Shari, Jill headed home to relax and prepare for her date. She popped in a John Coltrane greatest hits CD, lit a gardenia-scented candle and drew a warm bath. Easing into the water, she imagined Darren sitting across from her, drawing her into his arms. Did he have a hairy chest, she wondered. If he did, she'd twirl his damp curly hair around her finger as she brushed her lips against his. Darren would slip his hands underneath her thighs, spreading her legs apart and stroking her softness with his thumb. Her body throbbed at the thought. Jill couldn't remember the last time her body had been caressed and touched by a man. She'd become skilled in the art of pleasing herself, so skilled that without realizing it, Jill inserted her finger in the realm of her sexual heat, stroking her pleasure and making her legs shiver with delight. Though it was her own hand bringing her to the brink of an orgasm, in her mind it was all Darren. Would he use his tongue or his finger to warm her up? Maybe both as he pushed her back against the wall of the tub, diving into her face first, tasting her sticky sweetness. She rubbed herself harder and faster. Her nipples hardened as she took her free hand and ran it across them. Every nerve in her body stood on end as she reached her climax. And when she opened her eyes, part of her expected to see Darren there. All she saw was her satisfied reflection in the mirror.

Quickly, she washed her sensitive body, got out, and smoothed an apple-scented lotion over her damp body. It was nearly time to meet Darren, though she wasn't sure if she would be able to look at him without blushing this evening. They had made plans to meet for lunch, but since Cleveland was being released from the hospital, they had turned their date into dinner and a movie. She didn't care what they went to see as long as she was with Darren. Jill was falling for him hard and fast.

By the time Jill had dressed in her new Marc Jacobs dress, bumped the ends of her hair and wrapped herself in a full-length leather coat, she was ready for Darren. Instead of going to the Three Dollar Café, they had decided to go back to Red and sample their dinner menu before going to Phipps Plaza to catch a late movie.

Fortunately, Red was still a low key spot. The last thing Jill needed was a business associate to walk up on her and blow her cover before she told Darren herself.

Taking a cab to the restaurant, she ended up stuck in a traffic jam and she was late. If she hadn't had on a pair of three-inch high heels, she would have walked the four and a half blocks to the restaurant. When she arrived, Darren was standing out front looking at his watch. Her heart skipped a beat at the sight of him. She wondered how many women he'd had to fight off standing there looking like at Twenty-first Century Billy Dee Williams in his navy blue slacks, cream turtle neck and brown leather bomber jacket. She hopped out of the cab almost before it came to a complete stop.

"Darren," she said as she strode over to him. "Sorry I'm late. You know how traffic can be."

He leaned in and kissed her on the cheek. "Could have been avoided if you'd allowed me to pick you up. They're holding our reservation."

The couple scurried into the restaurant, and the maitre d' led them to a secluded table in the back of the restaurant with a bird's eye view of the dance floor, bar, and front door. Out of habit, Jill reached into her purse and tipped the man twenty. Darren raised his eyebrow but didn't say anything.

"This is nice," Jill said as the maitre d' started to pull her chair out.

"Thanks, guy, but I got it from here," Darren said possessively.

"All right," the man replied. "I'll send a waitress over right away."

Jill sat down, smiling at Darren. "You wanted him to leave, didn't you?"

He answered by gently kissing her lips. "I didn't need an audience for that."

Warm from the burning desire inside her, Jill took a sip of the water.

"How's your brother?" she asked when she found her voice.

"Great, but a little upset that Ma has moved in with him for a while. He values his independence."

"Most people do."

Darren shook his head from side to side. "Cleveland was potty trained at two because he didn't want anyone changing his diaper."

"Are you serious?"

Darren chuckled. "No, but he was two and a half. I'm just glad his injury wasn't more serious. I wish the city would realize that we need more money in the fire department budget. Maybe the right equipment could have saved him from this injury. Sometimes I wish the city would let some corporation underwrite us so we could get what we need."

"But what happens when that corporation tries to tell you what fires to fight?" she asked, thinking that some businesses would have the fire department running the hose at company picnics.

"I know it isn't realistic, but our budget keeps shrinking and shrinking."

"And what's the money going to? Definitely not the roads," Jill said, thinking about the huge pothole she'd hit the other day, which had bent the rim of her tire.

Darren brought her hand to his lips. "That's why I enjoy spending time with you. You're just as cynical as I am."

Did this man understand what the feel of his lips against her skin was doing to her? Jill tried to downplay the rage of lust that came over her.

Just then, a waitress, dressed in a red uniform, walked over to them to take their cocktail and dinner orders.

When the waitress left, Darren inched closer. "So, Jill, tell me more about yourself."

"What do you want to know?"

"Everything."

She smiled nervously. What should she say? "There's really nothing to tell. I'm a simple person."

"That I find hard to believe. Where did you grow up?"

"Macon. Told you, simple."

"I never would have guessed that. I thought you were from up north or something. How did you get into marketing?"

"It was something that kind of fell into my lap. I really wanted to do something with computers and marketing so DVA was a natural fit. Computer consulting, you know."

"I knew it had something to do with computers. I'll never forget the way you gripped that laptop the night of the fire."

She blushed as she thought back to the night that had changed her life. "Well, all of my important files were on that laptop and I couldn't let it go up in flames."

"Did your place get damaged any? What floor do you live on?"

"Uh, no, no damage. I live on one of the higher floors."

Darren reached out and grabbed her hand. "You can tell me where you live. I'm not a stalker or a killer."

"I know that. All right, I live in the penthouse on the fifteenth floor."

Darren's face registered shock. "Maybe I should get into marketing if you can afford the rent on that."

"Actually, I own it," she said in a voice barely above a whisper.

Still looking surprised, he didn't say anything and Jill offered no explanation. She prayed that he wouldn't question her on how she could afford such a lavish home.

Jill gripped the bottom of her water glass and tried to think of something to say to change the subject. Luckily, the waitress returned to the table with their drinks.

"You orders will be out shortly. Can I get you anything else?"

"I'm fine," Jill said as she turned to Darren.

The waitress looked at Darren. "And you, sir?"

"Everything is fine, thank you."

When the waitress left, Jill started talking about the Atlanta Falcons and their playoff chances.

"As long as Vick stays healthy, we should make it to the Super Bowl," Darren said. "But I'm not too concerned about the Falcons right now."

"Really?"

"What are you hiding, Jill?"

"Hiding? What do you mean?"

"I feel like you're holding something back. Or are you afraid to let me get to know you?"

This is it, Jill, just tell him the truth. "I am afraid," she said. "Don't get me wrong, I'm not saying you're a bad guy, I think the opposite, but when you've been burned, it's a little difficult to jump back in the fire."

Darren nodded, showing his understanding. "Even though I know how you feel, you can't judge everybody by a sorry standard. Whatever that other man did to you, know that I won't."

"Is that a promise?"

Darren made the Boy Scout sign. "I never make a promise that I don't intend to keep."

Tell him, her conscience screamed. *You know he doesn't want anything from you. You have no reason to keep up this lie.* Jill formed her mouth to say the truth but the words wouldn't come out.

"I'm going to hold you to that," she finally said.

Darren reached across the table and stroked the back of her soft hand. "You don't have to be afraid with me. After my divorce, I never thought I would let another woman get close to me again. I thought all women were evil, but meeting you blew that theory out the water."

She blushed like a school girl being told by the high school quarterback that she was pretty.

"But," Darren said, "you have to let me in. I want to get to know you from the inside out."

"Okay," she said. "Because I want to get to know you, too. So far, so good."

When dinner arrived, they ate in a comfortable silence, stealing glances at each other and sharing warm smiles. After they ate, Darren suggested that they go dancing instead of going to the movies.

"All right, but where?" Jill asked, hoping to stay below the radar.

"Do you like the blues?"

"How can we dance to the blues?"

Darren stepped closer to her, placing his lips close to her ear. "Slow and close. Come on, I know the perfect place off the beaten path."

"All right," she said, ready to feel Darren's body pressed against her love-starved one.

Darren led Jill to his Nissan 300X, opened the passenger side door for her and held it open until she slid into the sports car. "Nice," Jill said. "I guess you like speed, huh?"

"Occasionally. Truthfully, this is my date car. You know what they say about women and sports cars."

Jill smiled. "Well, it's not the car; it's the man driving it."

Darren leaned back in his seat. "So, what do you think about the man driving this car?"

"He definitely makes the car."

Darren peeled out of the parking lot and headed out Interstate 85 South to a small blues club near the airport.

"What is this place?" she asked. It actually put her in the mind of the juke joint in the movie *The Color Purple*.

"A little hole in the wall with none of those pretentious folk from downtown or overpriced drinks. Just music, a dance floor, and dim lighting." Darren pulled into a parking spot, hopped out of the car and opened the door for Jill.

"Thank you," she said as he took her hand. "You're such a gentleman."

"I try."

They walked up to the front door of the club and there was no long line as there often was at many of the clubs in midtown where people went just to be seen. No one paid attention to them as they entered and took a seat at one of the wooden tables in the back. They were just two more in the crowd. The lighting inside was almost non-existent, a few candles and dim lamps. B.B. King was blaring from the speakers, singing about the missing thrill.

"We didn't come here to sit, did we?" Darren asked as he stood up and extended his hand to her. Closing her fingers around his hand, Jill allowed him to lead her to the middle of the tile dance floor. The song changed to an artist she didn't recognize singing about a wicked woman whose love was so good.

Darren wrapped his arms around her waist and just as he'd promised, pulled her close and danced really slow with her, pushing his pelvis against hers. She felt his arousal as they wound their bodies together in rhythm with the deep bass of the song. Jill nestled her head against his chest. Dancing with him was quite erotic. From the way her body was responding to him with her clothes on, Jill knew he'd make her explode touching her bare skin.

The song ended, but they didn't separate; they danced to their own melody.

"Are people staring at us yet?" she asked.

"Who cares?" His lips brushed against her neck as he spoke.

Jill couldn't tell if he was doing it deliberately or not, but she sure enjoyed it. "This is nice."

"Yeah, and you feel so good. What are you wearing? It's intoxicating."

"I could say the same thing about you," she replied. The truth was, being so close to Darren made her forget the name of the jasmine-scented perfume she was wearing.

Another slow, bluesy song started playing, and a few other couples joined then on the floor, but all they could see was each other.

CHAPTER SEVEN

Darren didn't want his night with Jill to end. He wanted to take her home with him and lay her down on his cool cotton sheets, peel her clothes from her body and explore every inch of her with his tongue, then wake up with Jill nestled in his arms, her soft lips grazing his neck. But as the house lights came up in the club, he knew he had to take her home.

"I had a wonderful time tonight," Jill said as they exited the club.

"So did I," he said with a smile on his face. "I'm glad you opened up a little tonight."

Jill cast her eyes down and smiled. "You made it easy to do that. And I don't want you to think that I'm judging you by my past experiences, but it's just hard to…"

Darren didn't let her finish her statement; her lips just looked too delectable not to kiss. He captured her lips and tasted her sweetness. "I'm sorry, I had to do that. It's not that I'm not listening to you, though."

Jill didn't respond immediately. It was as if Darren had kissed all the words away.

"I guess I'd better get you home," he said.

"Yeah, it's getting late."

Darren opened the car door for her, and they stood against the car, eying each other with unspoken desire and longing. "We'd better go home," he said, finally finding his voice. As much as he wanted to take Jill home and make love to her, he knew she wasn't the kind of woman who would give in to lust and hop into bed with a man she barely knew. If she did, he'd be disappointed. Not that he was putting Jill on a pedestal or anything, but she had a certain grace and class that he hadn't seen in a woman in a long time. Many times, women threw themselves at him, offering him sex on demand. That took the fun and mystery out of dating for him. He didn't want a woman who had served more people than an all night diner. He wanted class and grace and he was looking right at it.

"Why don't we get some coffee and dessert before we call it a night," Jill suggested. "Krispy Kreme is open."

Darren grinned broadly. "Now I would have never taken you for the doughnut type."

She pointed to the doughnut shop directly in front of them. "The light is on."

"Then we'd better go before the hot ones are gone." Darren wrapped his arm around her shoulders and led her to the shop. As they walked, the couple jokingly argued about which doughnuts were the best. Darren like the chocolate glazed with sprinkles on special occasions and Jill was an original glazed girl all the way.

"I guess we lucked up," he said, holding the door open for her. "Now I'll have you all to myself and hot doughnuts to boot."

While they sat at the bar and waited for the clerk to return from the back with fresh doughnuts, Darren clasped Jill's hand, forcing her to face him on the stool. "You don't want this night to end any more than I do," he said.

"Maybe not. Could it be that I just like spending time with you?"

"I hope so because you can expect to see a lot more of me." He brought Jill's hand to his lips and placed a butterfly kiss on it.

"Aww!" the counterwoman said as she approached the couple. "That is so sweet. What can I get for y'all?"

"Two glazed and two coffees," Darren said. Jill nodded her approval.

The woman stared at Jill, narrowing her eyes as if she knew her. Jill turned her head to the side.

"Someone you went to high school with?" Darren whispered as the counterwoman moved away.

"What?"

"She was looking at you as if she knew you, and you turned away from her as if you didn't want to be recognized."

Jill laughed hollowly. "I don't…I had something in my eye. Besides, she doesn't look that far removed from high school herself."

He eyed her suspiciously as the woman placed the doughnuts and coffee in front of them.

"Have I seen you somewhere before?" she asked Jill.

"I don't think so," she replied politely.

The woman shrugged it off. "You just look so familiar."

"I get that a lot," Jill said as she gripped her cup of coffee.

"Sugar or cream?" the counterwoman asked.

"Cream, please," Darren said.

Jill sipped her coffee black. "This is good," she said.

Darren stirred his coffee and watched Jill chew her doughnut. Her demeanor changed after the counter-woman inquired about her. *What is she hiding?* He wondered. *Maybe I'm just being too suspicious, but she definitely didn't want that woman to notice her.*

They finished their doughnuts without any further conversation. Jill began to yawn.

"That's our cue to leave," Darren said, putting money on the counter.

"I guess I'm a little drained," she said.

"Coffee gives most people a second wind," Darren said as they stood up.

"I think I've developed a resistance to caffeine. When I was a freshman at Spelman, I pulled too many all nighters with pots of coffee."

"I can see you now, fresh-faced college student up to her ears in notes and books and shaking from too much coffee."

"That was me," she said as they walked out the door. "Sometimes I'd go a few days without sleeping."

"It's always been all work and no play for you, huh?"

She shrugged her shoulders. "I guess I didn't have a suitable playmate."

"Has that changed?" he asked as he opened the car door for her.

"I certainly hope so."

❧❧

When Darren pulled up to Jill's building, she gave him a quick kiss on the cheek and told him what a wonderful time she'd had and prayed that he wouldn't follow her inside. She was afraid that she would invite him in and they'd end up in bed. But Darren was too much of a gentleman to let her walk inside alone, even though the building had a security guard and there was an electronic key required for entry.

"I can't let you walk up there alone this time of night. I'll just walk you to the door." Darren pulled into a visitor parking spot.

When he opened the car door for her and she stood up, their lips brushed. She instantly pulled back because she wasn't sure she would have the will power to stop the kiss if it went too far.

"Thank you for a wonderful evening," she said breathlessly. "We'll have to do it again soon."

"We certainly will," he said before giving her a quick peck on the cheek.

Her breath caught in her chest as his lips touched her skin. She wanted that man to wrap his arms around her and hold her until the sun and the stars blurred together and there was no difference between day and night.

"I'll call you tomorrow," he said, then turned and headed for his car.

Jill waved to him as he drove down the street. Part of her wished he had asked to come inside, but at the same time, she was relieved that he hadn't. There was no telling what might have happened.

She'd dodged more than one bullet tonight. The woman at the doughnut shop had probably seen Jill's picture countless times and read all about her in *Essence* and the *Atlanta Journal-Constitution*. The next time someone noticed her, she might not be so lucky. What if some of the students that she'd spoken to at Spelman had spotted her out with Darren and put her on blast? Or what if a business associate had seen her? Jill was glad Darren liked to go to places off the beaten path, but in Atlanta, it was only a matter of time before you saw someone who knew you. And for Jill, everybody knew her.

Walking into the building, Jill knew that it wasn't going to be long before she'd have to come clean about everything. The longer she put it off, the more she'd look like a liar in Darren's eyes. *Just a little more time. I need a little more time to make sure he is as genuine as he seems,* she thought.

As she headed upstairs, Jill prayed that Darren was the real thing.

❧❧

The next morning, Jill did something she hadn't done in years. She slept until eleven-thirty on a Saturday and awoke only when the phone rang. Rolling over in the bed, she picked up.

"Hello?"

"Jill, it's Malik, I'm at the office and you aren't. I just wanted to make sure that you were all right."

"How many times have you told me that I need a life outside of DVA? As soon as I try to get one, you call and interrupt it," Jill joked.

"Is that dude there?" Malik asked excitedly.

"No! God, Malik, everyone is not like you, always trying to get into a woman's pants."

"You know I'm not like that anymore. I don't even have to try to get into my wife's pants, those are mine."

"What are you doing at the office anyway?" she asked as she sat up in the bed.

"Well, Shari and Evelyn are doing the mother-daughter thing this morning and I had to get out of there. I'm glad that they are getting along these days, but when the Walker women get together there's a lot of laughing and estrogen flowing. It's too cold to play golf, so I decided to do something productive."

"You are so funny. But to answer your original question, I feel better than I have in years. Darren and

I had a wonderful time last night and we're supposed to hook up today for a little something. Maybe catch that movie we missed last night."

"Jill, I'm really glad that you've met someone who makes you this happy. You remind me of what it's like to fall in love again. But why did you all miss the movie last night?"

"We went dancing. Malik, you sound down. Is everything all right with you and Shari?"

"We're fine. All marriages have their ups and downs. I think I'm spending too much time at work for her taste but when she's jet-setting across the country for *Essence*, I don't complain. We'll figure something out," he said with a sigh. "Nothing major. I love my wife and that isn't going to change."

"You and Shari mean too much to each other to let something this petty come between you. Besides, I can cut your hours if you want me to. Learn to delegate your work."

"It hasn't become a problem, yet. But you know how you can feel something building?"

"Yeah," she said, thinking of her own situation. "Malik, how do I tell Darren the truth?"

"What do you mean?"

"I still haven't told him that I'm not a DVA employee that I own the company."

"Are you serious?"

Jill could hear the incredulous tone in his voice.

"You're walking a tight rope with no net," Malik warned. "What are you so afraid of?"

Jill rubbed the back of her neck. "I just don't want to find out that Darren isn't perfect. Malik, you don't know how hard it is to trust someone enough to unwind with them and let them see the real you. I've been there and done that. It didn't turn out too well."

"And you're going to let one bad experience from your past ruin your future?"

"That's not what I'm doing," Jill protested. But she knew in her heart that was specifically what she was doing. Jill wanted to trust Darren, believe everything he said and promised, but the last time she'd done that, she'd almost lost everything. Deep in her heart, she knew Darren was nothing like David. But she'd also thought that she and David would marry. "Malik, I don't know what I should say or how to even bring it up."

"You just speak from your heart. That's how I got my wife."

"I've bent your ear enough," she said. "I'm probably going to do some work from home now since you made me feel so guilty. Can you e-mail me the Bluetooth information I requested?"

"I'm sending it now."

When Jill hung up, she lounged in the bed a little while longer, squeezing her pillow tightly, wishing it were Darren lying in her arms.

Darren sat on the floor in Cleveland's living room waiting for their mother to finish cooking breakfast. He felt thirteen again. When his mother called him at seven-thirty Saturday morning, he knew he'd be spending much of his day in Lithonia.

Cleveland, who was stretched out on the sofa behind him, popped his brother on the back of the head. "How was your date with baby girl last night?"

"It was great. Jill and I stayed out until two-thirty."

Cleveland raised his eyebrows in Charlie Chaplin fashion. "And what were you two doing out that late?"

"I'd like to know that, too," Margaret, their mother, said as she appeared in the living room. "What kind of woman gallivants in the streets like that? There's nothing but trouble out that time of night."

Darren sighed, knowing his mother's heart was in the right place. "Ma, Jill wasn't bouncing from club to club. We were on a date. We had dinner, went to a little blues club, and then had doughnuts."

"Um," she grunted. "Breakfast is ready. You boys want to eat in here or come to the table?"

Darren stood, crossed over to his mother and ushered her to a chair near the coffee table. He kissed her on the forehead. "You cooked, I'll serve you guys."

She smiled at her son and patted his hand. Cleveland rolled his eyes and laughed.

Yeah, Darren thought, *this is fourteen at best.*

Margaret had cooked a smorgasbord of food, scrambled eggs, home fries, blueberry pancakes, grits, oatmeal and fresh-baked cinnamon buns dripping in sweet icing. The aroma in the kitchen took Darren back to the Saturday mornings when his father would come in from his overnight shifts. His mother would greet Walter at the door with a hug, kiss and a bite of one of those sweet buns. She'd let him take one bite and tell him to take a shower so that she could bring him breakfast in bed.

Darren and Cleveland would eat their breakfast in the kitchen while their parents flirted with one another upstairs. Hours later, their parents would come into the living room and shoo the boys outside.

Darren wondered if Jill could cook. He decided that he would call her after breakfast and see if she wanted to catch a matinee and early dinner.

"Damn, Darren, did you have to re-cook the food?" Cleveland bellowed.

"Watch your mouth, Cleveland!" Margaret chastised. "I don't care how old you are, there is certain language you don't use around your mother."

Darren walked into the living room balancing three plates on his arms. "You should just feel lucky that I didn't eat all the cinnamon buns," he said as he set the plates on the coffee table.

"I knew that's what you were in there doing," Cleveland said as he slowly sat up to take his plate. "He's always done that, Ma. Always eating the buns before anyone else."

"Whatever."

Margaret slid her plate to the end of the table. "I want to hear more about this woman."

Darren groaned. "Ma, please don't start this."

Margaret waved her hands. "I know you think I'm meddling, but you're my son and I love you. The last thing I want is to stand by and watch another woman play loose and fast with your heart."

"Jill and I are just getting to know each other. She's not…You want to meet her, don't you?"

"I'm so glad you offered, because I wouldn't want to overstep," Margaret said demurely.

Darren looked at his brother, whose face had turned red from the laughter he was holding back. He'd been set up and had fallen for it, hook, line, and sinker. Margaret caught the look between her sons.

"Have you met her, Cleveland?"

He nodded and mumbled. "Yes, ma'am."

"You don't say. Well, obviously, Darren, you plan to get serious with her because your brother has met her. This is looking like Rita all over again. And it's not you I don't trust, it's the new millennium women I have a problem with. Their career first, family whenever attitude is appalling. 'You can have it all if you know how to balance things.' I worked, but I was also able to cook dinner for the two of you almost every day, be home before you arrived home from school and…"

"We're just friends, I have not asked her to marry me," he said, deciding not to reveal too much to his mother. But he had every intention of getting serious with Jill. Of course he would need time to get to know her better. He wanted to know everything about her, especially all of the areas that she tried to shade from the light.

At first Darren thought she might have been married or living with her boyfriend. But last night she'd proved that wasn't true when she allowed him to take her home.

She could still be lying, his mother's voice screamed in his head. But Jill wouldn't lie to him. *She has no reason to do that,* he surmised. Still, too many questions nagged at him.

"I'll call her and we can have lunch. Then Ma, I don't want to hear anything else about it."

Margaret smiled but didn't reply.

"I've got to see this," Cleveland said. "Where are we going for lunch?"

"Did I invite you?" Darren asked as he tossed a napkin at him.

Margaret stood up and cleared the empty plates. "You boys aren't going to grow up, are you?" she said. "Cleveland, of course you are welcome to come to lunch. We're going to my favorite place too."

"Houston's," Darren and Cleveland said in unison.

"That's right; I want a Biltmore so badly I can taste it and those delicious red cabbages." She closed her eyes and clasped her hands.

Darren knew exactly where they had gotten their love of food from. Their mother. She loved to cook and eat. Growing up, Darren and Cleveland had felt like going to McDonald's was a punishment. Processed food was not their friend when Margaret made the best hamburgers and fresh cut fries a little boy could want. She even made vegetables taste good.

Rita had been a good cook, too. That was one of the reasons Darren had made her his wife. These days men didn't run across too many women who cook.

If Jill can cook, I just might be in trouble, he thought.

"Anyway," Cleveland said. "Why don't we go to a downtown Houston's? The one on Lenox Road has much better service than the one out in the burbs."

"I'll call Jill and find out what she wants to do," Darren said as he took the dishes from his mother's hands and kissed her on the cheek. He placed the dishes in the sink, and then called Jill.

"Hello," she sang into the phone.

"Good morning, gorgeous."

"Darren. How are you?"

"A lot better now that I've heard your voice. I went to sleep a very happy man last night and had some great dreams."

"Really?"

"Oh yeah. You mind hanging out with me again this afternoon?"

"Not at all. I was going to go into the office for a few, so what time are you looking to hook up?"

"On a Saturday? You must want employee of the month or something."

She laughed.

"Listen," Darren said. "My mother is here and we're going to Houston's for lunch. I think Cleveland is driving her crazy and she doesn't want to admit it. She overheard me talking about you and now she's curious. So, she wants to meet you."

"Really?"

"Yeah. We're going to Houston's on Lenox Road around one-thirty. After lunch, you and I can go catch a movie. That is, if you want to. You are under no obligation to let my mother meddle in my life," he said.

"No. I mean, you have to love a man that wants to make his momma happy," Jill said.

"See you then," Darren said.

When he hung up, he knew his mother would like Jill and if she didn't, too bad, because he did.

CHAPTER EIGHT

Jill couldn't remember the last time she'd met a man's mother. Maybe that's why she felt as if she was going to toss her cookies when she hung up with Darren. What if his mother didn't like her? Worse yet, what if his mother recognized her?

She'd heard people talk about the bond between mother and son being like a lifelong umbilical cord. She'd seen friends' marriages end because of a meddlesome mother-in-law. She'd seen guys walk out on their girlfriends because Momma didn't approve. Maybe it was a southern thing. But she knew today she was going to have to impress Mrs. Alexander.

She stood in front of her closet trying to figure out what to wear. She didn't want to be too dressy nor did she want to be too casual. But she had to make a good impression on Darren's mother. She knew from previous conversations with Darren that they were close.

Please don't let her be an Essence *reader,* Jill thought.

Maybe it would serve her right for lying to Darren if his mother knew her true identity.

Finally, Jill decided to wear a pair of black slacks and a lime green turtleneck. She livened up her turtleneck with a rose-colored starburst pendant, pulled her hair back in a ponytail and glossed her lips with a neutral tone lipstick, trying to look like the kind of girlfriend a mother would like. Inside, though, she felt like a fraud.

She didn't know what to expect when she walked into Houston's. What would the implications be if Darren's mother didn't like her? Would that nip her budding relationship? Maybe his mother's approval was that important to him and he needed her to rubber stamp their relationship.

This isn't high school, she thought. *No grown man is going to ask his mother for permission to have a girlfriend.*

Jill sighed as she fumbled with her broach. "Just walk in there and close the deal. How bad can his mother be?" she mumbled as she placed her hand on the restaurant's door knob.

The door swung open. "Welcome to Houston's. Party of one?" the hostess asked.

"I'm meeting someone here, a gentleman and a woman."

"Are you Jill?" she asked.

"H-how did you know?"

The hostess smiled. "Mr. Alexander left your name up here with us. I'll take you to the table."

Jill followed her to a booth near the window, overlooking Lenox Road. When she saw Darren and his mother and brother, she smiled at them warmly, but inside she was screaming. This was a family lunch and her lying ass had no right to be here. Whatever Darren had told his mother about her wasn't true. She wasn't the woman that he'd said she was.

"Jill," Darren said as he rose from his seat and took her hand. "How are you?"

"Good, hello Mrs. Alexander, Cleveland."

Darren and Jill sat across from his mother and brother. "Jill, this is my mother, Margaret. Ma, this is Jill."

Margaret extended her hand. "It's nice to meet you. I'm glad Darren talked you into joining us."

"I was happy to come. This is one of my favorite restaurants."

Cleveland snickered, and then said, "Jill, you look stunning as ever. I still can't figure out why you're hanging out with this clown."

Darren glared at his brother while Margaret smiled at Jill and shook her head.

"These boys have always acted like this, in case you're wondering."

Underneath the table, Darren held Jill's hand, gently stroking it with his thumb.

Margaret leaned back. "So, Darren tells me you're from Macon. I have people down there. Sure we're not related?"

Jill inhaled sharply. "I hope not." Her face flushed and her heart skipped a beat at the thought of being remotely related to Darren. The things she wanted to do to him, with him and to certain parts of his body weren't familial thoughts at all.

"Who are your people?" Margaret asked.

"Ma," Darren said. "This isn't the time to dig up people's family trees."

"Well, if you want to know how good the fruit is, you have to look at the roots," she said so sweetly that it made Jill shiver. Margaret's comment was telling. This woman didn't play and she hid her tenacity behind a candy shell like an M&M.

"My mother was an Adams before she married my father," Jill said.

"Adams? Do you know Flozzie Mae?"

Uh oh, Jill thought.

"Yes ma'am, she was my grandmother. I guess it's true, everybody in Macon knows the Adamses."

"She and my mother were good friends before I was born and my father moved us to Atlanta. She must have been pregnant with your mother when we left. How is she?"

Jill dropped her head slightly. "She passed away three years ago."

Margaret placed her hand to her mouth. "I'm so sorry to hear that. What about your crazy uncle Stewart? Girl, back in the day all of the young girls in Macon wanted him. Every time I would go visit for the summer, he would look better and better."

"But not as good as my dad, right?" Cleveland interjected.

Margaret shot him a silencing glance.

Jill smiled at the thought of her uncle, whom the family called Sweets. The legend was that Sweets could talk a drowning woman into buying a glass of water if he wanted to.

"Uncle Sweets is just fine. He retired to Florida and I don't know how many times he's been married."

Margaret and Jill laughed and talked as if they were old friends, but the question came.

"So, what do you do for a living?"

Darren, who had been silent while the conversation had been benign, cleared his throat. Margaret ignored her son and leaned into Jill as if she wanted to capture her answer like the first flakes of a southern snowstorm.

"Marketing research. Nothing quite as exciting as what your sons do. You must be so proud."

"Oh, I am. They're just like their dad. Everybody's hero."

Jill glanced at Darren. "Darren is certainly mine." She squeezed his hand underneath the table as if to tell him he was a hero in more ways than one.

"How did the two of you meet?" Margaret asked.

"My building caught fire New Year's Eve and Darren saved me and my laptop."

"All right, enough talking," Cleveland said. "Let's order so that we can eat." He waved for the waitress while Darren slowly fingered Jill's inner thigh, drawing his awe and affection with his digit.

Jill struggled to keep a straight face, but somehow she didn't let on as to what was going on.

After lunch, Darren and Jill headed to Phipps Plaza to see a movie. As they walked up the block to the theater, he spun her around. "I've never seen anyone win my mother over like that. She usually hates every woman with the audacity to date one of her boys."

"Overprotective?"

"Understatement. But her heart is in the right place and I should have listened to her about my first wife."

Jill shuttered inwardly. In a sense, she was no better than his first wife, telling him half truths and lies. And it was only going to build and build until the initial lie become unrecognizable.

"Darren, do you think you could forgive someone if they were dishonest with you about something trivial? I mean, if I said this was my natural hair color, would you consider that a lie?"

Darren looked at her deep brown tresses. "No, besides, I see dark roots. Don't get me wrong, I'm not the morality police. I'm not going to say I've never told a lie, but one lie leads to another and before you know it, you have no idea who the person is you're looking at."

Jill forced herself to smile and pretend everything was all right.

"I have a little confession to make," she said not knowing what would come out of her mouth next. "I don't want to mess this up," Jill said. "I like you."

"I like you too," he said. "We sound like some school children. So, Miss Atkinson, now that we know we like each other, what's next?"

She wrapped her arm around his waist. "I say we pick the longest movie up here, sit in the way, way back and make out like we're high school students cutting class."

He leaned over and kissed her on the cheek. "I think I like the sound of that."

And they were in luck; there was a three and a half hour epic that was just about to start.

❧ ❧

The darkness of the theater seemed to embolden Darren as he held Jill against him. Her body was so soft and she smelled like a slice of heaven. His hands followed her curves as if they were on an expedition. And what a topography her body was, round hips, long legs and smooth feet. She had slipped out of her shoes and in the glow of the light from the screen; he could tell she believed in getting pedicures regularly. Immediately he wanted to take them into his mouth. He had a foot fetish and Jill was fueling it.

She moaned softly as he slipped his hand underneath her turtleneck, gliding across her taut stomach. Darren felt her shiver as his hand danced up to her breasts. Through her thin lace bra, he felt her nipples spring forth, rock hard and begging to be kissed. Of course, he couldn't do that.

But those lips. He feasted on them as he massaged her nipples. He took her bottom lip between his teeth, nibbling gently as if her lip were a delicate pastry. Jill ran her tongue across his top lip, sending chills down his spine. He reached between her thighs, resting his hand on her crotch. He could feel the heat radiating from her body. Was she wet? He couldn't help wondering as he rubbed his hand up and down. Jill moaned in delight as his hand moved faster and faster.

"Excuse me?" a voice said before a bright light shone on them.

Darren and Jill looked up at the usher and broke apart. The fresh-faced teenager looked as if he had just walked in on his parents making love.

"Um, we've gotten a few complaints about the two of you. Can you stop what you're, uh, doing?"

"Yeah, yeah," Darren said.

"Sorry," Jill said.

When the usher walked away, the couple burst out laughing. "My goodness," Jill said. "Were we that bad?"

"Yeah, I guess we need to watch the movie."

Jill smoothed her ponytail. "What's this movie about again?"

Darren draped his arm across her shoulder, stroking her breast back and forth as they attempted to watch the film about a Roman emperor and the wars he waged.

"What do you say we get out of here?" she whispered.

Darren turned to her and smiled. "Where do you want to go?"

"Wherever you want to take me."

He wanted to take her back to his place and straight to bed. He wanted to take her clothes off, unhook her bra and give those nipples the kisses that they so deserved. He wanted to kiss every inch of her body, starting with those toes.

"Do you really want me to decide that?"

One of the movie patrons in front of them turned around. "I hope you two find a hotel room so the rest of us can watch the movie in peace."

Jill and Darren stood up, but they weren't embarrassed by their passionate display. But was it too soon for sex? Would that change everything between them?

When they made it to the lobby, Jill turned to Darren. "So, Mr. Alexander, where are you taking me?"

"My place." His voice was low and seductive. "I want to make love to you. If you'll let me."

"I want you to make love to me."

They nearly ran to his car. The anticipation of making love hung in the air like the sweet stickiness of a humid Georgia summer. Darren sped to his townhouse, disregarding the speed limit and the work zones.

"We're not rushing into anything, are we?" Darren asked, glancing over at Jill.

"No," she said.

"Because I don't want you to have any regrets about what…"

Jill placed her hand on his thigh. "Darren. We're going to be fine. Do you have any doubts?"

He glanced at her hand. "Not at all. But I don't want you to feel pressured into doing something that…"

"This isn't high school and you're not forcing me into something that I'm not ready for. I want you just as much as you want me."

He turned into his driveway and put the car in park. His libido was in overdrive, and his heart pounded like a marching band's drum line. Darren hadn't felt this nervous about being with a woman since his prom night. His palms were sweaty, but he had to play it cool. He walked over to the passenger side and opened Jill's door. When she looked up at him, he didn't feel anxious. He felt amorous. Her eyes seemed to be filled with the same desire that he felt. Darren clasped his hand around hers and led her inside.

"Be it ever so humble, there's no place like home," he said as held the front door open.

Jill looked around his living room, which was decorated in a classic style, with mahogany wood and burgundy leather. The only thing on his wall was a family portrait that showed a young Darren, a younger Cleveland and his parents.

"That's a lovely picture," she said.

"Thanks."

They stood in the middle of the living room looking at each other, each waiting for someone to make the first move. Darren wiped his sweaty palms on his pants legs before taking her hands, bringing them to his lips and kissing them.

"You are so beautiful."

She cast her eyes down. Darren pulled her closer to him, wrapping her arms around his waist. He could feel her heart racing. Jill was a take charge woman, but this time, he was going to be in control. He was going to take charge of giving her pleasure and showing her that he was her rock, that she could lean on him because he wanted to take care of her. He'd never hurt her, betray her or do anything that some other guy had done to scar her heart.

Darren moved her hands above her head and lifted her turtleneck. When he pulled it off, her ponytail holder slipped off and her hair cascaded down to her shoulders. He ran his finger down the valley between her breasts. "Soft," he said.

Next, he spun her around and unsnapped her bra, slipping the straps down her shoulders. He brushed his lips against her neck as he unbuttoned her slacks then zipped them down.

"Umm," she moaned as he dipped his hand inside her panties. His fingers teased her juicy lips, inching their way to her hot button of love. Her hot wetness made him swell with passion. With his free hand, he slid her pants down to her ankles. Her body quivered against his as he rubbed his hand across her thighs. Jill lifted her legs to step out of her pants. Then Darren spun her around again, drinking in her sensual image—nearly naked and totally unabashed about her body. And what a body! Her breasts were perfectly shaped and looked as delectable as mounds of chocolate. Her stomach was flat and flawless; her hips round and ready to climb on top of him. And that onion behind her…Darren couldn't wait to clutch it while she rode him.

"Wow. Beautiful."

"You have me at a disadvantage," she said teasingly. "You're still fully dressed."

Darren pulled his sweater over his head, tossing it into the pile of Jill's clothes. Then he unzipped his pants slowly, like a male exotic dancer. Jill laughed.

"That wasn't the reaction I was going for," he said, then reached out and pulled her against him. His manhood poked out of his boxers and rested against Jill's thighs.

She moaned as she felt him against her. Darren kissed her neck, running his tongue down the length of it. She melted against his body, moaning slightly with her mouth agape.

"Yeah, that's more like it," he said before lifting her into his arms.

"I want you," she breathed.

"You got me." Darren carried her into his bedroom. He laid her on the bed and drank in her image against his soft white cotton sheets. She looked like a sex goddess beckoning him to partake in the pleasures of her body without saying a word. Could she possibly know how sexy she was, tousled hair and all?

Easing into the bed, Darren took his time kissing every inch of Jill, starting with her toes. Then he worked his way up her ankles and calves before spreading her legs, leaving a trail of kisses on her inner thighs. She groaned and gripped the back of his head as he kissed her sex, wrapping his tongue around her throbbing clitoris. Darren savored the taste of her feminine juice as it flowed down his throat. She tightened her hold on his head, indicating that she was near climax.

"How does it feel?" he asked.

"Good, gr-eat."

Wanting to make her feel even better, he kissed and sucked harder, drawing more of her essence into his mouth. Screams of passion filled the air. Jill wrapped her legs around his neck, shivering uncontrollably as Darren made her love come down like rain.

The satisfied look on her face aroused Darren even more. If he didn't feel her around him, he was going to explode. When he took her legs and wrapped them around his waist, he felt her heat against his manhood. Jill sat up, pressing her hips into his. She leaned in and kissed him, hard, long and deep. Their tongues wrestled for position in each other's mouth. Darren placed his hands on her breasts, kneading them as they kissed, and felt her nipples expand underneath his touch. Jill threw her head back, breaking off their kiss as he massaged her breasts. Falling back on the sheets, Jill made it easy for Darren to position himself on top of her. His erection pressing against her thighs, feeling her smoothness against him, nearly brought him to his own climax. It had been so long since he had touched a woman, been this close to a woman and smelled the sweetness of a woman.

Darren hadn't thought that he'd make love to another woman again. Sure he'd had sex since his divorce, but he hadn't felt the connection with any woman that he was feeling with Jill.

Unlike some men, he didn't sleep around with a woman he didn't have feelings for or someone he didn't see a future with. Sex was about more than reaching a climax; it was about sharing your soul and spirit with someone. He felt he could share that with Jill. He could allow her to come into his heart, take her to bed and make love to her because he knew she was special. She was a woman that he wanted to build with, that he wanted to take care of. A woman unlike any he'd ever known. He hadn't even felt this strongly about Rita and he'd married her.

Darren reached into his nightstand drawer and grabbed a condom. He pulled back from Jill and slid the latex sheath in place. He looked at Jill, who had a look of nervous anticipation on her face, and gently stroked her cheek.

"Are you all right?" he asked.

"It's just been a while since I've…"

"We can stop," he said, though his body was ready to have her.

"No, please don't stop," she replied, and then pressed her hips into his. "I want you."

Darren dove into her pool of sex, surprised at her tightness. The sensation nearly pushed him to the brink of an orgasm. He realized that this moment was special. Jill's body was practically untouched. Being with her made him feel as if he'd won a prize. She wasn't having a casual fling, this was pure lovemaking.

Darren leaned against her ear. "Do you feel good, baby?" His hips moved up and down slowly as she tightened her love around his manhood.

Jill and Darren fell into a sensual dance, rocking back and forth like an ocean wave. Their pace quickened and slowed, quickened and slowed until Darren felt his release coming. He opened his eyes and saw the lush look of satisfaction on Jill's face. Knowing he'd satisfied her and filled her with his love, he allowed himself to reach his climax.

Jill wrapped her arms around him as he buried his head in her bosom. "Baby," he whispered. "You are amazing."

"You're not so bad yourself," she replied, stroking the nape of his neck.

Darren rolled over onto his side, propping himself up on his elbow, and stared down into Jill's face. She wore a look of contentment. He pushed a stray hair from her forehead. "Thank you."

"Huh?" Jill asked.

"For sharing yourself with me. The first time I saw you, I knew I wanted to make love to you and take care of you. I could tell you weren't used to letting someone else take the lead. But you trust me and I can appreciate that. I'll never do anything to betray your trust in me."

Her eyes misted as he spoke. "Darren," she said barely above a whisper. "I-I…"

He silenced her with a slow, sensual kiss, hoping to remove any doubt that she had in her mind about him and what she meant to him.

Jill broke the kiss off by placing her hand on his chest. "Darren, I'm not the woman you think I am."

"What do you mean?"

Jill closed her eyes. "I'm not perfect and I'm not sure that I won't make mistakes."

"I don't expect you to be perfect. Hell, I'm not perfect. And mistakes, I'm sure we're both going to make plenty. Don't be nervous about us. We're going to be fine."

She wrapped her arms around him and hugged him to her body. "I'm going to hold you to that."

He brushed his lips across her neck. "Trust me, babe. We're going to be just fine."

CHAPTER NINE

As she held Darren, Jill knew she'd blown her chance to tell him the truth and not worry about the consequences. There was something about the afterglow of love making that absolved almost any sin. But how could she ruin such a beautiful moment. Making love to Darren had lived up to every one of her fantasies and then some. He was a gentle lover, a tender lover and when he kissed her, his kisses made her melt. If she could bronze his tongue she would because it was magical.

"What's on your mind?" he asked, taking note of her silence.

"You."

"Really? And what are you thinking?"

Jill arched her back, jutting her breasts upward. "The way you kiss me, the way you touch me. I feel so alive."

"Then," he said as he took one of her breasts in his hand, "let me make you feel alive."

As Darren suckled her hard nipple, he massaged her other breast. Cries of passion escaped her throat as he moved from breast to breast. She wrapped her legs around his waist, pulling his erection against her thighs.

After they made love again, Jill took a shower and dressed. Darren ordered some Chinese food and they had dinner and watched an old movie on AMC. Darren fed her lo mein noodles as they lounged on the sofa.

"Are you going to the game tomorrow?" he asked.

"I was thinking about it. But I'm sure my boss will use the playoff tickets himself."

"Good, you can watch it with me. ESPN Zone?"

"Why don't you come to my place?" she suggested.

Darren took a noodle into his mouth. "The inner sanctum. Your house isn't decorated in Falcons colors is it?"

"You'll see tomorrow."

"Can you cook?"

"Yeah," she said, and then regretted it. Jill was skilled at a lot of things, but cooking wasn't one of them. But she could make a mean salad and microwave with the best of them.

"What's your specialty?" he asked.

"What do you want to have tomorrow?"

Darren leaned back on the sofa and smiled. "You know I'm a country boy. I would love fried chicken, macaroni and cheese, some greens and homemade biscuits."

Jill chewed on her bottom lip and envisioned her kitchen filled with smoke as she tried to cook. How was she going to pull this off?

"I don't want you to go to too much trouble, though," he said, noticing the look on her face. "We can just pick something up if you don't want to cook."

"No, it's the least I can do. I don't cook a lot and I was just going over what I needed to buy to pull this off."

"Then don't worry about it."

"No, I'm going to cook for my man," she said.

"Well, I'm going to enjoy my lady's repast."

Jill beamed, but inside, she knew there was only one thing she could do. She had to call Shari and get her help. Glancing down at her watch, Jill told Darren that she needed to go home so that she could prepare for tomorrow.

"All right, let's get going then." Darren closed up the containers of Chinese food and Jill placed them in his refrigerator.

She was surprised that his place felt so much like home to her. Being with him was so easy. Twinges of guilt pricked at her like a thousand straight pins. If everything was all good with Darren, why was she still lying to him? Why didn't she just tell him the truth about who she was and why had she told him that she could cook?

ॐ ॐ

When Darren dropped her off, Jill rushed into the house, grabbed the phone and called Shari.

Malik answered the phone. "Hello?"

"Malik, it's me. Is Shari there?"

"Yeah, hold on."

A few seconds later, her friend was on the line. Jill explained her dilemma and begged for assistance.

" 'Oh, what a tangled web we weave'," Shari sang.

"I don't need a lecture. Are you going to help me or not?"

"I'll help you because it's good to see that Jill Atkinson isn't perfect. But how long are you going to keep up with this charade?"

"Not much longer. Darren may actually be the one," Jill admitted.

"Don't say another word; I'm on my way over there."

Knowing that it would take Shari about 20 minutes to get to her penthouse, Jill changed into a pair of yoga pants and a sweatshirt. When she touched her body as she dressed, she relived the passion she'd felt when Darren touched her. That man made her body sing and hit all the right high notes too.

If I don't tell him the truth, the whole truth and nothing but the truth, I'm going to lose him.

The shrill ringing of the phone jarred Jill. She grabbed the phone from the wall.

"Hello?"

"Jill, how are you?" a voice from her past said.

"David?"

"I'm surprised you remember my name."

"What the hell do you want?"

"Can't an old friend call to say hello?"

"I would hardly call you an old friend. You're more like a back stabbing bastard."

"That's harsh and totally uncalled for."

"Let's see, you tried to steal my company, you lied to me to get into my pants and pretended that you loved me. Back stabbing bastard suits you just fine."

"We don't need to be nasty, Jill. We had some good times, didn't we?"

"If you call betrayal a good time, then I guess you're right. What do you want?"

David cleared his throat. "Well, I'm trying to launch my own business, a magazine actually."

"You have some gall calling me about a business."

"I want to feature you in our first issue."

Jill slammed the phone down and cursed David. "That son of a bitch!"

Of all the people from her past that she would help, David was nowhere on that list and if he thought that she was going to help him with his rag, he could just go to hell.

She was shocked that hearing his voice had cut her as deeply as it did. That dull ache reminded her of why she was playing a game with Darren. If he turned out to be another David, she would swear off men forever and join a convent.

Her door bell chimed and Jill stomped to the front door.

"Whoa," Shari said. "Who stole your candy?"

"Come in, girl," Jill said. She and Shari took a seat on the sofa.

"Did something happen between the time we hung up and I got here?"

"You know, since I started my business, I've never had a real girlfriend before, someone I can talk to. So I'm grateful that you and I are friends," Jill said.

"All right, what's going on?"

Jill crossed her legs and looked at Shari. "I know you think what I'm doing with Darren is wrong, but before you got here, I got confirmation as to why I'm doing this. David Branton called me tonight."

"Who is he?"

"The last man I let use me. When I first started DVA, the vultures were circling. Concurrent wanted my company, IBM and all the big boys. David worked for Concurrent and he wooed me, made me love him and stabbed me in the back. He was a mole for Concurrent. But I flipped the tables on them. I raised enough capital to buy Concurrent and I fired everyone, including David.

"But my heart has never truly healed from what he did to me. I would go out to the Shark Bar and meet men who had a business plan in one hand and a loan application in the other. That's why I went into a self-imposed seclusion. No dating, just work. It wasn't all about trying to smash stereotypes, as I said in the article you wrote. I was lonely."

Shari placed her hand on top of Jill's. "I know how you feel. Gosh, after my fiancé died several years ago, I did the same thing. But if you want happiness, you have to take risks. Every man isn't David. And what the hell was he calling you for anyway?"

"That sorry piece of… He's starting a magazine and had the nerve to ask me if he could do a feature on me. I need whatever he's smoking."

Shari snorted. "We all do. After what he did to you, he has the audacity to ask you for help?"

Jill nodded and laughed to keep the tears that sprang into her eyes from falling. "You know what's sad, though? For a split second in the deepest recesses of my mind, I considered it. I loved that man and I thought he loved me too."

"Sometimes the people we love aren't the right ones for us. But you can't let David's call be an excuse to continue lying to Darren. And this cooking thing, one shot deal, sista."

Jill rose to her feet and laughed. "All right, all right. But I get the feeling that if Darren is going to be in my life, I'd better take some cooking lessons. He's a country boy through and through and you know what that means."

Shari nodded. "Brother man can eat, huh? We'd better get to Publix before they close."

Jill reached out and hugged Shari. "Thank you for listening to me and being my conscience even when I don't want you to be."

"Anytime," she replied. "Besides, I think you might be a godmother soon."

Jill brought her hand to her mouth. "Are you?"

"I don't know for sure, but I'm two months late and Malik's cologne makes me sick now."

"That's because he bathes in it," Jill giggled. "The running joke at the office used to be that you could smell Malik coming."

"Don't say anything to him yet. I'm going to the doctor next week to find out for sure," Shari said as they headed out the door.

They entered the grocery store laughing about Malik changing diapers at three A.M. Though she was happy for Shari, Jill wondered if she would ever get married and have a family of her own. Could she have that with Darren?

Not if you keep lying.

"Jill, where did you go?" Shari asked.

"I was just thinking about Darren."

"You're smitten. This is beautiful. You deserve to be happy in your business and personal life. Darren makes you glow."

Jill grinned. "He does. He's so sweet and compassionate. He treats me like a woman, not a business-woman or a meal ticket, but a sensual being that he's attracted to."

"Have you made love?"

Heat flushed her cheeks. "I'll never tell."

"That rosy glow on your face tells it all. So this is serious. You'd better hurry and tell him the truth. The man that you've described doesn't seem like he's out to take anything from you but your heart."

"I'm willing to give that to him, but I'm just not sure that things won't change."

"I hate to belabor the point, Jill, but if you think Darren will have a problem with your status and your success, and then you should walk away before it becomes an issue."

"You don't know what it's like to be lied to and hurt the way David did me."

Shari folded her arms across her chest. "Oh, no? Try this on for size. The man I thought was the one true love of my life did lie to me. He cheated on me and produced a son."

"Malik has a son?"

Shari shook her head. "My high school sweetheart and I were engaged right before we went off to college. He was killed the night he was driving to Atlanta to tell me about his one night stand and the baby that was on the way."

"Oh my God. When did you find out?"

"Years later, as a matter of fact, right after I met you. In my head, Tyrell was the perfect man and I never thought I would find someone I'd love the way I loved him. Then to find out that he lied to me, cheated on me…I was hurt beyond words. But I put it behind me and if I hadn't done that, Malik and I wouldn't be together now."

"I had no idea."

She waved her hands. "It's not something I talk about a lot. I'm over it, but that first heartbreak takes time to put behind you. The point is, in order to move forward, that's what you have to do, put the past behind you."

Jill nodded as she picked up a package of chicken legs.

"Uh, what's that?" Shari asked.

"Chicken."

"Is this man anorexic or something? You need to get a whole fryer." Shari pointed to what Jill thought looked like a flesh covered bowling ball.

"And what am I supposed to do with this?"

Shari shook her head. "Cut it up, season it, batter it and fry it."

"Chicken comes cut up, right?"

"Trust me, this will taste better. How in the world did you get roped into cooking dinner?"

"Open mouth and insert foot. I did this to myself."

Shaking her head, Shari said, "You've become skilled at telling tall tales."

Jill dropped two bricks of cheese in the cart. "Sounds like the beginning of a lecture and I don't want to hear it."

Shari threw her hands up. "You're going to need more cheese than that. One last thing, and I'm going to leave it alone. David might be a problem for you and your little ruse. New magazines go out to a lot of people and I'm sure he'll do a story on you with or without your consent."

"That weasel probably will. I'll just have to cross that bridge when I get to it," she said. "But I will not let David dictate how I live my life."

After they finished shopping, Jill and Shari headed back to the penthouse to prepare the dinner.

Maybe over this dinner I should come clean, Jill thought as the doorman unloaded her packages. *That's what I'll do.*

❧❧

When Darren's phone rang around ten-thirty Saturday night, he wished it were Jill. He wanted her to come back and spend the night in his arms. Her scent lingered in his house, adding to his longing for her touch, the feel of her breasts against his chest and the warm wetness of her closed around his manhood. The desire he felt for her was like nothing he'd ever experienced.

"Hello," Darren said in his sexiest imitation of Barry White.

"This isn't Jill, so you don't have to try and sound like a quiet storm DJ for me," his mother said.

"Hey Ma, what are you doing up so late?"

"Well, you and Jill got away so fast after lunch that I didn't get a chance to talk to you guys."

Darren leaned back in his recliner; he knew this was going to be a long conversation. "What do you want to talk about?"

"I like her. She seems nice and I can see that she makes you happy," Margaret said. "All I want is for you to be happy. Jill might be good for you."

"Might be?"

"You never know what will happen, but so far, so good. Besides, she has a good family. That Rita came from bad people. What kind of mother would help her daughter lie to her husband about killing a baby?"

"Please, I don't want to think about that." Every time Darren thought about receiving that letter and learning the truth about Rita's pregnancy, he cringed. He'd never told his mother that the child she mourned wasn't her grandchild. He didn't want her to go off the deep end about what kind of whore Rita really was. His mother would use that exact term.

"Are you sure you're over that? I know you're a grown man and you don't have to run to your mother about your problems, but you never talked about your divorce or the fact that she robbed you of your chance at fatherhood."

"That's because what's done is done. Talking about it isn't going to change the fact that Rita was a liar and I never should have married her."

"Holding that in isn't helping, though."

"Ma, it's been five years. I haven't seen Rita and I hope to God that I never see that woman again."

Margaret sighed. "Am I meddling?"

"Bordering on it."

"Well, I'm a mother and that's what we do. When you have children, you'll understand that. And I know your brother thinks I'm going to drive him crazy while he rehabs, but I'm not. I love you boys so much. Every time I look at the both of you, I see so much of Walter. Especially with your hard headed brother. Walter really put his shine on Cleveland."

Darren stifled a laugh. She had already driven him to the edge of crazy but he would never tell her that. "You know we love you, too."

"You'd better. I worry about you and Cleveland. I never wanted you two to become firefighters, not after what happened to your father. You would think that one of you would have rebelled and become a school teacher or something. I was so scared when you called me and told me about Cleveland's accident." Margaret's voice dropped to a whisper. "All I could think about was the day I got the call about your father."

"Ma," Darren cooed. "We're going to be fine. Cleveland and I are going to stick around and give you a couple of grandkids to spoil."

"You think Jill would give you a child? Or is she one of those 'I'm climbing the corporate ladder' type of women? Can she cook?"

Darren laughed. "I'll find out tomorrow. We're watching the game together."

"After you and Cleveland go to church with me first, right?" It wasn't really a question; it was more like a statement.

"Yes, ma'am."

"Good. Now, go to sleep and meet us at Voices of Faith for the eight A.M. service. I know how you two do during football season."

"I love you, Ma."

"I love you too."

Darren hung up the phone, happy that his mother had admitted she liked Jill. Not that it mattered what she thought, but Darren felt as if his relationship with Jill was going to grow and flourish.

Why wouldn't it? Jill was the kind of woman that Darren would like to see standing at the altar in front of a pastor declaring her love for him before God and witnesses. Still, there was something Jill was holding back from him. He knew in his heart that she didn't totally trust him with some aspects of her life.

But after sharing her body with him, he knew things would change. It would take time for Jill to trust him. Whoever hurt her had done a number on her heart, but Darren was going to heal her and show her how much she deserved to be loved and how much he could love her.

He picked the phone up and called her despite the lateness.

"Hello?"

"I hope I didn't wake you."

"No, you didn't," Jill said. Darren visualized her standing there smiling. He could hear it in her voice.

"I was thinking about you and I had to hear your voice before I went to bed."

"I wanted to call you, but I had to get everything for dinner tomorrow."

"Oh, that I am looking forward to. I wish you could have spent the night. Waking up with you in my arms would be heavenly."

"Maybe you can spend the night tomorrow. We can catch the Late SportsCenter together," she said.

"We'll have to see. By the way, you made quite the impression on my mother."

"What? What did she say?"

"That she likes you and coming from her that's a high compliment."

"Well, your mother loves her sons and protects them. I can't say that I blame her," Jill said.

"Now, you're the first girlfriend I've ever had that understood my mother." When Darren said 'girlfriend' he couldn't help smiling. He'd gone from having no woman in his life to having a girlfriend, a budding relationship that made him warm inside. Jill was definitely the kind of woman that you planned for the future with.

"I understand your mom because if you were my son, I wouldn't want some woman sinking her claws into my son, especially if he looked like you," Jill joked.

He could hear pots crashing in the background. "You're putting it down in the kitchen tonight, aren't you?"

"Uh, yeah. I wanted to make sure everything is perfect. What time are you coming over?"

"Game starts at four-fifteen, so about three-thirty?"

"That works for me," Jill said.

"I'm going to say goodnight and let you get our dinner ready."

"Sweet dreams."

Darren licked his lips. "If they're of you, I'm sure they will be." With that, Darren said goodbye and hung up the phone. He went to bed, all night long dreaming of making love to Jill.

CHAPTER TEN

Jill woke up Sunday morning feeling more than a little anxious about her dinner with Darren. Shari had prepared the meal, and all Jill had to do was place the macaroni in the oven, flour the chicken and place it in the deep fryer and bake the biscuits. Still, she felt that something was going to go horribly wrong.

"How did I get myself into this," she thought aloud as she preheated the oven as Shari had instructed.

While the oven was heating, Jill went into her bedroom, flung her closet open and agonized over what to wear. Her dilemma was simple: She didn't want to overdress, because all they were going to do was sit around the house. But she didn't want to look as if she'd been sitting in the house all day, dressed in ratty sweats and a ripped tee-shirt. After all, she did want to make a good impression on the man.

Finally, Jill decided on a pair of well-worn jeans and an Atlanta Falcons tank top. She laid the outfit on the bed, and then headed for the bathroom to take a long hot bath. Soaking in the tub would give her a chance to think about what Darren meant to her and how important this dinner was.

"I'm going to come clean," she said aloud. "Darren doesn't want anything from me but my heart and he can freely have that." Easing into the water, which was filled with scented oil and salts, Jill relaxed her shoulders. But just as she got comfortable, she remembered the oven was on. She leapt from the tub in rush, splashing water all over the floor, and nearly slipped.

Naked and dripping wet, Jill walked into the kitchen, which was hot as July. She was glad she hadn't put anything in the oven because it would have been burnt to a crisp. Checking the dial on the oven, she saw she'd set the temperature on 500 degrees. *Got to be more careful,* she thought, turning the oven to 350. She took the casserole dish from the refrigerator and set it inside, then went back to the bathroom, took a quick shower, and wrapped a towel around her body before heading back to the kitchen.

Shari had told her to bake the macaroni for 30 minutes and the biscuits for 15 minutes, or until they were golden brown. Going about her preparations, she forgot about the time, and when three o'clock rolled around, she was naked, save her towel. She began heating peanut oil to fry the chicken in. Peanut oil, Shari said, gave the chicken more flavor.

"Fifteen minutes on each side," she said as she dropped the breaded chicken into the hot oil.

Just then, the voice of the doorman came over the intercom. "Miss Atkinson, your guest, Mr. Darren Alexander is here."

Jill suddenly realized she wasn't dressed. *Ohmigod!* "Uh, send him up," she stammered. What to do? She couldn't leave the chicken, but she didn't want Darren to see her like this.

Seconds later, there was a knock at the door. Jill lowered the heat on the chicken, wiped the flour from her hands on a dish towel and walked to the door. Her face was warm from embarrassment even before she opened the door.

"Hell—whoa! Am I too early?" Darren asked, leering at Jill in her towel.

"Come in and never speak of this again. I was cooking and time got away from me."

"You always cook like this? Because if you do, you can come to my house and cook anytime."

"I have to get dressed," she said, her face now burning like an inferno. "Can you watch the oven for me? The biscuits and the macaroni should be done."

"It smells good in here, but oh my, it looks a lot better," he said, winking at her as she dashed into her bedroom.

&

Darren was impressed. Jill didn't do the buy-the-food and hide-the-boxes thing like another woman he'd dated had done. But when he looked around for a pot holder, he found only a dish towel and used it to take the biscuits and casserole out of the oven. Then he checked on the chicken as it sizzled in the fryer.

"I'm back," Jill said. She was dressed in a pair of faded jeans with a small hole in the knee and a black Atlanta Falcons tank top, but still Darren couldn't get the vision of a nearly naked Jill out of his head.

"You look great, but the towel has to be my favorite outfit."

"Shut up." She walked over to the stove and placed a chicken breast in the oil.

Darren noticed the way she held the chicken in disgust. "All right, Jill, it's time to come clean."

"What? What are you talking about?"

"You really don't want to do this, do you? If cooking isn't your thing, I can live with that. You don't have be something that you're not to try and impress me. I'm already impressed." Darren walked over to her and took the chicken from her hands and placed it in the oil.

Jill cleared her throat and said, "All right, I can't cook. I make salads. I had help with all of this because I wanted to impress you. When I talked to you on the phone last night, my friend Shari and I were in here doing the preliminary work on this meal for you. A little while ago, I almost burned my house down preheating my oven. That's why you caught me in my towel."

Darren threw his head back and laughed, then took her face into his hands. "Baby, I like you just the way you are. I don't need to be impressed. You did that the night you met me at the MARTA station."

He ran his lips across hers. "So, can this Shari woman cook?"

"Don't I get some credit for putting the food in the oven?" she asked.

"Yes, you do." He playfully smacked her bottom.

Once the food was done, Darren and Jill took their plates and planted themselves in front of the TV to watch the game.

Truth be told, Darren could have cared less about the moves Michael Vick made on the football field. Instead, he was mesmerized by the way Jill kicked her legs when the Falcons made a mistake, by the way she cheered when Vick broke a tackle and by the way she sat on the edge of her seat every time a flag was thrown by the referees.

"How can they make that call? That was encroachment!" she barked, then turned to Darren. "Are they blind?"

He smiled and shook his head. "I tell you, this is amazing. Never have I known a woman that loves football like you."

"Football was how my father and I bonded when I was growing up. He would never admit it, but he wanted a son. When I was five, I'd sit on his lap watch the game with him and when he nodded off to sleep, I'd sip on his Miller High Life."

Darren wanted a son, but he wouldn't mind having a daughter with a smile like Jill's. He placed his hand on her knee.

"Dinner was great, but Shari can't cook for us every night."

Jill blushed. "Well, I can take a cooking class or you can cook and I'll do the dishes."

He took her hand into his and held it up for inspection. "Looks like you've never washed a dish in your life."

"God invented the dishwasher so that I wouldn't have to touch you with dishpan hands." She stroked his cheek softly. "Doesn't that feel good?"

Darren answered her by pulling her against his chest and greedily kissing her. Jill pressed him back on the sofa, positioning her body on top of his engorged sex. Soft groans escaped his throat as she sucked his bottom lip.

From the sound of the cheers on television, the Falcons had done something spectacular, but all Darren cared about was the hot and wet kiss that Jill delivered as she pressed her luscious body against him, nearly making him climax through his jeans. He sat up, wrapped her legs around his waist, took her lip between his teeth and nibbled slightly.

She pulled back from him, staring into his eyes. Darren slipped his hands underneath her shirt, stroking her back. "You feel so good," he said.

"Darren, I-I," she said.

Her lips enticed him so much that he couldn't let her finish her statement. He kissed her with such zeal and passion that she melted against him. Darren could feel her trembling against his chest. He was going to explode if he didn't have her.

"I want you," he moaned.

"But I have to say something."

Darren lifted her shirt over her head, exposing her breasts because she wasn't wearing a bra.

"Yeah?" he said before taking one of her perky breasts into his mouth. Jill threw her head back in ecstasy. Her intention was forgotten as she gripped the back of Darren's neck and pressed against him. He reached for her fly, but Jill grabbed his hands and pushed him back on the sofa. She undressed him slowly, as if she were opening a sexy Christmas present. She ran her tongue down the center of his chest until she reached his waistband. Using her hands and her teeth, Jill unbuttoned his jeans and stroked his manhood until it throbbed with anticipation. She surprised him by pulling his boxers down and taking his penis into her mouth. The wet warmness of her mouth nearly pushed him over the edge. He dropped his hands into her hair as her head bobbed up and down. The pleasurable sensations that flowed through his body were indescribable. With one hand, she massaged his shaft, milking his essence from him.

Darren tried to hold his orgasm back, but Jill made that impossible when she took his hand and placed it inside her jeans. Heat radiated from her middle and when he stuck his finger inside her, she was wet and ready. As she pulled her lips off his manhood, he exploded with a groan.

Jill snaked up his body, rubbing her breasts, her stomach, against his sex, arousing him all over again. When she straddled him, he plunged right into her. Jill gripped his shoulders as she rode him, allowing his thickness to fill her.

He kneaded her breasts as she bounced up and down, tightening her walls around him. Darren had never experienced such raw passion, such desire and longing. Jill was a fire he couldn't put out, but he was having fun trying. Her body thrashed and flailed against his like that of a flamenco dancer. She was in control of his body. Whatever she wanted him to do, he did it. She pulled him deeper and deeper into her, as if trying to merge their bodies into one.

After they were spent from their lovemaking, Darren clung to Jill, kissing her on her forehead. "And what did you want to talk about?" he asked.

"I don't remember," she breathed.

He ran his finger down the valley of her breasts. "Don't remember, huh?"

She shivered and inhaled sharply. "Ooh, you made me miss the game."

"I didn't hear you complaining," he said. They didn't unwrap themselves from each other for the next few moments.

"I'm going to take a shower," Jill said, as she stood up. "Care to join me?"

Darren leapt to his feet and followed her up the stairs. "You wash my back and I'll wash yours."

Jill and Darren were squeaky clean and sexually satisfied when they returned downstairs to catch the second playoff game. She had changed into an over-sized tee-shirt and a pair of boxers, a simple outfit that was incredibly sexy on her. Darren fought with himself not to rip her clothes off and make love to her all over again. As they snuggled on the sofa, Darren took a look around her place. Jill had excellent taste. Her walls were painted a pale yellow and decorated with nouveau art, including a portrait of herself.

"That's lovely," he said, pointing to the portrait.

"Thank you. That was the first time I ever spent $1,000 on myself for a picture of myself."

"Wow." Darren wondered, though he would never ask, how much money she made. *Does she even need a man in her life? She has everything.* "How important is your career to you?"

"It's been my focus for a number of years. Some people say I hid behind my career and used it as an excuse not to date."

"Really?"

Jill sighed. "Not that most women haven't been, but I've been hurt before and instead of letting it happen again, I threw myself into my work, early mornings, late nights, weekends. All I did was work."

"Has that changed?" he asked.

"Somewhat. I mean, having you in my life has definitely shown me that there is a lot more to life than work and football."

"I'm glad I could help, because there is more to life than work and football."

She stroked his arm. "What about you? Why is a fine, hard-working man like yourself still single? You live in a city filled with beautiful single women."

"Beauty is only skin deep and beauty may open the door but it takes a lot more for a woman to enter my life and my heart."

Jill propped herself up on her elbows. "And what more does it take?"

"I want the total package. Brains, compassion, and if she looks like you, then I'm a lucky man." Darren held her face in his hands. "In other words, you're the one I've been looking for."

Jill cast her eyes down and Darren knew she was blushing.

"How do you know you've been looking for me?"

"Because when you collapsed in my arms New Year's Eve, I knew you were an angel and meant for me."

Her eyes glistened with tears, a reaction that confused Darren. He was opening his heart to her and she seemed sad.

"Are you all right?" he asked.

"Darren, I'm overwhelmed. I know we've known each other for only a short time, but I feel such a connection with you that it scares me because I don't want to be hurt. I don't want to give you my heart and have it crushed."

"I'd never do that. I've been on the other side of heartache and I wouldn't wish that on my worse enemy."

"Sometimes things happen that we don't plan for."

Darren placed his hand on her thigh. "I'm planning not to hurt you. I'm planning to have you in my life for a long time. You know, my ex-wife robbed me of happiness. She cheated on me, got pregnant and had an abortion. I don't know if it was my baby or if it was her lover's child. For a long time I didn't want anything to do with a woman. Well, I wouldn't say I didn't want anything to do with a woman, but I didn't see a future with a woman. And then I met you."

"What if I'm not the woman for you?" she asked.

"Why would you say that? Jill, you're damn near perfect, self sufficient, a woman that isn't looking for a man to carry her. Hell, maybe I'm not worthy of you."

Jill looked away from him and started gathering their dinner dishes. Darren stood up and grabbed her arm. "What's wrong?" he asked.

"You would make any woman happy and for you to think that you're not worthy of me, that's crazy."

"Well, I am crazy. Crazy about you, whether you can cook or not."

Jill disappeared into the kitchen and Darren sat on the sofa, turning the television up as the highlights from the Falcons game began to play.

"Michael Vick had a great game, rushed for more yards than Warrick Dunn," Darren called out.

Jill dashed into the living room. "Go Michael! We're going to win the Super Bowl this year."

Darren wrapped his arms around Jill's waist, feeling as if he had already won the big game. He had her in his life.

CHAPTER ELEVEN

Jill walked Darren to the front door at the end of the evening. She wished he could spend the night, but Monday marked the beginning of a seven day shift at the fire station. A week without Darren. Jill didn't know how she was going to get by.

"Sorry you missed the game," he said, leaning in to kiss her good night.

"Being with you was better than watching Vick run."

"Ugh, I'm going to hate working this week. You're going to have to come to the station and bring me some more of Shari's cooking."

She playfully slapped him on the shoulder. "Maybe I'll get Shari to teach me one of her signature dishes and make it for you. Let me know when."

Darren pulled her into his arms and rubbed his nose against hers. "I'd better go before I can't leave. I'll call you later tomorrow unless Sherman is resurrected and Atlanta burns." He let her go and headed out the door.

"Good night," she said. When Jill closed the door, she leaned against it, thinking that she shouldn't have let Darren walk out of this house without telling him her true identity. *I can't worry about that right now. Maybe it doesn't even matter. Obviously he knows I'm wealthy, and he hasn't tried to get into my bank account. He doesn't need to know; we're just fine. But how can I fall in love with him and still lie to him?*

The revelation that she was falling in love with him excited her. She'd finally put David in her past and was able to open her heart to another man and let him love her. The hurt that she'd held on to for so long wasn't shackling her anymore. She was a woman renewed by love and if she had to learn to cook to please her man, then that was just what she'd do. Jill pushed back as far as she could the nagging voice that said she was making a mistake by not being completely honest with him, that if she waited too long, someone else was going to tell him and make her look like a big liar.

❧ ❧

Monday morning was a frigid day in Georgia. Snow clouds hovered in the sky and there was a threat of an ice storm, according for the weather forecasters. This meant the fire department had to be on standby. Ice storms in Atlanta meant car accidents, downed power lines and chimney fires. No one seemed to think about their fireplaces until it was cold outside. With all the built up gunk in the chimney, fires were a given. Darren wished they weren't shorthanded at the station because he knew they were going to be busy if the forecasters were right.

He and the fifteen other firefighters planted themselves in front of the television hoping for the best but expecting the worst.

It didn't take long for the forecasters' predictions to come true. Three and half inches of snow and sleet blanketed Atlanta. The city was paralyzed and all Darren could think about was Jill. Was she safe? Had she stayed off the roads as the governor had recommended.

I hope Ms. Goal Oriented stayed home today. DVA doesn't need her as badly as I do, Darren thought as he drove extremely slowly to an accident scene that was less than a block from Jill's workplace.

Luckily, no life had been lost, but the *Atlanta Journal-Constitution* was going to have to replace their vending machine. When the police arrived, Darren was tempted to go check on Jill and drag her out of her office if she had braved the elements to go to work. But a call on his radio stopped him. There was another weather-related accident about three miles up the road.

What a day, Darren thought as he got into his car to follow the fire truck. The sight of another mangled car made his heart lurch. *I've got to call Jill and check on her.* If he happened upon an accident and Jill was involved it in, he didn't know what he was going to do.

❧ ❧

The lights in the office flickered on and off, then popped. Everything was pitch black.

"Damn," Jill swore. She hadn't saved the document that she'd been working on.

The back-up generators kicked on for about ten minutes, giving Jill enough time to recover her work, save it and shut down her computer. She was going home just like the rest of her employees had. Jill hated southern snow. Atlanta didn't get white and fluffy snow like the Weather Channel showed. Atlanta got a combination of snow and ice. The roads were treacherous and driving could mean sudden death if you missed a slab of black ice.

I'll stay here, she thought, when the generators kicked on again. Pulling out her battery-operated space heater and two blankets, she set the heater near the sofa in the corner of her office, and then settled on the sofa, wrapped in the blankets.

She was about to drift off to sleep when her cell phone rang. "Hello," she said.

"Are you all right?" Darren asked. "And please tell me that you're at home."

"That would be a lie. I'm trapped in my office."

"Do you have power?"

"For now. The back-up generators are on and I have small heater."

"Why did you even go to work today?"

"How many times have the weathermen been wrong this winter?"

"I'm coming over there."

"What about your shift? I know you guys are busy."

Darren sighed into the phone. "I'm going to make some arrangements so that I can keep an eye on what's going on and check on you. I know you're safe, and that's good. Traffic has died down a lot and most people have returned to home. I'm going to wait a few hours and see if some other guys can make it in so that if I leave I won't leave the station in a lurch."

"Darren," she said, "you really don't have to do this."

"I know but I'm doing it anyway. Stay warm," Darren ordered.

"Yes, sir," she said. Hearing his voice had already warmed her, at least between her legs.

A few hours later, her phone rang again. "Hello?"

"I'm at your front door."

"I'll be right down," she said. She had to walk down ten flights of stairs because she didn't want to risk the electricity going out while she was in the elevator.

Darren looked like an Eskimo in his fur-lined parka and snow boots. As she opened the door, to usher him in, she saw that more snow was falling. "Ugh! Why is it snowing here?"

"Hey, Atlanta gets snow sometimes. I think when all of those northerners moved down here they brought old man winter with them."

Jill unzipped his coat. "We've got climbing to do," she said, leading him to the stairwell. Once they made it to her office, Darren was a little winded.

"You make this climb every day?" he asked.

"No, I prefer going to the gym, but I don't really have a choice today. These back-up generators are flaky and the last thing I need is to be stuck in the elevator."

"You mean to tell me that you braved the ice-covered Atlanta streets but you're afraid of a little elevator ride?"

Jill sat on the sofa and wrapped up in a blanket. "There was no ice when I left home."

Darren slid beside her. "But there was the threat. I hope your boss realizes what an asset you are to this company."

"I think that goes without saying."

He looked around the office and let out a low whistle. "Yeah. How did you snag such a big office?"

"A lot of hard work," she said, feeling guilty with every word she spoke. Of course she had the big office, she'd built the company.

"Hopefully, the ice will melt by morning and we can get out of here."

"Morning? Are you going to be able to spend the night here?" Jill asked.

"Three more guys came in, and I delegated some authority. I'm only a radio call away." Darren held up his radio as he removed his heavy coat and tossed it on Jill's desk. "I just didn't like the idea of you being her alone without any security."

"You're too good to me," she said with a smile. "But how will we pass the time?"

He touched his chin thoughtfully. "I can think of about fifty things we can do, but it's too cold for that." He wrapped his arms around her and pulled her against his chest. "You know you should have stayed home."

She stroked his cheek. "Shoulda, woulda, coulda," she replied. "Maybe I just wanted to be rescued again."

"You know I'm your personal hero," he said. "Honestly, I was so worried about you. Those last two accident scenes I worked; all I could think about was you. The last thing that I wanted was to roll up on a scene like that and find you mangled by a crash."

"You really care about me?"

"That goes without saying. Jill, you are the most intriguing woman that I've met in a long time. I think, no, I know I'm falling in love with you."

Heat rushed to Jill's cheeks, her face flushed and she held him tighter. *I'm already in love with you,* she thought, but was too afraid to say it.

"Darren," she said.

He drew her face into his hands. "I'm not trying to rush you into anything and if you don't feel the same way right now, I understand. But I know you're the one for me."

The lights flickered again then went out. Jill searched for the right words to say. She searched her heart and it told her to tell him that she loved him. But the doubts and fears in her head told her to keep her mouth closed.

Darren kissed her cool lips, sending a warm sensation down her spine. Who needed a blanket when she had Darren, a man who was falling in love with her?

"Jill, I'm not scaring you off by putting my feelings out there like this, am I?" he asked, misreading her silence.

"No," she said, blinking back her tears. "Not at all. Darren, it's just…you're the kindest man I've met in quite sometime. You give and expect nothing in return. You don't care about what I have, just who I am."

He held her hand. "I know you have a lot. Financially, you're probably set for life, so I know you can't be bought. But whatever you're lacking, I can take care of for you. When you need a shoulder to lean on, someone to hold you and someone to love you, I'm here. All of this other stuff doesn't matter. It doesn't make me think any more or any less of you. You're the woman I've wanted to come into my life. I've dreamed of you and here you are."

"I'd given up on love and finding someone that I could be myself around. Then you came through the fire, literally."

He pushed her hair back off her face, "Everything happens for a reason. Best fire I ever put out. And to think I was upset that I had to work New Year's Eve."

"Did you have a hot date or something?" Jill asked.

"Nope and it's a good thing, too. She would have been heartbroken when I dropped her for you."

Jill wrapped her arms around his waist, "Good, now I don't have to bump her off."

He brushed his lips across her neck. "Umm, I like this aggressive side of you."

She pounced on him, pushing him backwards on the sofa. "You haven't seen aggression yet."

"Treat me like I'm from Missouri, show me."

Jill climbed on top of him and lifted his sweatshirt over his head, all the while kissing every inch of skin she exposed. First his shoulders, a smooth chocolate treat if she'd ever tasted one. Then she moved to his neck, using her tongue to heat him up in her lukewarm office. She unbuckled his belt as she suckled his nipples, which were as hard as diamonds. Darren arched his back, pressing his hips into hers. He reached up and slid his hands underneath her layers of clothing. At first, his hands were cold and made her tingle but it didn't take long for her body to feel as if it were on fire from his touch as he sensuously peeled each article of clothing off her upper torso.

Jill had never experienced this kind of sexual awakening with a man before. But Darren allowed her to release all of her inhibitions. She wanted to please him in every way possible. She pushed his corduroys down to his ankles and found him standing at attention in his boxers. Jill kissed his stomach, allowing her tongue to dance in and out of his navel.

"Oh Jill," he moaned as she drew his most sensitive muscle into her mouth.

She wanted to taste his essence, have him on her lips as he'd had her. She wanted to push the thought of his ex-wife's betrayal out of his head. She wanted to atone for her lies by giving him toe curling pleasure.

But how long would it be before the truth came out? On the other hand, with all that he'd just said to her, the truth didn't matter, did it? Jill pulled back from him, when the look on his face showed her that he was near climax.

She pulled her pants off, rubbing her wetness against his manhood. Darren moaned as he felt himself sink into her warm valley and he gripped her hips as she gyrated against him. Then Darren sat up, holding Jill on his lap, and kissed her with a sizzling passion that made her forget it was freezing outside. Suddenly there was a whiff of smoke in the room. She and Darren broke off their kissing and lovemaking and found that one of the blankets had fallen on the space heater.

"Oh my goodness!" Jill yelled.

Darren leapt into action, pulling the blanket off the heater and beating the small flames out with one of his discarded boots. Jill burst into laughter when he held up the blanket.

"I should have moved that heater," he said. "Do you know how many times we tell people not place blankets and articles of clothing next to these things?"

"We didn't take your advice, did we?" she asked, grabbing the other blanket and wrapping it around herself.

Darren moved the heater away from the sofa and pulled Jill into his arms. "Don't tell anybody about this. How would that look? Fire captain almost burns down office while making love to his sexy girlfriend."

She kissed his nose. "Umm, that would look kind of bad," she said.

"Do you have a weather radio?"

"I have a battery operated radio in my desk." She bounded over to the desk, opened the bottom drawer and pulled out the small radio.

Darren tuned in to the weather station.

"Sleet and snow continue to fall throughout the metro area," the announcer said. "Motorists are urged to stay indoors. Conditions are expected to worsen as temperatures plummet to the low teens overnight. Police have reported over 100 accidents on metro roads and two deaths have been blamed on the weather."

Darren shut the radio off. "You heard the man, we have to stay inside."

The generators started again and the lights flicked on. Jill smiled wickedly.

"Whatever will we do to pass the time?" she said as she seductively lowered her blanket.

Darren smiled at the sight of her naked body. "Oh, I have a few ideas that will keep us busy for hours." He pulled her into his arms and kissed her with fervor that made her knees buckle.

CHAPTER TWELVE

Darren woke up with Jill in his arms, his back stiff from sleeping on the tiny sofa. As the sun trickled in through the window, he took in the grandeur of the office: lush burgundy carpet, a huge mahogany desk, a large, deep brown leather chair and a view of the Atlanta skyline. A full closet, a bathroom and a massive file cabinet were also part of the office.

Darren wondered how much work she had put in to get an office like this. Surely the CEO of the company couldn't have a bigger office than this. His eyes roamed the walls, taking note of Jill's degrees, her photos of her parents and friends.

I wonder how she would look in a wedding dress, he thought, then immediately dismissed such thinking. It was way too soon to be entertaining thoughts of marriage. The last time he'd rushed into marriage had turned out to be a disaster. How could he even consider doing it again?

Jill isn't Rita, he reasoned. *And how do I even know Jill is ready for marriage? I can't see her giving up her career to settle down and start a family right away.*

But that's what Darren wanted, a family. Rita had robbed him of that chance but he was going to make sure it wouldn't happen again. But how was he going to have that conversation with Jill without pushing her away?

Darren ran his finger up and down Jill's forearm, contemplating what his next move should be. She already knew what was in his heart, but to tell a woman like her that he wanted to marry her might push her away. As he gazed at her slumbering body, he knew in his heart that Jill was the woman he wanted to spend the rest of his life with.

She stirred slightly in his arms as he gently kissed her on the forehead. She was beautiful when she slept. Darren wondered what she dreamed of. Was he a part of those dreams? She was the star of his dreams every night. He smelled her as he slept, felt her soft hands touching him in the night, felt her lips brushing against his, kissing him and giving him pleasure beyond imagination.

The real thing was no disappointment. Jill captured his body and spirit in ways that he'd never imagined could happen. He'd come close to making a commitment to another woman he was dating shortly after he divorced Rita. They'd rushed into sex and their intense passion had soon burned out like an oxygen-deprived fire.

What he and Jill had was destined to last. At least that's what he'd hoped was happening. His radio went off, waking Jill.

"Yeah, this is Alexander," he said.

"Captain, we were just checking on you. You didn't come back to the station last night and Harrison is letting the illusion of being in charge go to his head," one of the firefighters said.

"Yeah, I got stuck at an office building overnight. How are the road conditions?"

"Improving, slightly. Do you need us to send someone for you?"

"No, I'm cool. I should be back at the station by noon," Darren assured him.

"All right, cool. I mean, 10-4."

Darren laughed at the rookie, and then turned to Jill. "Good morning, beautiful."

"I seriously doubt I look beautiful this morning," she groaned.

"Not a morning person, I see."

Jill sat up, running her fingers though her hair. "Not until I've had some coffee."

"If you don't mind slipping and sliding, we can go out and see if anything around here is open," Darren said.

"Okay. But I have to take a shower first."

"I'd better go check in at the station. Why don't I come back in an hour?" he suggested.

"Good idea and maybe tonight I can go home."

They listened as chunks of melting ice crashed to the street. "We've got to be out of here by sundown before the roads refreeze," Darren said. "You're not traversing icy roads. Staying in isn't so bad."

"And I loved being in with you last night," she said.

Darren read the duality of her words and blushed. "I loved being in you, I mean in with you, last night too." He kissed her on the cheek, and then headed for the stairwell.

❧❧

Jill wrapped her blanket around her shoulders as she headed to the bathroom. The air was still cool in her office, but the memory of the night she and Darren shared there warmed her. As she turned the shower on and the water sprayed out, she was happy that she had gone for the gas water heater instead of the electric one.

This has gone on long enough; I have to tell him the truth. He's probably put two and two together already. What lower echelon employee has an office like this?

Jill had always had a fantasy about making love in her office, but she'd never thought it would come true, not considering her luck with men. But Darren seemed to be in the business of making her dreams come true. She would never be able to look at her sofa the same again.

Stepping into the shower, she closed her eyes, reliving the passion and intensity that she and Darren had shared as the tepid water beat down on her. He played her body like a master musician. She'd never felt so desired, so wanted. Last night, Darren had made it clear that he wanted to take care of her needs and wants. But would it all come to a screeching halt when the truth came out?

Jill stepped out of the shower, shivering from the artic air in the office. She grabbed her robe and headed for the file cabinet where she kept her work-out sweats and sneakers. She wished she had purchased a pair of Timberland boots but it was the Deep South, for goodness sakes. Grabbing her cell phone, she headed downstairs. As she dialed Malik's number to find out if he and Shari were all right, she wondered if Shari had shared her news about the baby with him yet.

"Hello?" Shari said in a frustrated tone.

"Hey, it's Jill."

"Please tell me you're open for business today, because your boy has to go."

Jill laughed. "Is it that bad?"

"Let's see, he's thrown snowballs at me and he will not leave me alone. He's worse than a child," Shari said, then burst out laughing. "This man has got to get out of my house."

"You know the roads are still bad. I was stuck in the office overnight," Jill said. "The power went out and we almost started a fire."

"We? Either you're learning French or you're talking about Darren."

"He was here. When I sent everybody home, I didn't take my own advice to leave. Next thing I know, the power goes out. The back-up generators were acting sketchy and Darren called to check on me."

"That was nice of him," Shari said.

"It was. He ended up coming over and spending the night." Jill couldn't help blushing as she talked about the previous night. Without giving Shari all of the details, she let her know that she and Darren had a good time and that she was meeting him for coffee and he was taking her home.

"So, how did you explain why you have the big corner office?"

"I didn't. He didn't ask."

"Don't ask, don't tell didn't work for the army. Do you think it's going to work for your relationship with Darren?"

"I really don't want to think about this right now," she said. "I know that I need to tell him the truth, but then again, after last night it might not matter."

Shari sighed. "It will matter, Jill. This man has no idea what he's getting into. He's going to be Atlanta's version of Stedman Graham and you know that. You should at least prepare him for that."

"Shari, we're just regular, ordinary folk. His mom knows some of my family in Macon," she said.

"But this isn't Macon. You're digging a hole that you won't be able to climb out of."

When Jill reached the first floor, Darren was standing outside waiting on her. "I have to go, Shari."

"Remember that tangled web," she said before hanging up.

Jill opened the door, took Darren's hand and off they went in search of coffee and breakfast.

"It seems warmer today," Jill said.

"Hopefully some of this ice and snow will melt," Darren said. "Luckily we haven't had anyone pull any charcoal grills into their house to heat themselves."

Jill nearly slipped on a patch of ice but Darren quickly grabbed her before she hit the ground.

"You all right?" he asked.

"Embarrassed but fine," Jill replied. "Where are we going again?"

"Sunrise Café is the only place open. I think they were stuck overnight too."

Jill looked at the usually busy Peachtree Street. It was eerily still, frozen and quiet. "Hard to believe that this is the heart of the city. Cover it with a little ice and snow and southerners stay inside."

"Which is what we're supposed to do," he said as he opened the door to the restaurant.

The inside of the restaurant was filled with people who looked as if they had cabin fever. They had only been stuck inside for one day, but people in Atlanta were used to being in constant motion.

"I see we're not the only ones who braved the elements," Darren said as he waved for the host to seat them. It took about ten minutes for a table to open up.

"Well, at least someone is making money in this weather," Jill said. "All of the people I needed to meet with and talk to aren't in the office."

"How dedicated to your job are you? Does every-thing else, including your safety, come second?"

"No, but I can't flip a switch and not be a busi-nesswoman one minute, and then the next minute become one. When computers are off, my company isn't making money."

"You act like you own the place," Darren said.

Jill froze in her seat. Once again she had the opprotunity to come clean. She did own the place, she did focus on growing DVA a little too much, but the words to confess didn't come. She couldn't say, "Yes, I do own it."

Darren mistook her silence for her being offended. "I'm sorry; I didn't mean it like that."

"I do take my job seriously, and maybe I am a little territorial about it all, but damn, your career is impor-tant to you. But all of a sudden when a woman values her career there's a big problem."

"I'm not saying that," he said.

Jill waved her hands. "All I'm saying is, my job is a part of who I am and if you have a problem with that, then I don't know what kind of future we're going to have."

They sat in an uncomfortable silence as the wait-ress came over and took their orders. Jill hoped that coffee would take the edge off her attitude. She didn't know why she was picking a fight with Darren. Was she subconsciously trying to sabotage her relationship to be sure it wouldn't end in heartbreak?

Darren stared at Jill as she smoothed a napkin across her lap. "Is this going to be a recurring argument?"

"Are you going to have a constant problem with my career?"

"I just wonder where I fit into your life. If your career comes first, where does that leave me?"

Jill sighed and blew on her nails. "Has my career been a problem so far? I've made time for you and I don't see that changing. And what about your career, Darren?"

"Touché. I guess I didn't realize how driven you are. But after seeing your office, I get it. You work hard."

"Why has this become an issue today?"

Darren shrugged his shoulders. "It's not an issue, let's just drop it."

"Fine."

The waitress brought Jill her coffee and Darren his orange juice. The chill between them was colder than the wind blowing outside. Jill sipped her coffee, looking around at the other restaurant patrons and ignoring Darren.

"Your food will be out shortly, the kitchen is a little backed up," she said.

"Thank you," Darren said.

Jill turned to him with a frown on her face. "You know what I don't understand? You men claim to want a woman who is independent, can take care of herself and when that woman is staring you in the face, you have a problem with her. Do you even know what you want?"

"I want you. But I don't know if I can compete with DVA."

Jill rose to her feet, knocking her chair backwards. "Guess what, nobody asked you too." She dashed out of the restaurant, nearly knocking over a family walking in.

She knew this argument was bogus, but she had to get away from Darren.

CHAPTER THIRTEEN

Two days after the city was blanketed by ice and the temperature barely rose above freezing, temperatures peaked in the mid 60s, melted the ice and brought Atlantans out in droves. Even though the sun was shining, Darren wasn't in the mood to celebrate. He hadn't heard from Jill since she bolted out of the Sunrise Café.

What's her problem? he wondered. *I don't understand women and I guess I never will.*

"Hey, Captain, your brother's here," one of the fire-fighters said from the doorway of Darren's office.

"I'll be out in a minute," Darren growled.

The young fireman threw his hands up and backed out of the office as if avoiding a minefield. Darren had been giving attitude to everyone in the station all day. No one wanted to talk to him, look at him or breathe near him for fear of an angry outburst.

That was just fine with Darren because he wanted to be left alone. And he certainly didn't want to see Cleveland. Why wasn't that man at home resting his back? The sooner he got better the sooner he could return to active duty. But Darren knew why his brother was there. Someone had probably called him, given him every detail of Darren's rampage and asked Cleveland to help them.

Seconds later, Cleveland was sitting across the desk from Darren, who hadn't acknowledged his presence in the office.

"Man, what's wrong with you?"

"Nothing. I'm working. Is there something you want?"

"Damn," Cleveland said. "Did somebody steal your box of corn flakes this morning and replace it with haterade?"

"Don't you have something that you can be doing? Physical therapy, perhaps?"

"The last time I saw you like this was…Where's Jill?"

"Working, since that's her priority."

Cleveland nodded knowingly. "I see."

"What do you mean, 'I see'?"

"You and Jill had your first argument, huh?"

"Whatever."

"Oh well, big bro, guess she wasn't perfect after all," he said sarcastically. "Still on that never-ending quest for perfection, aren't you?"

Darren rolled his eyes. "Can't you see I'm working? I don't need you to pretend you're a psychologist and try to analyze my life. And I don't want to talk about Jill."

"What did she do?"

"Are you deaf?"

"Nope, I hear everything you're not saying. What are you two fighting about?"

"It's stupid, really." Darren threw his pen on the desk. "She thinks I have a problem with her focusing on her career."

"And you don't?"

Darren rolled his eyes and picked up his pen and twirled it between his fingers. "You know, women kill me. One minute we're shiftless and tired because we don't take care of them and the next minute they're beating us over the head with how independent they are."

Cleveland leaned back in his seat and folded his fingers under his chin like a psychologist. "So, Jill doesn't want you to take care of her and you feel unneeded."

"Shut the hell up!"

"Didn't you spend the night with her in the ice storm?"

"And?"

"Just asking, damn."

"Why don't you mind your business? Where's Ma?"

"On her way home. The doctors said I don't need supervision anymore. I might be back to work in a few weeks."

"Good. We need you around here."

"Yeah, and you need to call Jill. Stop being so hard-nosed about everything. That woman probably needs to hear from you. Make up with her."

Darren waved his brother away. "Just go and stay out of my love life."

Cleveland stood up. "Keep that attitude and you won't have a love life for me to meddle in."

Before Darren could snarl back, Cleveland was out the door.

❧❧

Jill buried herself in work, overseeing deals that she normally trusted her executives to finalize. She scrutinized every detail of plans that came across her desk, even those from some of her top executives. If a comma was in the wrong place or a word misspelled, Jill made the person rewrite the document.

Malik burst into her office and sat down. Jill was busily typing at her computer and didn't notice him sitting there for a few moments.

"What are you doing in here?" she asked.

"I could ask you the same question. You've been on a tear since the ice melted. I haven't seen you act like this since the early days."

"And your point is what? I told you all at the beginning of the year that I was going to make this a banner year for DVA. Do you think that's going happen without hard work?"

"Hard work is one thing, but you're being an unyielding taskmaster."

Jill turned around in her chair and peered at him over her reading glasses. "*Unyielding*?"

"Yes."

"You're overstating things. I just want to make sure that we do the best that we can to increase revenues and our presence."

"Uh-huh," he said.

"What?"

"Jill, I know you. What's going on?"

"Nothing," she lied.

Malik raised his eyebrow and nodded. "How's the firefighter doing?"

"If you are referring to Darren, I'm sure he's fine."

"When was the last time you talked to him?"

"Why are you worried about it? This is a place of business, not a speakeasy where the topic of discussion is my love life."

Malik hissed like a cat. "Let me leave you to your work." He stood and walked out of her office, tiptoeing across the floor as if it were eggshells.

When he left, Jill stood up and looked out of the window. *What have I done? Maybe I pushed Darren away. He hasn't called and I don't think I can call him. I don't know why I made such a scene in that restaurant. He didn't deserve that.*

Jill had been waiting for the phone to ring and to hear Darren's voice on the other end. She absentmindedly stroked her headset, hoping that the next call that came through would be from Darren. Then the familiar buzz sounded in her ear and Madison said, "Jill, you have a call on line one."

"Who is it?" she asked hopefully.

"Mr. Covington."

"Voice mail," she replied detachedly. Sitting down, she returned to her tasks and tried to force herself not to think about Darren. It didn't work, because five minutes later, she was looking longingly at the phone.

She buzzed Madison. "Can you get Carl Covington on the line, please," she said.

Jill didn't have time to act like a love sick teenager; she had a business to run.

When the work day came to an end, Malik and Shari walked into Jill's office. She was hunched over her computer, rapidly typing up a draft of a contract to acquire Covington's new technology. The legal department was going to have make sure there were no loopholes that would leave DVA open to a lawsuit or anything.

Shari cleared her throat, causing Jill to look up at them. "What? Is it intervention time or something?" Jill continued typing.

Malik pointed to the door, and then walked out, leaving Shari alone with Jill. "What's really going on?" Shari asked as she sat down across from Jill.

"I'm working, that's all. I always work."

"Jill, did something happen with Darren?"

Jill stopped typing and turned to her friend. "He's just the same and I don't regret not telling him that I'm the CEO of DVA."

"What happened?"

"We had a fight about my career," Jill said. "In a roundabout way, he accused me of basically caring more about my career than our relationship."

"What did he say exactly?"

"It doesn't matter, he hasn't called and I don't have time to worry about him."

Shari sighed heavily. "Couples argue. You can't expect everything to be roses and sunshine."

"I'm not that naïve," Jill answered. "But Darren can't expect me to change my work schedule to please him. He can go to hell."

"You don't mean that."

Jill folded her arms across her chest. "Are you walking around in my head, reading my thoughts?"

"Testy, testy," Shari said. "Jill, why don't you call him and talk to him and this time let him know the true reason why you spend so much time here."

Jill waved her hands as if to say no. "If he wants to talk to me, he has my number. Do you think I'm going to chase some man down?"

"It's not about you chasing him. You said you cared about him. He makes you happy, so why let a misunderstanding come between the two of you?"

"Who said it was a misunderstanding? Darren obviously wants a woman who needs him and needs to be taken care of."

Shari folded her arms and shook her head. "It's not that. Sometimes people just say things in the heat of the moment and regret it later."

"That's not what happened here and I don't care to talk about it. Darren and I aren't meant to be, that's all." Her voice was low and not convincing at all. Both she and Shari knew that the last thing Jill wanted was for things to be over between her and Darren.

"You're not telling the truth to me or yourself. You don't give up that kind of glow for no reason and I'm sorry, but you're going to have to try harder to convince me and yourself that you want that man out of your life."

Jill stood up and gazed out of the window. "I guess you're right," she replied. "But what am I supposed to do?"

Shari picked up the phone from Jill's desk. "Call him. That's all you have to do."

"What if he doesn't want to talk to me?"

"I doubt that's that case. But hey, I'm a hopeless romantic and I want to see everybody happy."

Jill turned around and gave Shari a weak smile. "Have you heard from the doctor?"

"Yes, Malik and I will be parents in about eight and a half months."

Jill walked from around the desk and hugged Shari tightly. "I'm so happy for you and Malik. This is such a blessing for the two of you."

"I know. I just haven't been able to tell Malik yet. I'm sure he'll be happy, at least I hope so."

"Haven't you all talked about starting a family?"

"Yes, but not this soon. I wanted to make sure that I had my writing career in order and of course, Malik wants to see how far he can make it here in his career. There never is a right time to start a family, though. And love doesn't come into our lives every day. You'd better not let that man go."

Jill waved Shari away. "You'd better go tell your husband that baby makes three."

Shari winked at Jill, and then headed for the door. Stopping, she turned to her friend. "I bet Darren is waiting on your call."

When Jill was sitting in the office alone, she turned her computer off and took Shari's advice, dialed Darren's number and held her breath until he answered the phone.

"Hello?" he said.

"D-darren, it's Jill."

"How are you? I'm glad you called because I was sitting here looking at the phone trying to figure out what I was going to say when I called you."

"Have you figured it out yet?"

"I just want to know why we're fighting."

"Because I'm pigheaded, and I took you completely out of context?"

He laughed nervously. "Jill, I really don't have a problem with you being career-oriented. That's who you were before you met me and I don't expect you to change."

"Really?"

"Yeah. I have an idea; let's start over. Meet me tonight for a drink. You pick the place and I'll be there."

"Okay, my place and I'll make the drinks."

"Sounds good to me. Have you had dinner?"

"No, I haven't even left the office yet." Jill could imagine Darren frowning, furrowing his brows at her statement.

"I'll pick up some Chinese. How about that?"

Jill smiled. "That works for me."

When they hung up the phone, Jill couldn't get out of her office fast enough. She headed to the liquor store and picked up the ingredients for margaritas— tequila, sweet lime mix and salt. Cooking might not be her forte, but Jill could mix a hell of a drink. When she was a student at Spelman, her nickname had been "the bartender." She was the one who poured the drinks for her sorority sisters when they crossed into the sister- hood of Alpha Kappa Alpha Sorority, Inc.

She was the one who poured the drinks when she and her friends had their *Waiting to Exhale* viewing party whenever one of her girls was going through something with her man or ex-man.

Tonight she was going to lay a blockbuster of a margarita on Darren. And if she found the right outfit, the alcohol wouldn't be the only thing that went to his head.

"If it isn't Jill Atkinson," David said as he approached her.

The smile on her face disappeared like the Atlanta snow. "What do you want?"

"Just looking for that interview," he said. "By the way, you look awesome."

"And you look like lying pond scum. Excuse me."

"Drinking to combat the loneliness?"

"I'm far from lonely. Did you think I was going to roll up in a ball and die because you betrayed me?" Jill snarled at him. "You have some nerve to think I'd agree to an interview with your rag. If I didn't tell you before, let me tell you now, go to hell!"

"Do you really want to make an enemy of me?" David asked, his tone threatening.

Jill fought the urge to hit him with a liquor bottle. "We're not friends and if you print anything about me or my company in your paper and there is a misspelled word, dangling participle or a misused adverb, I will have my entire legal department swoop down on you like a pack of vultures and we will pick your sorry carcass until there is nothing left."

David shook his head, and then leaned into Jill. "You don't scare me, Ms. Atkinson. And I don't appreciate your threats."

"I don't make threats, I make promises," she said before turning on her heels and heading for the register.

❧

Darren loaded the last of the Chinese food in the back seat of the car. He'd probably bought way too much food. Maybe Jill would get the hint and they would hide away in her place until the food was gone.

He wanted this relationship to work. Maybe it was time for him to put aside some of his hang-ups about working women. Why shouldn't Jill put her all into her career? It was harder for women to get ahead and judging from her office, she'd worked hard. *I can support her,* he thought as he started the car. *It's not like I have the easiest job in the world for someone to deal with.*

As Darren pulled into the parking deck of Jill's building, he saw her getting out of a silver Jaguar XLJ. She looked extremely sexy dressed in a dark red pantsuit that clung to each tantalizing curve of her body. Her hair was pulled back in a sloppy pony tail and a few strands of hair framed her face. Darren hopped out of the car and closed the space between them.

"Hello, beautiful," he said before pulling her into his arms and kissing her the way he'd been wanting to do for the last two days.

When their lips parted, Darren smiled and stroked her cheek. "I've got dinner in the car."

She held up the plastic bag in her hand. "I have the drinks."

"Then," he said as he backed to his car, "Let's get this party started."

They walked inside, nodding to the doorman as he held the door open for them. Darren possessively draped his arm across Jill's shoulder as if he wanted to tell the world that she was his woman.

Darren looked at her as the elevator rose to the top floor. Jill stirred his soul, made him swell with desire. There was more than sex that turned him on when it came to her. It was the way she was shy and powerful all at once. It was the way she was in total control one minute and unsure about herself the next. Jill might have a lot of control at work but he knew in the realm of love and romance she didn't give it her all because she couldn't control the matters of the heart. Darren knew it was his job to show her that she was safe with him. That all he wanted to do was love her.

"You're kind of quiet over there," Jill said as they stepped off the elevator.

"I was just thinking."

She unlocked the front door. "About?"

Darren grasped the knob and held the door open. "I'm going to be honest with you, I'm old-fashioned, I like to pamper my woman and I can be a little over-bearing. That's what the root of our disagreement was. It wasn't about the fact that you're a working woman. Every accident scene I went to during the storm, all I could think about was finding you. I was mad that you went to work and then when we went to the restaurant and you started talking business, it just made me think again how you risked your well being to go to your office. I can't have my woman doing that."

"Let's get one thing straight," Jill said as she walked into the kitchen. "I'm my own woman and I'm going to do what I have to do to when it comes to my career. Granted, it was a little foolish of me to go to work the other day, but how many times have there been calls for ice storms and nothing has happened?"

"I know, but I have an overwhelming urge to protect you," he said.

"Protect me?"

He nodded and walked over to her, drawing her into his arms. "I can't help it. The day I met you, I just knew you weren't the kind of woman who hadn't been taken care of, cherished like the queen you are."

She faced him, her eyes glossy with unshed tears. "How did you figure that out before you even talked to me?"

"I could tell, just from the way you acted. You wanted to hop off that gurney and get that computer."

Jill laughed. "I was working on my business plan for the new year."

"On New Year's Eve. That was a huge clue that you needed to be taken care of." He lifted her on the counter. "You're not going to do any work this New Year's Eve. You and I have a date."

"The year just got started good," she replied, wrapping her arms around his neck. "Our dinner is getting cold."

"Do you think I care?" he asked, then brushed his lips against her cheek. "I've missed you."

"Me too," she breathed. Jill turned her head to receive Darren's kiss.

Her tongue never tasted sweeter, her kisses had never been so urgent. When he heard her stomach growl, he pulled back from the kiss.

"I guess you really do need to eat," he said with a laugh.

She dropped her head and giggled. "I didn't have much time to eat today," she said.

Darren walked over to her dining room table and pulled a chair out for her. Jill sat down as if she were about to be treated to a meal in a four star restaurant. Playing along, Darren made exaggerated moves like a stuffy waiter as he opened the cartons of lo mien, sweet and sour shrimp and chicken fried rice.

"Would the lady like me to feed her?"

"That's quite all right, but would you care to join me, that is, if you can."

Darren looked around as if he were in the middle of a restaurant. "I'm sure the boss can spare me. Besides, I don't even know where the plates are."

Jill rose from her seat, grabbed two plates and filled two glasses with sparkling fruit juice and walked over to the table. "Here you go," she said as she placed the plates and a glass in front of him.

Darren spooned food into their plates with the plastic utensils. He slid a plate over to her. "Dinner is served."

Jill cast her glance upwards at him. "I really appreciate you and the time we spend together. Everything is so simple with us."

"I'm a simple man. Love doesn't have to be complicated. We make it that way when we want to run from it. I'm not going to let you run, though."

She took a small bite of her food. "I'm not going to run unless it's into your arms. For too long I let my broken heart keep me away from love and the chance of being with someone special because I thought...It doesn't matter. It's nice to know that I have you in my corner, being my protector."

Darren reached across the table and placed his hand on top of hers. "I'm glad you can see that."

"I don't like to fight," Jill said, placing her fork on the side of her plate.

Darren followed her lead, setting his fork down. "Neither do I. Are we going to keep eating or go straight to the making up?"

He'd been longing for her from the moment he saw her step out of her car. His erection was the reason why he'd stopped serving Jill. He didn't want her to see what she'd done to him just by walking past him and sitting down. Somehow, she made that simple act elegant and sexy.

"I vote for making up, but I want to change into something a little more comfortable first," she said, pushing away from the table. "Wait here."

Darren smiled as she walked down the hallway. Jill had put an extra twist in her hips because she had to know he was watching.

CHAPTER FOURTEEN

Jill pulled her sexiest black teddy from the deep recesses of her lingerie drawer. The last time she'd planned to wear this outfit was the same day that she found out what a weasel David was. But she didn't have to worry about that with Darren. He was everything she'd ever dreamed of, the kind of man who loved unconditionally and someone she could trust.

She stripped out of her business suit and pulled the satin and lace teddy on. Her body glowed in the light of the setting sun that streamed though her bedroom windows. The contrast of the midnight black material with her skin brightened her complexion, giving her an exotic look. Jill pulled her hair up in a loose ponytail, to show off her bone structure and brown eyes.

As she looked at herself in the mirror, Jill knew she could open her heart to Darren and she could love him with everything in her. He didn't want anything from her. He was a giver and she was ready to receive his passion, his love and everything else he had to offer. For once, she was the one getting more out of a relationship. Darren had no idea how his love was transforming her and restoring her fragile trust in men. He showed her that she could indeed have it all, man, money, career and love. She was one step closer to being one of those couples she'd envied on New Year's Eve, she thought as she smoothed mango-scented body butter on her skin, making it feel as soft as silk. Then she misted the mango-scented body spray in the air, letting its essence fall on her. She pulled a pair of nylon and lace thigh high stockings from the drawer and slowly rolled them up her long legs, eagerly anticipating the moment when Darren would take them off. Would he use his hands or his tongue and teeth? She hoped for both. Jill rose from the edge of the bed and headed for the bedroom door.

"Darren," she called out. "I think we have some making up to do."

He stood so quickly that he knocked his chair over. "Whoa." Darren closed the space between them and pulled her against his body, running his hand up and down her sides. "You feel as good as you look."

She took his hand and placed it between her thighs. "And it gets so much better," she wantonly whispered.

She could feel Darren shiver as she moved his hand to the snap away crotch of her outfit. He stroked the front snaps, slowly unsnapping them, exposing her throbbing womanhood. He rubbed his finger across her passion, making her knees buckle. He inserted his finger in her tight valley of wetness, stroking her ripe bud with his forefinger. Erotic sensations crawled up and down her spine, manifesting themselves in a satisfied moan. Darren backed her against the wall and prepared to feast on her body, starting with her breasts as he teased them out of her sexy outfit. Her nipples were like chocolate drops ready to be tasted and his mouth watered at the sight. Darren drew her nipple into his mouth, wrapping his tongue around her bead, licking her as if she were his favorite flavor of ice cream.

Jill held the back of his head as he fed on her. She could barely hang on as he reached between her legs, stroking her until her body purred. He dropped to his knees, kissed the wet folds of flesh between her thighs, nearly causing her to slip down to the floor. He scooped her into his arms.

"Maybe we need a change of scenery," he said as he backed into her bedroom.

Darren carried her to the bed as if she were a virginal bride on her wedding night. Jill closed her eyes, imagining that this was indeed the night that she became Mrs. Darren Alexander. He laid her on the king-sized bed, a bed she'd spent so many cold nights alone in. Sometimes Jill would go as far as sleeping on the sofa bed in the downstairs den because she had too much bed to sleep in alone. She stroked the sheets and silently wished for more nights with Darren in her bed.

Then she reached up and cupped his face in her hands before bringing his lips to hers. Darren kissed her palm.

"I just want to look at you," he said, "God, you're beautiful. I'm lucky you haven't been snapped up by some other man. I know I'm not the only one who's seen how beautiful you are."

Jill blushed. Most men saw her as a meal ticket, but Darren looked at her with desire in his eyes and his heart, making her feel special, dynamic and sexy, things that weren't associated with a businesswoman like herself. Darren made her feel that she was all woman.

"I need you," Darren said huskily. "All of you, mind, body and soul. I've never felt this way about anyone before."

His admission stirred her soul. He needed her as much as she needed and wanted him. She answered his request with a soul searing kiss, drawing his tongue into her mouth, sucking it and savoring the taste of his sweetness. Darren broke off the kiss and slid down her body, letting his tongue map a course to her treasure. He hoisted her legs onto his shoulders, clearing the path to her wetness, lapping her sexual juices, making Jill throw her head back in satisfied bliss. Her legs shivered and she whimpered with delight when Darren's tongue pressed deeper into her valley. But she needed more; she yearned to feel the throbbing of his manhood inside her. Reaching for his engorged sex, she stroked his erection to a near explosion. Jill wanted to melt with him, wanted to become one with him and bury herself inside his soul.

In one motion, he positioned his body between her legs, pressing his throbbing manhood against her softness. When he plunged into her wetness, Jill exclaimed his name and pressed her hips into his. Her body fell into his pulsating rhythm, and she allowed him to lead her down satisfaction's pathway.

Making love to Darren was indescribable, wonderful, and fulfilled her every want and need. He was the kind of man she'd dreamed of but never thought she'd have because she didn't know fairy tales still came true.

When they reached their climax, Jill held on to Darren tightly. He brushed his lips across hers. "Baby, I love being with you," Darren said. "I love you."

She kissed him gently. "I think I love you too," she replied. Jill had never felt more nervous than when she confessed her love to Darren. She was raw, naked and vulnerable and had no idea what was supposed to happen next. Was he supposed to say something else? Was she supposed to explain her feelings to him in a poetic fashion?

Darren stroked her cheek, silently easing her mind. Love didn't need an explanation, a caveat or an ironclad clause, she realized. All love needed was two willing hearts.

After they'd filled themselves with each other, Jill and Darren headed into the kitchen but neither of them wanted the leftover Chinese food. So Jill made the margaritas, pulled out some tortilla chips and a jar of salsa.

"Do you have any cheese?" he asked as he watched her put the salsa in the microwave.

"I think so," she said, then pointed to the refrigerator. "There should be some cheese in the crisper."

Darren opened the refrigerator, found a brick of cheese. "Grater?"

"What?"

"Cheese grater?"

Jill pointed to an assortment of cooking utensils on the wall. "There should be one over there."

Darren gently pinched her cheek. "I forgot, the kitchen isn't your favorite room."

"Maybe I need to spend more time in here," she said as she watched Darren turn generic salsa into something else.

He grated half a brick of cheddar cheese into the salsa, stirred it up and placed it in the microwave until the cheese melted. "Do you have any sour cream?"

"I seriously doubt it. You can check the fridge, though."

Darren looked but didn't find any. "I guess it will be all right without it," he said as he took the salsa out of the microwave.

"It smells good," she said. Darren set the cheesy mix in the middle of the chips.

Jill poured the margaritas into chilled glasses. "All right, to the living room," she said.

They carried their snacks into the living room and tuned the television to ESPN. Jill handed Darren his drink as they settled on the sofa.

"Thanks, babe," he said as she handed him his drink. She nestled against him on the sofa.

They fell into a comfortable silence. At that moment, Jill knew she should have opened up more about herself, particularly the fact that she was the CEO of DVA and not just an employee. But, she surmised, that shouldn't even matter now. *Darren loves me for who I am and not for what I have.*

But what about a future with Darren? If he became her husband, she couldn't hide it from him anymore.

"Where you a bartender in a past life?" he asked in between sips of his drink.

She nodded. "That's how I made it through college."

Darren took another sip. "I can see that. You must have made a lot of tips."

Jill smiled and dipped a chip in the salsa. "Maybe we should open a bar."

"Like you would leave corporate America to be the sexiest bartender in the state of Georgia."

"Maybe I would. It depends on whether you would leave the action and adventure of the fire department."

"So, why don't we do it? Give up our careers and start over."

Jill chewed her bottom lip. "Tempting, but I know you would never do it."

Darren feigned surprise. "You wound me, woman. I would quit, but the only way I'd go into business with you is if you worked as hard for me as you do for DVA."

"Oh, I would. I believe in hard work."

Darren drained his glass. "And where would we open this bar?"

"Definitely not in Buckhead. We don't want to get swallowed up by the other bars that are already there. And you know we would have to have plasma TVs to show all of the Falcons and the Hawks games."

"Maybe not the Hawks," he said. "We do want to make money."

Jill smiled and took another chip. "What's wrong with the Hawks? They're Atlanta's team too."

"The Hawks are losers and no one likes a loser." Darren stroked Jill's cheek. "I like dreaming with you."

"We could make this happen," she said. "Raising the capital would be easy. I could get someone to research an area that…"

"Honey, you can't be serious. We're just talking."

Jill nodded, even though she was in business-making mode. "You're right; I just let my business savvy get the best of me."

"So, you want to start your own business?"

"Uh, yeah," she stammered. "It can't be too hard."

"They say the small business sinks or swims in the first five years. I admire people that can see it through, but it has to be tough. Could you imagine keeping up this kind of lifestyle while depending on people to buy your product? What happens in the summer when people don't want to go into a dark bar because the action is all outside?"

"I don't know. Outside seating and a posh patio that overlooks the street so they won't miss anything?"

"You don't miss a beat, do you?" he asked.

Jill could tell he was impressed.

"Maybe you should stick around DVA. In a couple of years you're going to be running the place."

She laughed nervously. "That would be something."

"Your face all over the covers of magazines and newspapers. That would be something to see."

Jill stood up and began to clear their glasses. At least one thing was confirmed. Darren didn't pay much attention to business magazines.

"It's NFC championship weekend," Darren said, repeating the announcer on TV. "Think Vick can take McNabb down?"

"I sure hope so," Jill called from the kitchen as she placed the dishes in the dishwasher. "The Eagles might be tough this year. Philly is tired of wiping egg off their collective faces in the championship game."

Darren walked into the kitchen, catching Jill around her waist. "You know what else is coming up."

"What's that?"

"Valentine's Day."

Jill hadn't looked forward to February 14th since she found out that Cupid wasn't real. Every year, her employees would chatter in the office, excited about dates later that evening, gushing over flowers that everyone received. Jill would stay locked in her office, her nose buried in one file after another. Though the thought crossed her mind, Jill never sent herself roses and chocolates. That wasn't her style.

"Valentine's Day, huh?" she said.

"Yeah and I want to take you away from all of this—no work, no cell phones, no laptop computers, just me and you."

Jill smiled. If Darren sent her long-stemmed red roses she would be happy. "Where are we going?"

"That, my dear, is a surprise."

"I love surprises," she said.

He gently kissed the side of her neck. "And you will love this one. I have to go."

"Okay," she replied, then pouted like a little child being ushered to bed.

Darren pinched her cheek. "I'll see you later. Let's do dinner tomorrow night."

"All right, you pick the place," she said as they walked to the door.

"I love you."

"I love you, too."

Jill leaned against the door as she closed it behind Darren. The night had been perfect and she couldn't wait to close her eyes and dream about spending Valentine's Day with her man.

CHAPTER FIFTEEN

Darren sat at the computer in his office searching for the perfect weekend getaway for him and Jill. He wanted to take her away for a week, but knowing the way she felt about work, he knew that wasn't going to happen. He'd settle for a weekend. Nothing but the two of them wrapped in each other's arms. Darren knew by Jill's reaction when he mentioned Valentine's Day that she'd never been treated properly on the day of love. But that was going to change this year. Valentine's Day was going to be a day she'd never forget.

Darren made reservations at Charleston's McCrady's Long Room for their Valentine's Day party. Then he booked a room at the Battery Carriage House overlooking the Charleston Harbor.

"Knock, knock," Cleveland said as he walked into the office. "What happened to you last night?"

Darren looked up from the computer with a Cheshire cat grin on his face. "I went to see Jill."

"So, all is right with the world now?"

Darren rolled his eyes at Cleveland, but the answer was yes. Jill was slowly becoming the center of his universe and there was no way he could think about a life without her in it. The last thing he wanted was to hear his brother tell him that he was making the same mistake twice or that he was rushing into another relationship that was going end in heartbreak.

"Jill is good for you," Cleveland said.

Darren leaned forward in his chair. "Come again?"

Cleveland nodded and grinned. "I know this sounds strange coming from me, but Jill is nothing like Rita. She was scandalous and the wrong woman for you. All she cared about was herself. I could see that from ten miles away. Jill isn't giving off that kind of vibe. I can tell she cares about you. That's the stuff you don't find every day."

"Unconditional."

"Yeah, what Ma and Daddy had. Maybe you and Jill are building that."

"Maybe."

"I'd stand up for you at this wedding," Cleveland said.

Darren bit down on his bottom lip, remembering the knock-down, drag-out fight he and his brother had had when he announced his upcoming wedding to Rita.

❧❦

"You're a damned fool to marry her. You don't know anything about her," Cleveland said over a game of basketball that had suddenly gotten extremely physical.

Darren threw the ball into Cleveland's chest. "You don't know her either and if you would stop being so heartbroken over the end of your marriage, you'd see all women are not the same."

Cleveland bounced the ball, turning his back to his brother and throwing up his elbow to shove it in Darren's stomach.

"This has nothing to do with me and more to do with you being whipped by what's between her legs."

Darren shoved him hard in the back, making Cleveland stumble. Cleveland threw the ball against the wall and pushed his brother in the chest.

"What the hell is wrong with you?" Darren demanded. "All I'm asking is for you to support me."

"You're walking into this thing half-cocked and it's going to be the biggest mistake of your life. She ain't the woman you need to bring into our family. That woman doesn't love you."

Darren punched Cleveland in the face. Dazed for a second, Cleveland countered with a punch to Darren's breadbox, knocking him backwards. Darren steadied himself with one hand on the court and kicked his brother in the leg.

"Why are we doing this?" Darren asked. "If you don't want to support me, then to hell with you."

Darren pushed away from Cleveland and headed for his car.

ℵℵ

In hindsight, Darren knew Cleveland had been only looking out for him and if he had listened to him, it would have saved him an awful lot of heartbreak and pain.

He looked up at Cleveland. "I'm going to listen to you this time. Jill is going to be mine and we're going to build a life together. And maybe she has a single girlfriend that you can meet."

"Please don't play cupid. Big white diapers don't look good on you," Cleveland said. "Are we on for the game this weekend?"

"Jill is probably going to tag along with us," Darren said. "She loves the Falcons."

"Yet another reason to snatch her up right away," Cleveland said before standing and walking out of the office.

Darren pulled his credit card from his pocket and confirmed his reservations. He wasn't going to let Jill get away.

❧❧

Jill pulled her glasses from her face. She hadn't gotten one thing done all day because she had been fielding calls from one of David's reporters all day. She had to give him credit, he was creative. He pretended to be an investor, he pretended to be from the *Atlanta Journal Constitution*, and he pretended to be from *Time* and *Newsweek*.

"Madison, if you put another call through here that isn't one I'm expecting, you're going to be working in the mail room."

"Sorry, Jill, but you know you love the media spotlight."

She bit back a caustic comment that would have burned Madison's ears like hydrochloric acid. "Just do what I said."

"And who is on your 'do call' list?"

"Darren Alexander and that's it, unless it's someone from inside the company. Got it?"

"Yes, ma'am," she said sarcastically.

Jill slammed the phone down and tried to return to the document that she was working on. The phone rang immediately.

"Yes?"

"Hard day?" Darren asked.

"Very much so. How are you?"

"Okay, but I'll be much better when you're better. Let me take you away from all your stress, at least for a couple of hours."

"And go where?" Jill asked as she twirled the phone cord around her finger.

"Lunch and a little workout."

"Workout?"

"That's the best way to relieve stress, a vigorous workout, clothing optional."

Jill blushed like a teenager seeing a naked man for the first time. She rose and closed the door to her office. "Mr. Alexander, I do believe you are propositioning me."

"I am. Oh, do you want to join me and my brother and some friends to watch the game this weekend? It's a tradition that whenever the Falcons make the playoffs we watch the championship game, eat, drink and be merry."

"Are you sure you all want a girl to crash your testosterone party?"

"You're going to be a welcomed addition. Now, back to my propositioning. Can you leave in the next twenty minutes?"

"I sure can, I'm not getting much work done right now anyway."

"See you then," he said.

When Jill hung up, she dashed into the bathroom and freshened up, brushed her teeth and fluffed her hair. Then she dabbed a bit of jasmine perfume on her wrists and behind her ears.

As she walked out the door, she told Madison that she would see her the next morning.

"Well, well," Madison replied. "Have fun for me too."

Jill winked at her. "I will."

By the time she made it downstairs, Darren was walking into the building. "Perfect timing," he said.

"Yes. Let's get out of here."

They strolled out onto Peachtree Street hand in hand. "Where are we going?" she asked.

"I figured we'd have lunch at the Madison Grill," he said. "You wouldn't happen to have some gym shorts handy, would you?"

"Up in my office," she said, eyeing him with questions dancing in her eyes.

"Sneakers too?"

"Yes."

"Go get them."

"Why?"

"I told you we're going to work out and," Darren looked down at her heels, "I don't think you can perform in those shoes."

Jill folded her arms across her chest. "What kind of performance are we talking about?"

"On the court. You do have basketball skills, don't you?" he asked.

"You are asking for it now, buddy," she said as she turned and headed back into the office.

Jill dashed passed Madison who said, "I thought you were gone."

"I am," she said. "You're not seeing me."

Jill walked into her office and grabbed her gym bag. She always kept one in her office, but rarely had time to use her midtown gym membership at Gold's. *I'm going to cream him,* she thought as she hoisted her bag strap over her shoulder.

After lunch, Darren took Jill to the city's workout facility where all of the firefighters and police officers worked out and played. But at this time of the day, Darren knew the place was going to be deserted.

"You can change over there and prepare to take this whipping like the Eagles on Sunday."

Jill kicked off her shoes. "Please, I'm Michael Vick and you're the Eagles secondary, about to get scorched."

Darren looked at her feet. She was definitely a woman who believes in pedicures. Her toes were so perfect and were also about the only part of her body that he hadn't sampled lately. He reached into her bag and pulled out her socks. "Let me get those for you," he said, then eased each foot into the white socks. Next, he put her gym shoes on.

Jill stood and headed for the locker room. "Hope you're ready to lose."

Darren couldn't help smiling at her confidence, but when she got on the court, he was going to show her no mercy. Seconds later, Jill walked out of the locker room dressed in a pair of Lycra shorts that hugged her luscious curves like a second skin. The tank top that she wore pushed her breasts up and made him want to kiss them until she begged him to stop.

"No fair," he said.

"What? We haven't even started playing yet," she said.

"And I'm supposed to concentrate with you looking like that?"

Jill walked over to him and took the ball from his hand. "Don't make excuses for why you're going to lose." She dribbled the ball between her legs as if she were Allen Iverson.

Despite what a sexy distraction she was, Darren knew it was game time. "Take the ball out," he said. "First one to ten."

Jill tossed the ball to him. When Darren began to dribble, Jill stole the ball from him and shot it in the hoop.

"Two zip," she said as she tossed the ball to him.

"All right, you think you got skills," he said as he dribbled the ball, keeping his eye on her so that she wouldn't be able to steal the ball this time. Darren went up for his shot, but Jill altered his shot by putting her hand in his face. The ball bounced off the rim and Jill chased down the rebound and hit a shot from behind the arch.

"Five zip, where's the D, baby?" she asked slapping him on the behind.

Darren took the ball and drove to the hole, nearly knocking Jill over. "Two points, in your face, boo!"

Jill took the ball and dribbled around him, taunting him by hiking her booty in the air. "Come get it, baby, come on."

Darren wrapped his arms around her waist and brushed his lips against her sweaty neck.

"Foul," she said as she turned around to receive his full kiss.

Darren devoured her lips, sucking her tongue as if he were trying to suck it dry. She wrapped her arms around his broad shoulders and he lifted her legs around his waist. They backed on to the bleachers, clawing at each other's clothes as if they were in the privacy of their own home. Darren swelled with anticipation when he reached between Jill's legs and felt her body throbbing.

"Ahem," a voice said.

Darren and Jill looked up at a group of kindergartners and two police officers who were obviously giving them a tour. Jill covered her hand with her face. "Oh my God," she muttered.

"Uh, sorry," Darren said as he and Jill gathered their things and slunk out of the center.

Once they made it outside, Darren and Jill looked at each other and burst out laughing. "That was crazy. I just knew no one would be there today," he said.

Jill held on to his shoulder as she laughed. "I still beat you and if you hadn't distracted me with your lips, then I would have gotten to 10 first."

"Maybe, maybe not, I was just getting warmed up," Darren replied as he took her by the hand. "Let's find some place else to play."

"We can go to Gold's Gym. I have a membership there and I think they have a basketball court. I know they have a private sauna. The key is in my bag."

"I like the sound of that, but I don't think I want to play with you any more. Losing to a girl would bruise my ego beyond repair."

"I guess I should have told you, I played ball in school and I was an All American," Jill said proudly.

"You learn something new every day," Darren said as he led her to his car.

"Still want to play me?"

"No, Miss All American. I'm going to have to look up your stats on the Internet and see what other secrets you're hiding."

"I don't have any secrets, just ask me what you want to know," she said in a clipped tone.

"Calm down, baby, it was just a joke."

She sighed and squeezed his hand. "I'm not trying to be difficult. But you can't believe everything that a computer spits out and you have the source right here."

Darren kissed her hand but wondered why she'd reacted so strongly to his joke about the Internet. He had to wonder if she were hiding something. What could it be? *Maybe I'm just being paranoid. No one wants to have his or her privacy invaded.*

"We're off to Gold's, right?" he asked.

"Yes."

Darren looked at her, wondering why she couldn't open up to him completely. He felt like she was still holding a part of her life back from him. Was it that she didn't truly trust him? Darren knew he'd never do anything to hurt her or make her feel as if she couldn't put her trust in him. He gave her a little smile, wishing he could read her mind and see what she was hiding.

"What's that smile for?" she asked.

"Being with you makes me smile. That's not a crime, is it?"

"No," she replied. Heat rose to her cheeks. "I don't know what to make of you sometimes. You seem too good to be true."

"I'm no mirage. What you see is what you get."

"Darren, I-I…" Her voice trailed off as if whatever she had to say pained her.

He reached out and stroked her arm. "What is it, Jill?"

She smiled softly and said in a voice barely above a whisper, "I really care about you and I don't want to lose you in my life. Being with you has given me the chance to dream of love again."

"Sounds like there's a but in there somewhere," he said.

"No, there's not. I'm just not that great at expressing how I feel sometimes."

"And I thought women were supposed to be the emotional ones."

Jill folded her arms across her chest. "In the shark pool of corporate America, a show of emotions is like dropping blood in the water. It's hard to turn that on and off, especially after David, even though I know you aren't him."

"That's right, because I would never do anything to hurt you. The rules of business don't apply to romance."

Jill made a grunting noise as if she were remembering everything David did to her and everything that Darren was going to have to undo to truly have her heart. "I think I know that in my heart, but my head doesn't want to have my heart broken again."

"And it won't be."

Jill rolled her eyes. "You can't say that."

"With certainty and deliberation and even premeditation, I promise not to break your heart."

She beamed at his proclamation. "I'm going to hold you to that," she said as they slid into his car.

"Just let me sign my name across your heart."

She eyed him quizzically. "And how do you plan to do that, Terance Trent D'Arby?"

"That song was the jam, wasn't it? And I thought I was being clever."

Jill leaned over and kissed him on the cheek. "Don't ever try your hand at comedy."

"That was cold."

"But honest."

They rode in a peaceful silence to Gold's Gym and when Darren tuned the radio to an urban oldies station, Terance Trent D'Arby's song began to play. He and Jill looked at one another and broke out laughing.

"See, there's the confirmation. We're meant to be," he said before turning into the parking lot of the gym.

CHAPTER SIXTEEN

The agony of defeat was etched on every face in Cleveland's living room. Three minutes were left in the game and the Atlanta Falcons were down by 10 points. Michael Vick, usually Mr. Magic on the field, looked like an over-hyped quarterback and Donovan McNabb showed why he was making his third appearance in the NFL's Pro Bowl.

Jill chewed on her bottom lip, crossed her fingers and legs, and stared at the TV, hoping that Vick would create a miracle and the Falcons would win the NFC championship.

"Vick's pass is picked off," the commentator said.

"Ah! Man!" the small crowd said. Jill uncrossed her fingers and legs and stopped biting her lip. Darren rubbed her thigh.

"You all right, baby?" he asked.

"This sucks!" Jill said. "I was ready to go down to Jacksonville and cheer on Vick!"

Cleveland's friend Roland looked over at Jill and smiled. "You really like football, sista. I thought you were just trying to impress Darren."

Jill flashed him a fake smile. She'd had to check Roland the moment she walked in the door.

"Oh, halftime entertainment," he'd said when he spotted her.

"Man, chill with that," Darren warned.

Cleveland smacked Roland, who was short, round and bald, on the back of his head. "Jill knows more about football than you do."

With that comment, the battle was on. Roland threw out some trivial statistics about the NFL and some of the most popular teams, like the Dallas Cowboys and Washington Redskins.

The other men who had been in the kitchen began gathering around Roland and Jill.

"Emmitt Smith is the league's leading rusher and he made most of those yards with the Cowboys," Roland said.

"But Barry Sanders was on pace to break Walter Payton's record and had he not retired or had the O-line that Smith had with Dallas all of those years, he would have broken that record before Emmitt," Jill said. "And let's talk Payton. When the Bears won the Super Bowl in 1985, how many touchdowns did he score in that game?"

"One," Roland replied confidently.

Jill wagged her finger in his face. "Wrong. Walter didn't score one touchdown in the Super Bowl."

Ooh's and ah's were emitted from the small gathering. "Damn, took down by a woman," Cleveland ribbed.

"Now, Roland, can I sit down before kickoff?" Jill asked. "Or do you have some other football questions I can clear up for you?"

Darren proudly placed his arm around Jill's shoulders. With his free hand, he tapped Roland's cheek. "And she's an All American on the basketball court."

Now Roland seemed to have a newfound respect for Jill and her sports knowledge.

"You look familiar to me," he said.

Jill inhaled sharply. "Really? Maybe I have one of those faces." *Please God, don't let this man know me.*

"Maybe so. Did you go to Clark Atlanta?"

"Spelman."

"Maybe that's where I've seen you. I went to Morris Brown, before they lost their accreditation," he said. "You played ball for Spelman, right?"

"Sure did. Led the school in scoring, a record that has yet to be broken," Jill said proudly.

Darren returned to the living room with a platter of hot wings. "Roland, leave my woman alone."

"Aw, man, you caught me. I was trying to steal her away. Jill, you have got to be the perfect woman. Not only do you like football, you know your stuff," Roland said, then kissed her hand.

Louis, one of the firefighters that worked at the station with Cleveland and Darren, chimed in. "Most women spend half the game asking stupid question. 'Baby, what's a first down?'"

"Or," Cleveland added, "'How come they hit so hard?'"

Jill stood up, "Hey, hey, I can't let you all bash the sisters, because there are a lot of women out there who love football and get into it just as much as I do."

"Where are they hiding," Cleveland asked.

"You got sisters?" Roland inquired.

"Don't you want to leave Darren and run away with me?" Louis said.

Darren tossed a celery stick at him. "She's not going anywhere."

Jill wrapped her arms around Darren's waist. "That's right."

"So, who's hosting the Super Bowl party?" Roland asked, looking at Jill and Darren.

"Was that your not-so-subtle hint that Jill and I should throw the party?" Darren asked.

"I'm saying the two of you are the new power couple of the group," Cleveland said. "Besides, I'm tired of having your rusty Negroes all up in my house."

Darren looked at Jill as if to say it was up to her.

"Fine," she said. "We can all get together at my place for the Super Bowl and I'll even order some wings and stuff."

Roland stepped back and eyed her. "Order? You mean you can't cook? I knew you were way too good to be true."

Darren plunked him on the forehead. "You don't need to worry if she's perfect or not. She's perfect for me."

Cleveland held up the remote. "Does anyone care about the AFC championship game?"

"Of course," Jill said. "I hope the Steelers can take down New England. That way the Eagles will definitely win the Lombardi trophy."

"Man, whatever," Roland said. "Philly doesn't have an answer for that hamburger boy."

"Hamburger boy?" Louis said.

"He means Roethlisberger, the rookie quarterback who has never faced this kind of pressure. The Eagles will cream them," Jill said matter of factly.

"I got to agree with her," Darren said.

"You saw what the Eagles did to Michael Vick," Louis said. "Burger boy wouldn't stand a chance."

"So we're cheering for the Eagles now?" Roland asked.

"No, but I don't want New England to win again, because I hate dynasties unless there is a star or a falcon on the side of the helmet," Jill said.

"A star? As in the Dallas Cowboys?" Louis asked. "Man, I thought you were cool, Jill. I was about to give you a nickname and all of that. But you're a closet Dallas fan." Louis mimicked a kung-fu stance. "You are my mortal enemy."

Darren whispered in her ear, "He's from DC and only cheers for the Falcons because Washington, like the Cowboys, won't see the Super Bowl again in our lifetime."

Jill pinched Darren's arm. "Whatever."

Louis yawned and excused himself from the second game. "Some of us have to work tomorrow."

"That's right, you do," Darren laughed. "You've only had two weeks off, how sad."

Louis flicked his hand and headed for the door. Jill glanced down at her watch. She would have loved to spend some time alone with Darren, but he didn't look as if he was in any hurry to leave as he took a seat and a plate full of wings.

Her cell phone rang, shattering the silence in the room as they waited for kickoff of the next game.

"Hello?"

"Jill, it's David."

She rose and headed out the door. Darren watched her as she walked away.

Cleveland walked into the living room with a tray of drinks. "Where did Jill go?"

Darren pointed to the front door. "Someone called her."

"And she walked away from you? Man, that sounds like she's on the phone with another dude," Roland said with his mouth full of chicken.

"Shut up," Cleveland said. "It could be work."

Darren didn't say anything, but it was strange for Jill to just walk away because she got a telephone call. He wasn't going to think the worst, though.

"Come on, dawg, if it was Darren walking away with his cell, what would she think? Women cheat just like men, ain't that right, D."

"Shut the hell up," Darren bellowed. He knew the next thing out of Roland's mouth was going to be his situation with Rita.

When Darren and Rita were married, Roland was on the Atlanta Police force with her and knew of her affair but never told Darren, despite the fact that they were supposed to be friends. After Darren announced his divorce, Roland seemed to take extra pride in Darren's pain, telling him all about Rita's exploits and the man she was sleeping with. That's when Darren learned that there weren't many people you could count on in the world and Roland was definitely not someone he would consider a good friend ever again.

"I'm just saying, after what Rita put you through, you could stand to be more suspicious when it comes to womenfolk," said Roland.

"I asked you to drop it. You don't need to worry about me and my relationship. You weren't that concerned when you knew Rita was screwing around on me."

"You need to let that go. It's not like Rita was a prize anyway," Roland said. "Her nickname was 'Doorknob,' and it wasn't as if she was a locksmith."

Anger bubbled in Darren's stomach, partly because he hated to hear anyone denigrate a woman and partly because he didn't know why Jill felt the need to run outside and have her phone conversation.

Cleveland noticed the look on Darren's face. "Big bro, ignore Round-land. He's sour because he has no woman and no chance of getting one. You know Jill is a workaholic or that could be an Eagles fan."

"Whatever," Darren mumbled and grabbed a bottle of beer. Seconds later he heard Jill's high-pitched voice yelling. He dropped his beer and sprinted outside.

"I told you one time and I'm not telling you again. Call your reporter off or I will sue you! Yeah, whatever. Oh, grow up. You were fired because you were incompetent and a would be thief. People who I can't trust don't work for me. So, what is this, revenge? I wouldn't spit on you if you were on fire, so why do I want to help your magazine? You have a nerve calling me when I've told you on more than one occasion that I want nothing to do with you or your business venture. This is borderline harassment and I have the full power and capability of the DVA legal depart-ment to bury you with it."

She snapped her phone shut and turned around to find Darren behind her.

"What was that all about?" he asked.

Jill ran her hand over her face. "David, my ex, wants me to help him in his new business. Doesn't he have a nerve! After what he did to me, he actually has the gall to hound me about this and I've already told him, no, hell no, no way in hell."

Darren pulled her into his arms. "Next time he calls, you let me speak to him."

Jill looked up at him. "I don't need you to fight my battles."

He held her out at arm's length. "I didn't say you did, but this is what boyfriends do for their girlfriends without being asked."

"Darren, this isn't about us. This is someone from my past with an axe to grind with me: I'll handle it."

"But you don't have to handle it alone."

"What if I want to? I don't have to lean on you for everything; I don't have to play the damsel in distress. I can take care of myself."

"I'm not denying that, but I want to help you. Whoever that was on the phone seems like they're out to get you and I want to stop that from happening. What is he doing, blackmailing you?"

"Look, I can appreciate you wanting to be there and help me, but this has nothing to do with you."

Darren glowered at her. "So, what is going on? Is there another man or something?"

"Why would you even question me on that? Have I ever given you reason to believe that there was anyone else in my life besides you?"

He turned away from her. Neither had Rita. But in hindsight, he remembered the hushed phone calls, the moments when she'd get a call and leave the room, the secret e-mails and mysterious gifts. He had been blind one time, but he wasn't going to be this time.

"Are you sure it's over between you and David?"

Jill slapped her palm against her forehead. "Are you kidding me? That man cut me deeper than a butcher and you think something would be going on between the two of us? Darren, you are the only man in my life and if you don't trust that and feel that, maybe I don't need you in my life at all. I'll call a cab to get home." She started down the steps and he grabbed her arm.

"Don't go, not like this. I didn't mean to accuse you of cheating, but I just—it was strange for you to get up the way you did and it reminded me of my ex-wife. Besides, Jill, there are still parts of your life that are shrouded in mystery, whether you want to admit it or not."

"No, that's not true," she said weakly. "But even if it is, how can you expect me to trust you when you don't fully trust me?"

"I-I," he sputtered. Darren knew he had scars from Rita, but he thought they had healed. He thought that being with Jill was proof of that, but it didn't seem that way at the moment.

What in the hell am I doing? he thought. *I can't ruin the best thing that's ever happened to me.*

The front door opened and Cleveland stuck his head out. "Everything all right? The game has started and I know you football fanatics aren't trying to miss a down."

Jill turned away from him.

"We're going to take off," Darren said. "Jill's not feeling well."

She folded her arms across her chest, but didn't say anything. Darren knew Cleveland saw right through his lie, but was smooth enough to say, "All right, you all drive safely."

The silence in the car back to Jill's place was deafening. She wouldn't even look in Darren's direction and he gripped the steering wheel so tightly that his knuckles turned white.

"Jill, I'm sorry."

"Whatever."

"What does 'whatever' mean?"

"It means I'm tired and according to you, I don't feel well."

Darren pulled the car over on a side road and killed the engine.

"What are you doing?" Jill asked.

"I've got some explaining to do," he said, gazing into her eyes. "Like you've been hurt, so have I."

Jill cocked her head to the side as if trying to decide if his story would plausible.

Darren continued, "I fell hard and fast for my ex-wife. She was everything I thought I wanted, smart, sexy, and had goals that were more than just becoming someone's wife. She wasn't desperate for a man, but she made me feel wanted and needed. When I asked her to marry me I thought it was going to be forever. So you can imagine how excited I was when she came to me and told me that she was pregnant."

"You have a child?" Jill's eyes stretched like those of an owl.

Darren held his hand up. "Let me finish, please. Rita didn't want a child, because as a cop, it would have been hard for her to move up in rank. I didn't care. I would have been a stay-at-home dad if need be.

But Rita wasn't having it. We had a huge argument; she left and went to Savannah. When she came back, there was no more baby." His voice began to crack. "She initially told me she'd had a miscarriage from all of the stress she was under. But as it turned out, she'd had an abortion."

Jill covered her open mouth with her hand. "How could she do that to you?"

"It gets deeper. The child wasn't even mine. She'd been cheating on me. So, in the span of one day or so, I lost my child—twice—and my wife. When I looked back on the situation, I had all the signs that told me Rita was cheating. She left me with some deep scars and, honestly, they haven't all healed. Maybe that's why I had the reaction I had tonight, but it's not that I don't trust you or I have issues with you. Before the night of the fire, I'd sworn off women forever. I was ready to spend my life alone and then I met you. I don't want my insecurities to ruin what we have. I trust you, Jill. I know you'd never hurt me and that you're real with me."

Jill's eyes shone with unshed tears. "Darren, I…"

He silenced her with a tender kiss. "It doesn't matter," he said. "Now, let's go catch the rest of this game."

CHAPTER SEVENTEEN

Jill sat in her penthouse still digesting what Darren had told her and dealing with her own guilt. Yesterday had been the perfect time to tell him that she owned DVA and explain that the reason she hadn't told him in the beginning was because of what David and others had tried.

Today she hadn't gone into the office because she had decided this would be the day she finally told him the truth. Now she had to build up the nerve to do it. She'd planned to cook dinner and had done her best to follow the recipes in the *Cook'n to Keep Him* cookbook, but she'd burned everything except the dessert. Now the plan had shifted. She was going to ask Darren out to dinner, invite him over for dessert afterwards and then tell him the truth.

There would be no backing out this time, either. She walked into to her bedroom. She picked out a simple black sheath, a pair of black tights, black heels and a pink cashmere wrap.

Next she called Darren.

"Hello, beautiful," he said. "What are you doing at home?"

"Well, I have a lot of vacation and sick time banked, so I decided to take a day. Besides, I have something special that I want to do tonight."

"Really? Just what would that be?"

"Well," Jill said coyly, "it involves you, me, a little black dress, dinner, and homemade dessert."

"Homemade as in made in your home?"

"Yes, don't sound so shocked. But I burned dinner."

Darren laughed. "Why am I not surprised?"

"Meet me at Houston's on Peachtree about seven. Then after dinner, dessert's on me," she said suggestively.

"I like the sound of that," he said.

"See you later," Jill said, and then hung up. She didn't want to tell him over the phone that she had something important to tell him. That needed to be done face to face. Maybe with everything between them now, Darren wouldn't care. He already loved her, she already loved him. He knew she was wealthy and that hadn't changed anything between them. But she had lied to him over and over again. What if he didn't forgive her and walked out on her?

Then Shari would be proven right, she thought. She prayed that would not be the case.

At seven, Jill was sitting in Houston's, waiting for Darren to walk through the door. When he did, he took her breath away. He was dressed in a pair of navy blue slacks that hugged him in all the right places, a gold turtleneck that highlighted his beautiful skin and a navy sports jacket. She wanted to forget dinner and feast on her sexy boyfriend, but tonight was about far more than her desire for him, though she didn't know how she was going to concentrate on the purpose with Darren looking so delicious in front of her.

The hostess led him to Jill's table and Jill saw the looks of envy the women shot her when Darren leaned in to kiss her cheek.

"This is a nice way to start the week after our boys lost the championship. And you look wonderful."

"Look who's talking," she said. "You take wonderful to a whole new level."

Darren smiled and popped his collar like a young rapper. "When you said little black dress, I knew I couldn't come in here half-stepping."

Jill reached across the table and covered his hand with hers. "Darren, I've been thinking a lot about what you said yesterday."

"Jill, that's over and dealt with," he said.

"No, I have to tell you…" Before she could get the words out, flashbulbs temporarily blinded her. "What the…"

"Jill Atkinson, I'm from *Atlanta Scene* magazine. Care to make any comments?" the photographer inquired.

"Get away from me!" she yelled.

Darren stood to push the man out of Jill's face, but the photographer threw his hands up and backed away.

"What's that all about?" Darren asked.

"That call I got on Sunday from David. That jerk works for him."

"Why does he want you in his magazine so badly?"

Tell him, she thought. "Because I'm the reason David was fired from his job. He tried to use me to get inside information about DVA."

"Really?"

Jill sat down, picked up her glass of water and took a sip. Water wasn't going to cut it; she needed something stronger for this.

"David and I met at one of those networking meet markets. I was new in the business, so I went to see if there were some contacts I could make. And I'd received a technology award so I wanted to have a little fun. David and I made eye contact and I thought he was going to be something special. At first he was. Dinner, dancing and visits to the office when I worked late at night.

"Well, one night, I pretended I had to work late and I had a nice romantic evening planned. But when I left to get my surprise, I came back to the office to find David copying files from my computer to feed to his bosses at Concurrent."

"That was low. So, you turned him in and he was fired?" Darren asked.

"Not exactly. DVA took over Concurrent and everyone was fired."

"Wow. That was cold."

"Now he has this magazine and I'm sure it's not a business magazine. I doubt I'll be portrayed favorably in any story he writes. Don't worry, though, I'll take care of it."

"I'm sure you will, but I would like to give this David person a smack to the face and a big thank you. Had he not been such an idiot, I wouldn't be here with you right now," he said. "Your bosses must have a lot of confidence in you, because I know you made the recommendation for DVA to acquire old Davey boy's company."

She smiled nervously. She wasn't ready to confess, not just yet. "Uh-huh," she said, masking her discomfort by taking a sip of water.

"You still in the mood for dinner here or do you want to skip straight to dessert?" he asked.

Jill licked her lips. "We have to have dinner first, because my Better than Sex cake isn't for an empty stomach."

"Better than Sex, huh?"

"That's what the recipe said."

"Obviously that recipe has never had the pleasure of your lovemaking," he whispered seductively.

Jill waved for the waiter. "Can you make our meals to go?"

"Sure thing," he said. "But I have to take your orders first."

After quickly rushing through dinner the couple left the restaurant, quickly weaving through the midtown traffic to get to Jill's place. Following a short ride up the elevator, Darren and Jill were sitting on her sofa, silently eating chocolate cake. She fed him a forkful of the decadent dessert, watching as his eyes rolled back in his head with every bite.

"This is good," he said after a forkful. "And a wonderful surprise. I have one for you on Valentine's Day, as well."

"Really, what is it?" Jill asked.

Darren dipped his finger in the icing and placed his finger to her lips. "You'll have to wait and see, but you will need to pack a bag."

She licked the icing from his finger then smiled. "Where are we going?"

He dipped his finger into the icing and traced Jill's lips with it. "You're going to love it, but right now, I'm going to love this."

Darren kissed the chocolate away, sucking on her lip and treating her as if she were the dessert. As he kissed her, he took the plate from her hands and set it on the coffee table.

Jill was powerless to resist his kisses and his caresses, even though the reason they were at her place was to talk. But talking was the last thing on her mind when she tasted Darren's chocolate-covered tongue. When he slipped his hands between her thighs and massaged her inner thighs with his thumbs, the last thing that mattered was the conversation she desperately needed to have with him.

With his touch, Darren made her lose herself, made her forget that she'd ever been lonely and on her way to becoming a spinster. His touch made her forget that David was out to ruin her. Made her forget that when he ran that picture of her and Darren on the front cover of his magazine their relationship was going to be over.

"Darren," she murmured as he nibbled on her neck, still stroking her thighs and rubbing her wetness. "We need to talk."

"We can do that later," he replied before slipping his finger inside her throbbing vagina.

He moved his finger up and down, a promise of what was to come. Her brain was clouded with desire, wanting Darren to replace his finger with his hard manhood. Wanting Darren to take her and disappear inside her, make her womb shake from desire.

"Love me," she moaned as she began to strip his clothes off. "I need you."

Darren lifted her dress up to her waist, peeled her panties from her body and dove for her treasure. "You taste better than that cake. This is the chocolate I want."

Jill clasped her thighs around his head as his tongue tasted her, teasing her button of pleasure, making her love juices cascade down her thighs like a soft summer rain. He didn't stop but acted as if he wanted to make her lose herself with his tongue. And that's what happened. She shook and shivered as Darren brought her to a climax.

She reached for the zipper of his slacks, nearly ripping it apart to release his manhood. When Darren's erection sprang forward, Jill didn't say a word but rolled down his body to taste him as he had savored her body. She kissed the tip of his manhood before slipping him into her mouth. Darren moaned deeply and heavily as she moved her lips down the length of him. Her tongue rounded the head, and then went back into the depths of her warm mouth. He held the sides of the sofa, barely able to stop the explosion that was building inside him.

Slowly, methodically and with the rhythm of an African drum, Jill pleasured her man orally, tasting the essence of him as he began to explode. Then she pulled back from him and mounted his erection, taking him deep inside her hot body. "Love me," she moaned over and over, clutching his shoulders as they took each other to ecstasy.

Darren gripped her bottom as he reached his climax. "Oh, Jill, I love you!"

She slowed her hips, wanting to join Darren in his climax. Leaning into him, she kissed him slowly, as if to say, "I love you too."

When they were spent from lovemaking, they fell asleep on the sofa, clinging to each other as if they were magnetized by desire.

It was well after midnight before Jill woke up. It wasn't a dream; Darren was holding her. And she still hadn't opened up to him about DVA. She pried his arms from around her and went into the kitchen to pour herself a glass of water. She couldn't confess her secret to Darren right now; it would ruin his Valentine's Day surprise. But when those pictures made the cover of David's magazine, she was going to have a lot of explaining to do. Somehow, she was going to have to stop David from publishing them, even it it meant cooperating with that snake.

She sipped her water, hoping to get the bitter taste out of her mouth. The thought of dealing with David on any level was enough to make her sick. *I'll try to appeal to his human side, if the bastard has one.*

"There you are, I was wondering where you disappeared to," Darren said as he appeared in the kitchen. "Are you all right?"

"Perfect," she replied with a smile. Darren walked over to her and sipped her water.

"Jill," he whispered.

"Yes."

"I just like the way your name sounds in my mouth, almost as good as you taste on my tongue."

She tapped him on the chest. "Darren, I love you and I don't want anything to ever change between us."

He took her hand in his and kissed it. "It won't."

"But we can't be sure of that, now can we?"

"Am I missing something here? If we're in love, what can come between us?"

"My work, my enemies."

Darren waved his hand as if to say 'whatever.' "I get that your career is important to you. But from what I've seen, you haven't let that stop us from spending time together and getting to know each other. And speaking of your career…"

Uh oh, she thought. *He knows and he's going to dump me right here. That's why we made love. He wanted to make sure I'd miss him when he walked out of my life. I can't say that I blame him. I did what he said he couldn't forgive.*

"I know you probably have sixteen weeks of vacation time, but I'm only asking for two days. No cell phone, no PDA, no business talk, nothing but you and me. If your boss says no, call in sick."

"I think I can get the time off with no problem."

"Good, because I don't want anything to ruin my surprise for you. Make sure you pack that dress you wore tonight."

"When are we leaving?" she asked excitedly.

"Let's see," Darren said. "Thursday, that is if you can break away from your job."

"I can do that," she said without hesitation.

"All right, I'll meet you here at nine Thursday morning."

"I'll be waiting, but I hope this doesn't mean that you're leaving now."

Darren shook his head. "Not until the sun comes up," he said, and then drew her into his arms. "Why don't I go run us a nice hot bath?"

"Great, and I'll bring some wine," she said.

As Darren headed for the bathroom, Jill picked up the phone and dialed David's number.

"Hello," he said.

"It's Jill," she said. "I don't appreciate your photographer ambushing me."

"I was just going over those pictures. You look wonderful. Who was the guy with you? Doesn't look like the executive type."

"Don't worry about who he is. Can you just kill the story? If you hold it for a couple of weeks, I'll give you an interview, I'll even run an ad in your magazine, full page if you want me to."

"Why the change of heart? A few days ago I was a backstabbing bastard. Why don't you want the city to know about you and your new love?" he asked.

"Because it's no one's business. What kind of tabloid are you running?"

"Listen, you're asking for a favor. You could stand to be a little nicer. We're set to go to print in the morning and we're going to be on the street tomorrow. How soon can you get that full page ad in here?"

"First thing in the morning. How much?"

"For you, $15,000."

"I'll have a check messengered over to you."

"No. Meet me for breakfast at the Buckhead Bread Company and bring the check."

"Why?"

"Maybe I want to see you," David said. "Besides, you're the one asking me for a favor. I'm calling the shots this time, Jill. Seven-thirty and not a minute later."

"Babe," Darren called from the bathroom, "what's taking so long?"

"I have to go," Jill said, then hung up the phone. She grabbed a bottle of merlot and two glasses, and then dashed down the hall.

When she walked into the bathroom, Darren was in the tub, covered by bubbles. Candles surrounded the bathtub and cast a golden glow over the bathroom. Jill held up the bottle and the glasses.

"Sorry, I had to make a quick phone call," she said.

"Business this late?"

"I have a breakfast meeting that I needed to confirm. That's all." Jill set the glasses and the wine on the edge of the marble bathtub before slipping out of her underwear and joining him. Darren leaned over and wiped his hands on a towel before he took the corkscrew and opened the wine.

"You don't ever turn off, do you?" he asked her.

"What do you mean?"

"You're a twenty-four hour businesswoman. What's going to happen when you have a family?"

Jill shrugged her shoulders. "I think my biological clock is on snooze."

"Have you ever thought about having kids, though?"

She reached for a sponge and dipped it in the water. "I have. But I know I don't want to be a single mother. I would want my son or daughter to grow up in a home with a mother and a father."

"I know that's right. Silk and sandpaper."

"What?"

"That's what Cleveland and I used to call our parents. Dad was silk and Ma was definitely sandpaper. She doled out punishment, spankings and took away the phone when we were bad. Dad would come behind her and remind us how much she loved us and tell us that everything she did was to make sure when we grew up, we didn't wind up in jail or dead. And just when we thought he'd knock a day or two off our punishment, he'd always say, 'You know your mother is right, so I hope you learned a lesson.'"

Jill laughed as she squeezed the water from the sponge and rubbed it across Darren's pectorals. "I was spoiled," Jill said. "I pretty much got away with anything because I could talk my way out of trouble."

"Why am I not surprised?"

She giggled and dipped the sponge in the water again. "Sometimes my mouth got me in trouble, though. My mother was old school, children were to be seen and not heard."

Darren took the sponge from her hand and ran it down the valley between her breasts. "And you wanted to be seen and heard, huh?"

"Sometimes. I was quite the little diva growing up."

"Pigtails and all?"

She turned around and faced him. "I hated pigtails. They were one of the reasons I got quite a few spankings. My mother would take the time and part my hair, place it in what seemed like 10,000 pigtails, and I'd go to school and change my hairstyle. I could never get it right before I got home."

Darren wrapped his arms around her waist and she locked her legs around his. She could feel his sex growing against her. He leaned forward and kissed her on the neck.

"So what would happen when your mom saw your hair all remixed?"

It was hard for her to think as she felt the full swell of his erection dancing against her thighs. "Uh, that I,—," she stammered, then pressed her lips against his. She kissed him hard and long, slipping her tongue into his mouth, reveling in the taste of his kiss.

Darren pulled back from the kiss, smoothing her damp hair from her face. "I could be with you like this forever," he whispered, placing his hand on the back of her neck. "I love you."

"I love you too," she breathed.

They kissed again. Slowly their tongues jockeyed for position in each other's mouth. Darren eased her against the back wall of the garden tub, spread her legs apart and eased between them. Jill shivered with anticipation as Darren thumbed her hard nipples. He leaned in and nibbled her neck as if it were a delectable dessert. She closed her legs around him, felt his thickness against her thighs and drew his manhood inside her. Though her body was raw from their previous lovemaking session, she still craved more and Darren was more than willing to deliver the passion she desired.

He filled her with his love and made her feel more like a woman than ever. She wrapped her arms around his neck and tightened her body around him. Never before had she been so wanton and so filled with enthusiasm about a lover. No one had ever made her feel so feminine, so womanly.

But she couldn't help feeling guilty that she had been lying to him. That was going to end, though. She was going to tell him the truth as soon as Valentine's Day was over.

When they finally got out of the tub, Jill and Darren retired to her bed. When he wrapped his arms around her, she felt safe, secure and loved.

She wanted that feeling to last forever.

CHAPTER EIGHTEEN

The next morning, Jill rose, guiltily awakening before Darren. Why had she agreed to meet David, knowing the emotions that would come from the meeting? Though she'd put some of the pain he caused her in the past, she was still wounded.

I can't think about that, she reasoned. *I have to convince David not to run that story yet.*

She leaned over Darren and kissed his cheek gently. "Wake up, sleepyhead," she said.

Darren's eyes fluttered open. "What time is it?"

"Six."

"You have a meeting, don't you?" He sat up in the bed and rubbed sleep from his eyes.

"Unfortunately. Do you have to go into the station today?"

He shook his head. "Nah, but I'll probably go in anyway. This is Cleveland's first full week back and I want to make sure he's all right."

"You and your brother are really close, aren't you?"

"We are. He's my little brother and I have to look out for him."

"You know what, I'm the one who has a meeting, and you don't. Why don't you lock up when you leave?" Jill walked over to her jewelry box and handed him her extra house key.

"Where do you want me to leave it when I'm done?"

"Keep it." Jill couldn't believe she'd said those words. She'd never given a man a key before. Her home had always been her inner sanctum, which she didn't want to share with anyone. But Darren wasn't just anyone. He was her man.

He rose from the bed, still naked from the night before. "What time is your meeting?" he asked.

"Seven-thirty."

He playfully swatted her bottom. "Then you'd better get a move on."

She blew him a kiss as she disappeared into the bathroom.

❧❧

Darren eased back into the bed and stared up at the ceiling. Jill was the kind of woman that he didn't think existed anymore. She meant the world to him and it didn't matter that she worked too much for his taste, because she'd proved that she was a woman who could balance love and her job.

He watched her as she dressed, covering up that body that brought him so much pleasure in a black pants suit. She was supple, sexy and demure, enough to send any man's hormones into overdrive. It took every ounce of self-control in him not to rip her clothes off and make love to her again. Jill had awakened a hunger in him that he couldn't fill.

Darren sat up in the bed as she reached for a pair of black and red heels. "How can anyone concentrate on business with you looking like that?"

"You're silly." She eased her feet into the shoes as Darren rose from the bed and put his boxers on. He crossed over to her and wrapped his arms around her waist as she dabbed his favorite perfume on her wrists.

"You're going to make me late."

He kissed her neck. "I don't even want you to leave. But if you must…" He dropped his hands to his side.

Jill turned and faced him, a smile touching her cherry lips. "I could get used to this."

"Me too. You felt good in my arms last night, this morning and right now."

She kissed him and he inhaled her minty-fresh breath. Jill broke off the kiss. "I have to go. I can't be late."

Reluctantly, he let her go. "Do your bosses know how hard you work?"

"Bye, babe." Jill dashed out the door.

Before he left Jill's place, Darren made the bed, washed their wineglasses, cleaned the tub and emptied the trash. It reminded him of the days when he and Rita were married and he left the house after she did. Darren didn't mind helping his woman out; in fact, he enjoyed it. He wasn't the type of man who thought a woman should do all the cooking and cleaning. A few more nights with Jill and he knew he'd be waiting on her hand and foot like the queen she was.

Darren hummed a love song all the way to the station. When he walked in the door, he greeted everyone with a smile.

"What are you doing here?" Cleveland asked when he found Darren in the break room fixing himself a cup of coffee.

"Came to check on you."

"I called you this morning, but you must have been with your woman."

"Don't be jealous."

Cleveland pushed his brother in the chest. "Why would I be jealous? You still got that same face."

Darren pushed him back. "I look better than you on a bad day. Anyway, I was at Jill's this morning and man, I never thought I'd feel like this again."

"It's good to see you happy. You're a relationship man. Me, on the other hand, I have no use for all of that drama."

Darren took a sip of his coffee, which tasted more like day old espresso. "You never let a woman get close enough to you to find out if a relationship will even work."

"And you marry women before you even know their blood type."

Darren's eyebrow shot up. "Whatever."

"Man, I'm saying you and I are different. There's not a woman in Atlanta who could make me want to commit. Besides, marriage is an institution and institutions are for crazy people. I'm not crazy. Bought Jill an engagement ring yet?"

"Nah, not yet. But I can see that happening in the near future."

Cleveland smiled despite himself.

Darren knew his brother was happy for him. Now if he could only channel some of that happiness into himself. Darren wanted Cleveland to find what he had found in Jill. But he wasn't going to force the issue

"Let's go get some breakfast," Darren said. "My treat."

"All right, got to get the rover and I'll be right out," Cleveland said, referring to his radio.

Moments later they were headed to Buckhead Bread Company for fresh baked Danishes and orange juice.

❧ ❧

"Why can't you just make this disappear?" Jill snapped. She'd been sitting across from David for the last thirty minutes trying not to reach over and wring his neck.

"Why do you want it to disappear? You've never been camera shy before. You had no problem announcing your grand takeover of Concurrent and the firing of its executives in front of the cameras. And then there was your spread in *Essence, Black Enterprise* and the *National Business Journal*. What's the problem now?" He leaned back in his chair, picking an imaginary piece of lint from his crisply pressed slacks.

David had style, but that was about it. He was a user and liar. What she ever saw in him was a mystery to her. And as he sat there with her money in his hand, she realized what a blessing it was to find out that he was the scum of the earth when she had, rather than years down the road.

"My personal life is my business," she said. "I don't want it splattered all over the front of your magazine or anyone elses." She gripped her juice glass so tightly she was surprised that she didn't crush it in her hand.

"Who was he?"

"None of your damned business."

"You're in the public eye, people will want to know."

"People or you?"

David rolled his eyes. "I'm over you, Jill. I could care less who you're sleeping with. It's nice to know that you have finally stopped being so bitter."

That did it! Jill tossed the contents of her glass in David's face. "You slimy bastard. You have some damned nerve, after what you did to me. You used me to steal my company away and you want to talk bitter? You can-can…" Her voice trailed off when she looked at the door and saw Cleveland and Darren walking in. Jill sat down and smoothed her pants. "This meeting is over, David. For once in your life, do the right thing."

He wiped his face and glowered at her. "Go to hell, Jill. I'll run my magazine the way I see fit and if I want to run the picture of you and your lover, I'll do it."

"Then give me my check back."

"No. We had a deal."

"And you just admitted that you weren't going to live up to your end of it."

He shrugged his shoulders. "So, sue me."

She reached across the table and grabbed his damp tie. "You think I won't? Print a word about me or that picture and I will haul you into court faster than you can say stop the presses." Jill pushed him back into the seat.

"Won't that defeat the purpose of you trying to hide your lover? You'll be getting the bill for my dry cleaning as well." David stood up and dropped a couple of dollars on the table. "And I used to think you were such a class act."

"You wouldn't know class if it bit you on the end of your nose." She fought the urge to slap him with all the fiery fury that was building in the pit of her stomach.

David turned on his heel and walked out of the restaurant while Jill waved for the waiter and the check.

When she looked to her left, she saw Darren walking over to her. *God, I hope he didn't see that.*

"Jill, what are you doing here?"

"Breakfast meeting."

Darren surveyed the scene, the spilled juice and half eaten food. "Didn't go too well?"

She shook her head. "Nope."

"Want to talk about it?"

"No, I'll be all right," she said, though she knew that wasn't true. If Darren saw those pictures before she had a chance to explain herself, everything would be over.

"Don't beat yourself up, beautiful. You'll get them next time."

Jill stood and hugged Darren tightly. "You're right. I'm going to pay this check and head to the office." She let him go and stared at him pensively.

"Are you sure everything is all right?" Darren asked, holding her gaze.

She forced a smile that didn't quite reach her eyes. "Yes, I'm fine. I just hate starting the day off like this."

"How about we have lunch, then? Make today better?"

"I'd like that. I'll meet you in front of the building at noon."

Darren leaned in and kissed the tip of her nose. "See you then."

❧❧

For the rest of the day, Jill was a bear to be around, snapping at everyone who crossed her path. Madison didn't even want to ring Jill when she had a phone call.

When noon rolled around, Jill left down the back staircase because she didn't want to see anyone but Darren. He was waiting on the sidewalk when she went out. The smile she flashed him was the first genuine one since she and Darren had got out of bed this morning.

"There's that smile," Darren said when he spotted her.

Jill fell into his arms. "I'm so happy to see you."

"That meeting this morning really got to you, didn't it?"

"I don't want to talk about that. Let's just go grab something to eat and be together."

Darren draped his arm over her shoulder. "Come on; let me make you feel better."

"Can we go somewhere that we can be alone? I just want you to hold me."

"We can go to my place," he said.

Jill nodded. "Sounds good to me."

Darren whisked Jill off to his house, taking secluded side streets, avoiding the swell of lunchtime traffic. As he drove, Jill reflected on her meeting with David. She was sure he'd double-cross her, even after taking her $15,000 check. She glanced at Darren as he drove.

Please let David's magazine fail before the picture runs, she thought. *Please don't let him ruin my chance at love again.*

"Penny for your thoughts?" Darren said.

"Darren, I've never felt about anyone the way I feel about you. I just can't go back to the way I was before we met. You're the closest thing to Prince Charming I've ever known. I'm so afraid that one day I'm going to wake up and discover all of this was just a beautiful dream."

"Jill, I don't understand. You're talking like I'm going somewhere and I'm not. Baby, I love you."

Jill turned and looked out the window. "It's been my experience that love doesn't last. No matter what happens in the future, I hope you will remember all of our good times, how good it felt making love to each other and how we felt in each other's arms."

"Jill, why are you talking like this?"

"I-I don't know," she said, wishing she could find the words to tell him that she hadn't meant to lie to him.

I was afraid; I was scared to tell you about my job because I didn't want things to change between us. I didn't want this to end. I didn't want you to run or be like the others, I just wanted you to love me.

"Is there something you need to tell me?" he asked.

"No."

Darren pulled into his driveway. "You know we can talk about anything."

"I know and that's one of the things that I love about us. We do talk about everything and I feel like I can trust you with anything."

They got out of the car and walked inside. "Jill, I don't like seeing you like this. What was that meeting about this morning and why are you so rattled?"

"Because I don't like to lose."

"I get that things didn't go well, but did your boss give you grief over it or something?"

"I never have trouble with my bosses."

"Then who's giving you trouble?"

"David Branton."

"Your ex?"

"He's still planning to run that story about me and it's going to be something sleazy. He basically told me that he doesn't care if his story hurts me."

As they sat on the sofa, Darren held Jill's hand and forced her to look at him.

"I don't give a damn what lies this man prints about you. It's not going to change how I feel about you. To hell with him."

"I don't want to talk about it anymore. How's Cleveland doing back at the station?"

Darren smiled, "Back to his old self. Turn your back to me and lean into my chest. I'm going to help you relax."

Jill followed his instructions and let him remove her suit jacket. Then Darren slipped his hands inside the collar of her shirt and began massaging the tension from her shoulders. His touch relaxed her, at least for the moment.

His warm hands kneaded her shoulders as if her skin was dough. She closed her eyes and melted underneath his touch. Darren moved down her shoulders, down her back, then reversed himself and moved up to her neck.

"Better?" he asked.

She moaned affirmatively. He continued to massage her, this time unbuttoning her silk blouse and easing it from her shoulders, kissing her smooth skin as he unveiled it.

"You smell good," he said, with his lips close to her ear.

"Thank you."

"Just think, in a few days we're going to be away from all of this. No phones, no fires and no business to distract us from each other."

"Oh, that sounds heavenly."

Darren moved his hands down her sides and rested them on her thighs. Jill closed her eyes, holding back the fearful tears pooling in her eyes. She pretended to be asleep because she knew this could very well be the last time Darren held her like this.

CHAPTER NINETEEN

Jill kept a low profile until Thursday. She worked from home, telling Madison that she was battling the stomach flu. When Malik and Shari called to check on her, she assured them that she was fine.

"Can't I take some time off?" she asked Malik when he called her on Wednesday. "Yeah, since you own the place. I'm calling because Madison said there is a check that came through that seems suspicious."

"What check was that?"

"It was made out to David Branton. What's going on?"

"Don't worry about that check."

"I'm not; you're the one I'm worried about. Are you dealing with that fool again? Why would you be paying him for anything?"

"It was payment for an ad in his new magazine," she said.

"Jill, I'm not one to question your business technique, but why would you advertise with him? He's a snake and he has an axe to grind with you."

"I know what I'm doing. Why don't you take care of your work and your pregnant wife and let me handle this?" she snapped.

"My what?"

Jill's mouth burned. She was sure Shari had told Malik that she was pregnant. "You didn't know?"

"No, I didn't. Why wouldn't she tell me? Are you sure Shari's pregnant?"

"It wasn't my place to say that, I'm sorry. A couple of weeks ago she said she thought she was pregnant, but she hadn't told you because she didn't know how you would react and I just blew it."

"If she is pregnant, I'm happy, I want a child. I wasn't sure if Shari did because of all of the traveling she does with the magazine. Do you think she…" His voice trailed off and Jill knew what he was thinking.

"She would never abort your child. Talk to her," Jill said.

"Why would she keep this a secret?"

Jill silently prayed that she hadn't caused a rift in their marriage with her slip of the tongue. Was this how it was going to happen with her and Darren? A careless phrase thrown out when she least expected it?

"I'm going to wait her out," Malik said. "Maybe she's going to tell me when she comes back from New York."

Jill made a mental note to call Shari and give her a heads up. "I'm sorry," Jill said.

"See what happens when you keep secrets? I hope you've taught yourself a lesson." Malik hung up and Jill stared off into space, wondering what calamity awaited her next.

Thursday morning she called David once more to plead with him not to run the picture of her and Darren in his magazine.

"Branton," he said.

"It's Jill."

"Your office should have received my dry cleaning bill."

"That's not why I'm calling," she said. "It's about the picture."

"That again?"

"David, I don't want my personal business plastered all over Atlanta. Why don't you see that?"

"You're hiding something. The journalist in me wants to get to the bottom of it."

"Journalist? Don't make me laugh."

"Didn't you call me for a favor?" he snapped. "I tell you what, when I find out who that man is and why you're so hell-bent on keeping your affair a secret, I'll get back to you for another ad."

"Now you're blackmailing me? You slimy son of a..."

"Temper, temper."

"David, don't do this to me, okay?"

"Did you think about my feelings or anything when you fired me because I hurt your feelings?"

"You tried to steal my company. That was business. What you're doing now is a personal attack."

David sighed into the phone. "I did care for you. But I had to do my job. No one was going to replace you. But you took over Concurrent and made a point to fire me. I had bills to pay, a mortgage and you didn't give a damn."

"You don't look like you starved and I do recall giving all of you generous severance packages, so don't come at me with that bull about your bills. David, if you ever truly cared for me, you would stop this."

"I did care for you but that's past tense. I want you to feel the embarrassment I felt when you took over that company and put me out to pasture. Enjoy your Valentine's Day. Are you guys sticking around Atlanta? We're probably going to need more pictures for the article."

Jill slammed the phone down and cursed herself for putting herself at David's mercy. Tears spilled from her eyes.

"How could I have been so damned stupid? I can't trust that snake, I never could."

She rose from the sofa and headed up to her bedroom to gather her bags. She and Darren were still going on their Valentine's Day trip. *I'm going to have to tell him the truth,* Jill thought. *If I tell him the truth, then David can't hurt us.*

The buzz from the doorman startled her. "Yes," she said into the intercom.

"Mr. Alexander is here."

"Send him up," Jill said, wiping her face.

She met Darren at the door with a smile plastered on her face. Darren extended a long-stemmed white rose to her.

"Good morning, beautiful."

"Oh, Darren." She beamed as she accepted the flower. "This is beautiful."

"Not compared to you. But that goes without saying. Ready to go?"

"I just need to get my bags," she said.

"Are they in the bedroom?"

She nodded and Darren dashed down the hall. Seconds later, he was carrying Jill's luggage out the door. She locked up and they took off for the car.

"So," she said once they were seated in the car. "Where are we going?"

"You'll see when we get there," he said.

"Oh, please give me a little hint," she begged playfully.

"All right, it's not in Atlanta."

Jill folded her arms and pouted. "That's not much of a hint."

"You said a hint and that's what you got. Sit back and relax and enjoy the ride, darling."

"Fine," she said, paying attention to the route he was taking. "We're going to Savannah?"

"No, not Savannah. Stop guessing and relax. Do you want to stop for breakfast?"

"I guess. But why don't we do that when we get closer to our destination?" she said, still fishing for clues.

"You're not going to find out until we get there," Darren said, seeing through her smoke screen.

"Fine," she said.

Darren drove for about an hour before he pulled off the highway. Jill looked at the interstate signs. They'd been on I-20, passing through some small Georgia towns, which reminded Jill of why she'd left Macon. Since they were traveling east, she figured that they were going to South Carolina.

"Are you sure you want to stop here?" she asked as they pulled up to a restaurant advertising 'Countree Cookin'.'

"These are the best places to eat," he said. "These little restaurants still cook with lard and all the other good things that grandma used to cook with."

"And you get the heart disease that grandma died from too," she pointed out.

"Not if you eat like this only once in a while," he said. "Come on, live a little."

"All right, fine, but the first time someone calls me 'gal' I'm out of there."

"Come on, gal," he joked.

Inside the restaurant, a laid back hostess with a bright smile led them to the counter bar. "Good mornin', y'all. How're y'all doin' this mornin'?"

"Good," Jill and Darren replied.

"Y'all ready for Valentine's Day?"

Darren kissed Jill on the cheek. "Yes, we are, but we need to get a good start on the day with a good breakfast."

The woman slammed her hand on the counter excitedly. "I know jus' whut you need. A lover's break-fast."

"A what?" Jill asked.

"Lover's breakfast, I can tell y'all are in love."

Jill smiled proudly. She was in love and scared. "Yes, we are."

The woman clasped her hands together. "I got the perfect meal. Henry!" She headed back to the kitchen.

"See, it's not that bad," Darren said.

"I know," Jill said, wrapping her arms around Darren's waist. "It's good that people can see how much we care about each other. Where did you say we were going again?"

Darren kissed her on the tip of her nose. "I didn't. But you're slick, you almost got me."

Henry, who must have been the cook, walked into the dining area. Jill smiled when she saw the massive man with the grease-stained apron. "I hear you all are goin' to git married," he said. "And you need my gettin' hitched breakfast. I also do catering for weddings and such."

"But we're not getting marr…" Jill began, but Darren cut her off.

"Thank you kindly. We'll get in touch with you for our reception. That is, if you don't mind coming to Atlanta."

"Y'all big city folk, huh? Well, I hope you're ready for some good cookin' and not that fake stuff they serve down in Atlanta."

Jill spoke up. "I'm from Macon, so I'm looking forward to this meal."

Henry smiled and headed back to the kitchen.

"Looking forward to the meal, eh?" Darren said, reaching over and stroking her cheek. "Could have fooled me."

"Henry reminds me of my uncle who used to cook for us all the time at the family cookouts and everything. I couldn't hurt his feelings and tell him I don't eat this kind of stuff."

"You're so sweet."

Moments later, Henry was bringing out a platter of crispy bacon, buttery grits, toast bathed in honey, liver pudding and scrambled eggs.

"Looks good," Darren said, salivating over the spread.

Jill flashed Henry a smile and the thumbs up sign. They dug into the food and it was delicious. She hadn't eaten a breakfast like this one since she was a little girl in Macon.

After they were stuffed from breakfast and Henry had loaded them up with fried chicken, homemade biscuits and cole slaw, Darren and Jill were back on the road again.

"Comfortable, darling?" Darren asked as Jill eased into the car.

She smiled and nodded as he drove off. Instead of pressing Darren for information on where they were going, Jill closed her eyes and drifted off to sleep.

∾❧∾

Darren glanced at Jill as she slept. She looked like an angel with her head tilted back and her lips slightly pursed. He stroked her thigh as she slumbered. He couldn't wait until they were alone in Charleston. He was going to show her the time of her life. Over the last few days, Jill had been stressed out and Darren wanted to make sure that she relaxed again. Stress wasn't good for her and it was his job as her man to be her protector, a role he relished. With every beat of his heart, he loved her, cared for her more than anything else in his life.

Darren realized that after his relationship went sour with Rita, he'd spent a long time looking for someone he could live with. In Jill, he'd found someone he couldn't live without.

He tried to focus his attention on the road ahead, but, his thoughts kept drifting to a wedding with Jill as the bride and him as the groom. He wished he could make that come true this weekend, but it was too soon to ask Jill to be his wife. He'd messed up and married the wrong woman before, but he wasn't going to let the right one get away from him this time.

His cell phone rang and Darren grabbed it quickly so that he wouldn't wake Jill.

"Hello?"

"Darren, it's me," Cleveland said. "I got in touch with a friend of mine in Charleston and I did something nice for you and Jill."

"What's that?"

"Brian McKnight is having a Valentine's Day concert. You've got two tickets waiting for you for the eight o'clock show."

"Man, that is all right, how can I repay you?"

"By giving me the $80 for the tickets when you come back. This is your chance at real happiness and I got your back, bro. Besides, you're going to need something other than your ugly face to get that woman in the mood."

"I'm hanging up now," Darren said.

Jill stirred in the seat.

"Are you all right, baby?" he asked when her eyes fluttered open.

"We there yet?" she said.

"A few more hours."

Jill faced Darren. "Thank you. I can't remember the last time I looked forward to Valentine's Day."

"Too many thank you notes to return for all the chocolate and flowers?"

"Please, I usually didn't get a thing for Valentine's Day and watching everyone in the office get taken to lunch or have something delivered was just something I learned to accept. Don't get me wrong, I've had boyfriends around this time of the year, but I just never celebrated Valentine's Day."

"Well, this is going to be our new tradition. We'll celebrate Valentine's Day together from now on out."

Jill smiled. "All right, I'm going to hold you to that."

He tweaked her nose. "I never make a promise that I can't keep. If I said it, then it's true."

"That's what I love about you," Jill said. "I know I can depend on you."

"You sure can. Because you're all I need."

CHAPTER TWENTY

The look on Jill's face when they pulled up to the hotel in Charleston was priceless. He wished that he had a camera to capture her expression.

"How did you know Charleston was one of my favorite places?" she exclaimed as she got out of the car.

The hotel, which was a historic building, was beautiful and seeing Jill standing in front of it, Darren thought it was the perfect postcard.

"Let's go see if our room is ready," he said as he took her into his arms.

After they checked into hotel and placed their bags in the room, the couple went on a cobblestone carriage ride, taking in the sights of Charleston on an unseasonably warm afternoon.

Darren drew Jill into his arms as they sat in the back of the carriage. "Having fun?" he asked

"Yes. Thank you so much," she said. "What else do you have up that long sleeve of yours?"

"We're just going to have to see, aren't we?"

"All right, Mr. Secretive."

"Let's just say that you're going to like everything that I have planned for us over these next few days."

The guide highlighted the sights but neither Jill nor Darren listened to what he was saying. They were too busy kissing and caressing each other. When the tour was over, they went back to the hotel to eat lunch in the hotel restaurant.

They dined on authentic low country cuisine, shrimp and rice, stewed tomatoes and spicy corn-bread.

"Umm, this is so good," Jill moaned.

Darren loved seeing her so relaxed and enjoying herself in this manner. She wasn't bogged down by DVA business or worried about a meeting that went awry. She was just enjoying life, being happy and in love. Darren reached across the table and grasped her hand.

"I love you like this."

She smiled and placed her fork on the side of her plate. "Thank you for bringing me here. I can't remember the last time I came to this town."

"I had no idea Charleston was one of your favorite places. Who's your favorite singer?"

"There are several, Anita Baker, Stevie Wonder, Brian McKnight, Gerald LeVert," she said. "The list goes on and on."

"But you like Brian McKnight?"

"Yes, why?"

"Just asking, for when I set the mood with music tonight."

She gave him a 'yeah, right' look before returning to her meal.

After lunch, Darren and Jill took a walk around the historic neighborhood. Charleston was definitely a place he could see moving to after he retired. And with Jill by his side, he would be content to sit on the front porch of a plantation style house and rock back and forth while they watched people go by.

"Have you…" The shrill ringing of Jill's cell phone interrupted him.

"Sorry," she said as she pulled the phone from her purse.

Darren took the phone from her. "This is Jill's phone and she's on vacation, hundreds of miles away from Atlanta. This is a problem you will have to fix yourself."

He turned the phone off and didn't give the caller a chance to say a word.

"Darren," she pouted.

"I told you to leave this at home. No business until Monday."

"Yes, sir," she said, giving him a mock salute.

He slid the cell phone into his pocket. "And I'm going to hold on to this."

"Don't you think that's a little extreme?"

He shook his head. "Besides, where you're going there are no cell phones, PDAs or Blackberries allowed."

"And just where might that be?"

Darren pointed up the block to a colonial style building. "We're going to the spa."

"You're spoiling me," she said giving him a tight hug.

"That's the plan."

They walked inside and headed for their respective treatments.

❧❧

As the masseuse kneaded Jill's back and shoulders, she felt as if she were in heaven. All the stress she had been carrying around dissipated like water vapor. She didn't think about David, her secret, or what Darren's reaction would be to it. She was totally relaxed and she loved it. She was in one of her favorite places and no one knew who she was. All they saw was a woman spending Valentine's Day with the man of her dreams.

"All right, Ms. Atkinson, Jamie will be in here to give you a pedicure. You can lie here or take a seat by the window," the masseuse said.

"Thank you," Jill said, and then sat up. The masseuse helped Jill into a white terry cloth robe before leaving the room.

As she crossed the room to the leather recliner, Jill wished she had her cell phone so that she could call Shari and tell her about Darren's surprise. Then again, calling Shari might not be such a good idea. There was no telling what the fallout was from her spilling the beans about Shari's pregnancy.

I should've kept my mouth shut, she thought as she leaned her head back and closed her eyes. Jill knew she was going to have to apologize to Shari and Malik.

The door swung open and to her surprise Darren walked in. "What are you doing in here?" she asked.

"I came to get some tips. I hear rubbing a woman's feet is the key to getting her heart."

"You already have my heart."

"Then I want to make sure I keep it. I'm just going to watch."

The pedicurist walked in and smiled at the couple. "Good afternoon," she said. Darren moved out of her way and watched her as she washed and massaged Jill's feet.

Again Jill was in perfect bliss as the pedicurist smoothed grape oil on her feet. By the time her pedicure was over and the attendant left, she didn't think she could feel any better than she did at that moment. But Darren changed her mind when dropped to his knees and kissed her feet, sucking each toe as if it were covered in chocolate. Desire pooled between her legs and she thought she was going to melt away.

Before Darren could open her robe and feast on the rest of her body, there was a knock at the door.

"Hello? Ms. Atkinson, are you ready for your next treatment?"

"Oh yeah," Jill replied, her eyes locked with Darren's.

"You'd better go before we start something we can't finish," he whispered. He stood up and opened the door. "Ms. Atkinson is ready for her next treatment."

The woman smiled at Darren as if she knew what had been going on in the massage room.

About an hour later, Darren and Jill headed back to the hotel, walking hand and hand. "Are you enjoying yourself?"

"I am," she replied.

"The best is yet to come," he said, leaning closer to her ear. "We're going to order dinner in tonight."

Jill stroked his cheek. "I wouldn't have it any other way."

"And I have a special present for you."

She smiled like a kid on Christmas morning. "What is it?"

"You'll see when we get in the room," he said wickedly.

Jill wanted to run into the room and get her gift as soon as possible.

When they walked into the room, Darren went to the closet and retrieved a red box with a white bow on top of it. "You can open it now or wait until after dinner."

Jill took the box from him and shook it gently. "I'm impatient, you know that."

She ripped the ribbon off the box, and then ripped the wrapping paper. Inside, she found a short silk gown. Holding it against her body, she said, "This is beautiful."

Darren smiled approvingly. "Why don't you change into this and I'll order dinner."

Jill's reply was to dash into the bathroom to change into the gown. Moments later, she was walking into the room, looking breathtakingly sexy. Darren couldn't have picked a better present. The gown hit her at mid-thigh and the ivory color highlighted her brown skin. Darren watched her as she spun around so that he could get a view of the low cut back that melted down atop her behind.

"Wow," he whispered.

"This is lovely. A perfect fit."

Darren took her into his arms, capturing her ripe lips. Their tongues jockeyed for position. He slipped his hands underneath the straps of the gown and eased them off her shoulders. Her perky breasts spilled forward and Darren greedily took one, then the other, into his mouth, sucking her nipples and squeezing her breasts gently.

She shivered as he pushed the gown further down her body and slid his hands between her thighs. She started unbuttoning his shirt and he kicked out of his shoes, but before she could finish, there was a knock at the door.

"Room service."

Darren groaned and Jill ducked into the bathroom as he opened the door.

The waiter wheeled in a cart decked out with candles, two steak dinners, green salads, a bottle of champagne, and two slices of cheesecake.

"Would you like me to open the champagne?" he asked.

"Nah, I can handle that," Darren said as he opened the door in a not so subtle hint for the man to leave.

"Yes sir," the waiter replied and slipped out the room.

Darren turned to Jill, who had walked out of the bathroom when she heard the door close. "Hungry?"

She'd slipped the gown straps from her shoulders. "Starving, but what I'm craving isn't on that cart." The gown fell to the floor and Darren stared at her statuesque body as he unbuttoned his shirt.

Jill crossed over to him, ready and willing to assist him. She unzipped his slacks, pushed them down to his ankles with one hand and massaged his manhood with the other. Darren moaned excitedly as he stepped out of his slacks. Jill had his body primed and ready for action. He took her hand in his, and then scooped her into his arms.

They fell backwards on the bed and Darren removed the rest of his clothes. The sight of his nudity sent ripples down her spine. Darren spread her legs apart, finding her thighs moist with desire. When he tasted her, kissing the soft folds of skin between her thighs, Jill shivered with delight.

"Make love to me," she pleaded. With Darren, sex was about love. Jill had no doubt that Darren loved her and was the man she'd marry. She didn't have to question his motives or wonder if he was hiding a computer disc with DVA secrets on it. His love was real, dependable and oh so good.

When he wrapped her legs around his waist, she sucked him into her moist valley, relishing in the feel of his thickness against her G-spot. Leaning into her, Darren took one of her breasts into his mouth, sucking her hard nipple until she felt as if her body were going to explode. Soft moans escaped her throat as she held the back of Darren's head, urging him to go deeper and deeper.

For those blissful moments of lovemaking, nothing else mattered to Jill. Time stood still as orgasm after orgasm rushed through her body, making her feel as though she would evaporate into thin air. Darren pressed deeper into her pulsating body until he reached his own climax and collapsed on top of her, wrapping her up in his arms.

"Darren," she whispered.

"Yes, baby?"

"I feel safe with you and that's something I've never felt before."

He kissed her forehead. "I want you to feel that way because as long as you're with me, nothing or no one will hurt you."

She shivered as she thought of what waited for her when she returned to Atlanta. David would have plastered her picture all over the city and her secret would be out. That's why she was going to enjoy every minute of her time with Darren this weekend.

After they pulled themselves apart, they ate dinner under the covers, naked. Jill fed Darren a piece of steak and he spooned cheesecake into her mouth.

"So, what else are we going to do tonight?" Jill asked.

"Anything you want, although I wouldn't object to spending the rest of the night right here in bed with you."

She set the plate on the nightstand, and then took the cheesecake from Darren's hands. Straddling his body, Jill kissed him with urgency before she said, "I don't have any objections either."

She and Darren proceeded to make love all night.

CHAPTER TWENTY-ONE

The morning light bathed Jill in a glow that Darren thought made her look angelic. He ran his index finger down the length of her leg. Her skin was smoother than silk. Darren wondered what twist of fate had brought Jill into his life and what he had done to deserve her. Maybe she was his reward for all he'd gone through with Rita. He pushed her hair back behind her ear, peering into her lovely face as she still slept. Darren wondered when Jill had last slept past nine A.M. Knowing her, she was probably in the office at the crack of dawn. While he admired her dedication, he felt as if she were pushing herself too hard. Once they were back in Atlanta, she'd bury herself in work again. *What would the CEO of DVA do without Jill? She seemed to do more work for that company than the so-called owners.*

Her eyes fluttered open. "Good morning, beautiful," he whispered.

"Morning," she replied in a husky voice that sent chills down his spine.

Jill was even sexier this morning than she had been dressed in the silk gown that he had bought for her.

"Hungry? I can order breakfast."

She shook her head and nestled closer to him. "I'm fine just lying here. I can't remember the last time I slept this late."

Darren laughed. "I kind of figured that."

She toyed with the hair on his chest. "You know, I'm going to need my cell phone. I have to make a call."

Darren groaned and shook his head. "Remember our deal, no business."

Jill smirked and held her hand out. "I promise, I won't be on the phone long."

He propped up on his elbow and looked into her brown eyes. "All right, but keep it short. And I want the phone back when you finish. I can't have you sneaking off during dinner to make business calls."

"I won't, promise."

Darren reached down for his slacks and pulled Jill's phone from his pocket. She took the phone from his hand, kissed him on the cheek, then wrapped up in the sheet and headed to the private terrace to make her call. He couldn't help wondering who she was calling and why she had to go outside. Though he trusted her, Darren felt wary about what she was doing, even if it wasn't fair to her. Creeping from the bed, he walked over to the half-closed terrace door to listen in on Jill's conversation.

"Shari, I'm sorry, I didn't mean to let the cat out of the bag, but…I understand. That's not the same thing. Fine. What more do you want from me? That's not fair. I am your friend. Darren has nothing to do with this. I understand. I don't want this to affect our friendship.

Of course you can trust me. Are you pregnant? Congratulations, then. Shari, believe me, it was just a slip of the tongue. Malik and I were talking and he was telling me how I should live my life but I know it's no excuse. Are we still cool?"

Darren walked away, feeling like a complete jackass. *Jill isn't Rita.* He headed for the bathroom to take a shower, hoping that he could wash away all of doubts and distrust still lingering from his divorce. He couldn't continue to let his baggage cloud their relationship.

Jill returned to the room and tossed her phone on the bed. "Everything all right at the office?" Darren asked.

"I didn't call the office," she replied before slumping in a chair. "I messed up bad."

"What happened?"

"My friend Shari, you know, the cook, is pregnant and I accidentally told her husband before she had a chance to. She had told me that she wasn't sure if he was ready to start a family and when I told him, he immediately thought that maybe she was going to terminate the pregnancy. But she was just trying to make sure that she was pregnant."

"You told her husband?"

"I didn't do it maliciously, it just slipped out," she said. "Anyway, I think everything is fine between them but I don't know if things are cool between Shari and me."

"Maybe she didn't want to tell him," Darren said, thinking back to the events surrounding Rita's abortion.

"She was going to tell him, and the point is, she should have been the one to do it, not me."

"I hope you two work things out when you get back to Atlanta, but right now, you have to get dressed because I have plans for you."

She eyed him excitedly. "What plans?"

"You'll have to get showered and dressed to find out," he said as he ushered her into the bathroom.

While Jill showered, Darren ordered breakfast and tried to come up with those plans he'd mentioned. When he called room service to order breakfast, he asked the clerk for suggestions on how to spend half the day alone with Jill.

"Well," the man said, "there is the sunset trip which is a tour of the intercoastal waterways and the beautiful downtown Charleston skyline. Dining can be arranged at any number of restaurants accessible by boat."

"We won't need dinner. I have tickets to a show tonight."

"The tours have different hours. Would you like me to set one up for you?"

"Yes. I think we should be ready to leave in about an hour and a half," Darren said. He turned his head and saw Jill walking out of the bathroom, water glistening on her shoulders and the towel barely covering her ample breasts.

"Make that two hours," he said, and then hung up the phone. Darren crossed over to Jill and pulled her into his arms. "There ought to be a law."

"A law against what?" she asked.

Darren pulled her towel down. "Against you looking this damned good."

She smiled brightly. "What were you whispering about on the phone?"

"How would you like to take a little beach cruise?"

"Isn't it a little cool for that?"

"A good excuse for me to sit close to you and hold you."

"All right," she said. "When do we leave?"

Darren kissed her hand. "As soon as you get dressed and we have breakfast."

She stepped back from him. "Then I'd better go get dressed."

He reached for her arm but she moved out of his reach. "If I don't get dressed now, we're never going to leave."

As Jill walked into the bathroom, he almost wanted to cancel the cruise and stay locked up in the room with her until a search party came looking for them. But he couldn't do that. This weekend was about showing Jill a good time, though personally he always had a great time making love to her.

A few minutes later, Jill emerged from the bathroom fully dressed and their breakfast arrived. After eating, Darren and Jill headed downstairs for their waterway getaway. They climbed into the tour van and much to Darren's joy, discovered they were the only couple going on the Folley Beach tour.

When they made it to the boat launch area, Jill squeezed his hand and kissed him on the cheek. "Thank you. I love Folley Beach," she said excitedly. "How did you get into my head to know all of this?"

Darren shrugged his shoulders, glad he had stumbled on this fact.

"Good morning, I'm Captain Rocko. Looks like it's going to be just the three of us on the tour this morning," the boat captain said as he led them to the boat. Darren got in first, and then held his hand out for Jill. When they settled into the boat, Darren put his arms around Jill's shoulders. Although the mist from the river sprayed them in the face and chilled them, he saw that it didn't matter to Jill because they were together. He leaned in and kissed her lips.

She stroked the side of his face. "This is wonderful," she whispered. "I haven't had this much fun in a long time."

"Then let's start a new tradition. Every Valentine's Day, we'll come up here and do all of this and more."

Her lips curved into a smile. "All right," she said. "I'm really looking forward to the 'more' that we're going to do."

He lifted his eyebrows and gave her a Cheshire cat grin.

Jill rested her head against his shoulder and they listened to the captain describe the sights they passed.

Around noon, the captain stopped at a small soul food restaurant in the shadow of downtown Charleston. The restaurant didn't look as if it could hold more than fifteen people at a time and the takeout counter looked like a football team's huddle. Jill and Darren took the last open table, which was next to the large bay window overlooking the Cooper River.

Darren reached across the table and held Jill's hand. "I'm glad you're enjoying yourself, but I'm even more proud that you haven't once gotten on the phone and made a business call or even read the business section of the paper."

She twirled a strand of her hair around her index finger. "Who can think of business being with you? The only business I'm thinking about is the business we have together," she said seductively.

"I like the sound of that." He brought her hand to his lips and kissed it gently.

The captain must have sensed their impatience because he skipped some of the sights on the way back.

Darren was happy, happier than he'd ever been. Could he and Jill be this happy for the rest of their lives? Wait a minute; was he considering a marriage proposal?

Jill knew she was on borrowed time and wanted to savor every second that they were spending together. She made up her mind that she was going to tell Darren the truth as soon as they got into the hotel room. That way there would be nothing hanging over their heads, nothing that would ruin what they were building.

But the moment Darren opened the door to the hotel room, Jill knew the last thing he wanted to do was talk.

He pulled her into his arms, kissing her with an ardent fervor that made her knees shake. He unzipped her jeans, and then slipped his hand inside. Jill's body quivered as he slid his finger between her moist folds of skin. He backed her onto the bed and slowly removed her shoes, kissing her toes, using his tongue to inch up her calves and thighs as he removed her panties and hungrily dove in between her legs, tasting the sexual juices seeping from her body. Jill yearned to feel him inside her, but she decided to go with the flow and let Darren explore her body. He was in control and she was going to lie back and let him work. She had never been able to let herself go like this with any other lover.

She felt safe in his arms, felt as if she could trust him with her heart. But would he forgive her when he learned the truth? Her body froze. If Darren didn't forgive her, she'd be devastated, heartbroken and alone again.

"Are you all right?" Darren asked, staring down at her.

"Yes, yes," she said, hoping that she was convincing him. "I just…I want you so much."

"You got me, baby." He kissed her forehead as he parted her thighs. "You don't have to worry about me not being here." He kissed her cheek, then her lips. "I've got to be here to kiss these lips."

She lifted her hands and brought his face closer to hers. Their lips touched and she outlined his lips with her tongue. "Love me, Darren."

He dove into her awaiting body and she moaned with pleasure, clutched his back, pulling him deeper and closer. She wanted to lose herself in him, meld her soul with his. They rolled over so that Jill was on top. He reached up and pushed her hair from her face, then captured her lips as she rocked back and forth, tightening herself around his throbbing manhood. Would he stay with her when he found out the truth? Would he still want to make love to her when he knew that she didn't trust him enough to share everything about herself with him?

Jill threw her head back as she climaxed. Tears and sweat streaked her face and she collapsed against his chest. Darren stroked her back as he held her. "Are you all right?"

"Yes," she said, refusing to look him in the eye.

"Why the tears? Jill, what's wrong, honey?"

"Darren, tell me that this will never change, that nothing is going to change what we have right now."

"I don't know how many ways you want me to say, it Jill. I love you and nothing is going to come between us."

"I just like to be reassured," she whispered.

"Is there something you want to tell me? Something lurking in the background that you think will change the way I feel about you?"

She turned away from him. "I hope not," she replied in a voice barely audible.

"Let's get up and get something to eat or do we want to eat in bed?"

Jill forced a smile. "Now if we stay in this bed, only one of us will be eating something."

After they showered and dressed, Jill and Darren headed to the gift shop in the lobby of the hotel searching for chocolate. She noticed that he kept eyeing his watch.

"You need to be somewhere?" she asked as she picked up a bag of chocolate covered pecans.

"No, *we* have to be somewhere. You did bring that black dress, didn't you?"

She nodded and her eyes asked why.

Darren opened her bag of candy and popped one in his mouth. "We're going to a concert tonight. I need you to take your chocolate, go back to the room and relax. I've got to take care of one small detail."

"And just what might that be?"

Darren winked at her before backing out the door. "You're just going to have to wait and find out."

She pursed her lips but didn't say anything. Jill was getting used to Darren's little surprises and looking forward to them. Still, she couldn't help wondering what Darren had planned for tonight.

Darren knew he was asking a lot of Cleveland and his friend, Lynette, the Brian McKnight concert promoter. But Cleveland had called her and she'd agreed to meet with Darren. Now, he just had to find his way to the Charleston Civic Center. He hopped in the first cab that he saw outside the hotel.

"Can you get me to the civic center?" Darren asked.

"Sure," the man said. "Going to the concert alone and this early?"

"I'm just laying the groundwork for a surprise." Darren leaned back in the leather seat. "I fell in love with a woman who means the world to me and if I could scream it from the roof tops, I would."

The driver chuckled. "I remember when I was in love like that. You have to hold on to that kind of love, young man."

"Trust me, I'm going to."

CHAPTER TWENTY-TWO

Jill studied her reflection in the mirror. With her hair pulled up in a loose bun and just a touch of makeup on her face, she felt like the sexiest woman in the world. She planned to surprise Darren by wearing a black lace teddy underneath her dress so that she could strip for him after they returned from wherever they were going. When they returned to Atlanta, she was going to have to get him a gift. She bit her bottom lip as she thought of Atlanta. Would Darren even want anything to do with her?

Shaking her head, Jill decided not to worry about Atlanta and focus on what was in front of her: another night of pleasant surprises. As she stepped into her dress, she wondered where Darren was.

Just as she fastened the clasp of her bracelet, Darren burst through the door. "Sorry I'm late...Damn, you look good." He ran into the bathroom, shutting the door behind him.

"Where have you been?" she asked. "And where are we going?"

She was answered by the whoosh of the shower. Jill sat on the edge of the bed and slipped on her four-inch pumps. "He'd better not have me walking a long distance," she mumbled.

Darren walked out of the bathroom wrapped in a towel from the waist down. She smiled at him and fought the urge to rip the towel from his body and ravage his body. Instead, she stood up and walked over to the mirror and began restyling her hair.

"Where did you say we were going again?" she asked.

"Slick," he said as he pulled on his slacks. "I never said where we were going."

Looking at him over her shoulder, she smiled. "Doesn't hurt to try. Just tell me this. I'm not going to have to do a lot of walking, am I?"

Darren buttoned his black silk shirt and crossed over to Jill. Wrapping his arms around her waist, he brushed his lips against her neck. "You look wonderful and smell so good. I might want to keep you in the house for the rest of your life."

"One slight problem, we're not in a house and I didn't put these shoes on to sit in this hotel room tonight," she ribbed.

Darren spun her around and dipped her as if they were in a ballroom. "You're right. I guess I can share your beauty for one night." He let her go. "Ready?"

"Yes."

Darren walked over to the door and opened it as if he were one of Cinderella's footmen. "Madame, your chariot awaits you."

She nodded to him and headed out the door.

Downstairs, a black limo waited for them. Jill smiled at Darren as the driver opened the door. "This is too much," she said as they slid inside.

"Nothing is too much when it comes to you," he said, then kissed her cheek.

She held his face in her hands. "Sometimes I really think I don't deserve you."

"Why would you think something foolish like that? You were made for me." He brought his lips to her ear. "I know that because your body is a perfect fit for me."

Heat rose to her cheeks just thinking about the way his body fit with hers. "Darren," she whispered. "You're so bad."

"And you know you love it."

As the limo pulled up to the civic center, Jill squealed like a school girl. "*One Night with Brian McKnight*! How did you? Can you read my mind or something?"

Darren smiled. "I'm beginning to think I can. You're not just saying you're having a good time to make me feel better, are you?"

"No, not at all. This has got to be the best Valentine's Day of my life."

"You haven't seen anything yet," he said as the driver opened the door.

They walked into the center and took their seats in the third row from the stage.

Gerald Albright walked on to the stage and began blowing his saxophone. Jill felt like a kid in a candy store. When she stood up and began swaying to the beat, Darren followed her lead, stood and wrapped his arms around her.

"Having fun?" he asked as he dipped her.

"That's an understatement. Thank you so much for this."

"The night is still young," he said.

When Gerald moved into another song with a Latin rhythm, Jill and Darren sat down, still moving to the beat.

After about thirty minutes, Gerald took a bow and told everyone the man of the hour, Brian McKnight, would take the stage soon.

When Brian McKnight took the stage, Jill and the other women in the audience screamed like teenagers.

"Good evening, Charleston!" Brian yelled from the stage. "How you feeling tonight?"

"Good!" the audience yelled back.

"Before I took the stage tonight, this guy came up to me and said, 'Brian, I want to do something special for my woman.' I was like, bro, just bring her to my show."

Everyone laughed.

"But seriously, this man said, 'Brian, my lady is special and I want to let everybody know how much I love her, how wonderful she is and how I can't live without her.' "

A few women in the crowd slapped each other fives. Then a spotlight lit on Jill and Darren.

Brian McKnight scooted to the edge of the stage. "Jill, do you know how much this man loves you? Do you know that he dreams about you every night? Because the first time he saw you, he knew you would be the irreplaceable love of his life."

Brian began to sing his hit song, "Love of My Life," and Jill cried silently. Darren squeezed her hand as Brian sang to her.

Jill couldn't help wondering if Darren would feel all of those good feelings when her secret was exposed. She tried not to think about it and leaned her head on Darren's shoulder.

"I don't want this night to end," she whispered as Brian sang another of his hits.

Darren stroked her arm and held her hand. "Should I be jealous?"

"Not at all. I'd take you over him," she motioned to the stage, "any day. That was so sweet of you to get him to dedicate that song to me."

He kissed her hand and swayed to Brian's rendition of "Kiss" by Prince.

Before the concert was over, Brian tossed a single red rose to Jill. "You got a good man over there," he said before launching into his hit, "What We Do Here."

As Jill and Darren walked out of the concert hall, she could feel the envious stares of many of the other women. They should be so lucky to have a man like Darren in their lives. But in the back of her mind, Jill wondered how much longer she was going to have him in her life.

The weekend seemed to speed by after the concert. When they were standing at the front desk counter checking out, Jill reached for Darren's arm.

"Do we have to leave?" she asked, sounding like a child not wanting to leave Disneyland.

He kissed her on the cheek. "Yes, the real world is calling us." He reached into his pocket. "You can even have this back."

Jill took her cell phone from his hand but didn't turn it on. She had gotten used to not hearing the chirp of her phone and not being available to people twenty-four hours a day. Turning that phone on would be like reality slapping her in the face. Already she knew that her voicemail box was going to be full.

"Why don't do a little more sightseeing before we leave," she suggested as Darren settled the bill.

"All right," he replied, obviously not in a big hurry to return to Atlanta either. Darren turned to the front desk clerk. "Do you have any suggestions as to where we can spend a couple of hours?"

"Well, there's the *Porgy and Bess* tour," the clerk said, then slipped Darren a brochure. "You can sign up for a one hour or two hour tour."

With her eyes, Jill pleaded with Darren to take the tour. He nodded.

"Can you get us set up on the two hour tour?" Darren asked as he squeezed Jill's hand.

Great, she thought. *I can put off the inevitable for another few hours.*

After the tour of old Charleston, Darren and Jill headed home. As she slept in the passenger seat, he stole glances at her. What had he done to be so lucky to have her in his life?

Rushing or not, I'm going to ask Jill to marry me. I love her and I want to spend the rest of my life with her.

It was mid-morning when Darren and Jill happened upon the small restaurant where they'd stopped on the way to Charleston. The waitress smiled when she saw them cross the threshold.

"Y'all are back," she said.

"Yes, we had to have some more of that fried chicken before we headed back to the city," Darren said.

"Good thing y'all beat the lunch rush," she said, then pointedly looked at Jill's hand.

Darren knew she was looking for an engagement ring. "Come on, let's sit down," Darren said as he took Jill's hand into his.

After they ate Henry's famous fried chicken, they headed back to Atlanta.

"I really don't want to go back," Jill whispered.

"Aw, you know you missed being in the office and texting on your Blackberry."

She reached over and pressed her hand against his thigh. "No, I didn't. You kept me thoroughly occupied."

Darren couldn't help smiling under her praise. "I aim to please, ma'am."

"And that you did. Since tonight is actually Valentine's night, you have to please me again and again."

He winked, and then said, "I don't see that as being a problem."

Jill smiled and leaned back in the seat, though she didn't remove her hand from Darren's lap. "I knew you were going to say that."

CHAPTER TWENTY-THREE

Two days after Valentine's Day, Jill was sitting behind her high mahogany desk, looking over merger papers and reviewing messages she'd received while she was out of town, when Madison burst through her office door.

"Jill, have you seen this?" She plopped a copy of *Atlanta Scene* magazine on her desk. "You're on the cover and the story is scandalous."

Jill snatched up the magazine and her eyes bugged when she saw the headline, "The CEO and the Fireman."

Jill fumed as she read the story, which described her as a maneater, said she used men as pawns, that the only thing she cared about was business.

"When it comes to Jill Atkinson, everything is about business and there is no business of love," the article read.

"I can't believe this bastard!" she exploded.

"So who sold you out? The man in the picture or the person who wrote the article?" Madison asked. "I mean, what is this, a ghetto tabloid?"

"How did you get this?"

Madison flipped another page. "They're all over town, like *Creative Loafing.*"

Jill dropped her head into her hands. "This can't be happening."

"How did we end up running an ad in this trash?"

Jill snatched the magazine from Madison, then shooed her out of the office. Then she yanked the phone off the hook and angrily dialed David's number.

"Sorry, the number you have called has been changed to a non-published number," the recording relayed.

Jill slammed the phone down and opened the magazine to look for the office's address. It was a post office box. But Jill knew where she could find David. He'd be sitting at the Atlanta Bread Company, eating a bagel with lox and sipping decaf. She hoped to catch him in mid sip so that she could splash the hot coffee in his lying face.

Grabbing her purse, she stalked out the door. "I'll be out for the rest of the day," she barked on her way out. The thought of what Darren's reaction would be to the magazine took a backseat to taking off David's head.

She walked into the Peachtree Street restaurant and there he was, sitting at a table, surrounded by potential advertisers. Everyone was looking at the current copy of his magazine. Jill wanted to walk over there and turn that table upside down. Instead, she calmly walked over to the table and cleared her throat.

Every eye turned to her and the awkwardness that enveloped the room could have been filleted and fried.

"David, I'd like to have a word with you," she snapped.

"Jill," he said. "I'm in a meeting here."

"And you're about two seconds from a lawsuit. We can talk now or in court," she said firmly.

David stood up, straightening the lapels of his jacket. "Gentlemen, if you would excuse me."

Jill pointed to the front door. Outside, she turned and faced him with angry flames flickering in her eyes. Then she hauled off and slapped him. "You lying son of a bitch. And then you had the nerve to use my ad in this smut."

David stroked his jaw, which stung from her blow. "I warned you. So don't come in here acting all surprised about this magazine or my cover article."

"What about the money?"

"This wasn't about money, I told you that too. Jill, you can't go around embarrassing people and think that it won't come back to bite you. I'm sure your little fireman friend has seen this magazine and wants nothing else to do with you. And why would he?"

"Darren loves me and nothing you can say in this rag of yours is going to change that. You'll be hearing from my lawyers." She turned on her heel to walk away.

"Sue me all you want, but seeing that look on your face and watching those businessmen in there shrink away from the 'great and powerful' Jill Atkinson made it worth it. I wish I could see the look on your face when you try to explain yourself to your firefighter boyfriend. Maybe I should put another tail on you so we can capture the aftermath."

"You bastard. What perverse pleasure do you get from doing this to me? Do you feel like a real man? Did you grow an inch or two in your pants? You can write all the lies you want about me but I'll still be a better businessman than you will ever be and yes, I fired you when you were trying to steal my company. Why don't you write about that in your smutty magazine?" Jill stormed away from him, muttering curses under her breath.

This was far from over and David was going to pay.

⊷⊷

Darren walked into the fire station with a two and a half carat diamond engagement ring in his pocket. He'd made up his mind that he was going to marry Jill. Why should he wait when he knew he loved her and she loved him? The song "Maneater" by Hall and Oates was blasting from the speakers as Darren headed to his office. He furrowed his brows, wondering why someone was playing that old song. After entering his office, he sat down and started to pick up the phone to invite Jill to lunch. Cleveland burst through his office door.

"Darren, we need to talk," he said.

"What's with the music?" Darren asked as Cleveland closed the door behind him.

Cleveland sat on the edge of the desk. "Have you…"

"I'm going to ask Jill to marry me," Darren exclaimed.

"Don't do that, man. Jill isn't the woman you thought she was. She's a liar and good at it because she had me fooled."

Darren eyed Cleveland with questions flickering on his face. "What are you talking about?"

Cleveland shook his head. "You haven't seen it, have you?"

"Seen what? What are you being so cryptic about? You've met Jill, she isn't a liar. I love her and I'm not going to let your sour attitude ruin my chance at happiness.

Cleveland lifted his hips from the desk and handed a copy of *Atlanta Scene* to Darren.

"Man, I'm sorry."

Darren read the article. The one thing that stood out was that Jill was the CEO of DVA. She wasn't a dedicated employee, she owned the place. Why had she lied to him about that? Had she just toyed with him for her own perverse pleasure as the magazine suggested? What about all of those promises that they'd made? When she said she loved him had she been lying then? Seething with anger, Darren balled the magazine up. "What the hell is this?"

"I don't know, some new magazine. It's all over town, though. Even Ma has seen it."

Darren wanted to punch something, smash something against the wall. "I can't believe this," he muttered. He pulled out the black velvet ring box. "Why do I keep making the same mistake when it comes to women?"

Cleveland put his hand on Darren's shoulder. "It's not you. These women in Atlanta are just scandalous. They lie without a conscience and then call us dogs. This is why I'm not trying to…"

"Just cut it out. Why don't you just leave?"

"Man, don't do anything…"

"Get out!" Darren bellowed.

Cleveland left, knowing he was going to have let his brother deal with his heartache and disappointment in his own way. He didn't want to watch Darren go through this again.

Darren slammed his office door behind Cleveland, and then slouched in the chair behind his desk. How had this happened to him again? How had he given his heart to the wrong woman for a second time?

Am I such a fool that women feel like they can tell me anything and I'll fall for it? Jill, how could you?

He stood, pacing back and forth as he contemplated calling her. What would he say and why would he ever want to speak to her again? Jill had done the one thing he couldn't forgive her for: She'd lied and in so doing had made a fool of him.

Darren snatched up the phone, his heart thumping like a war drum.

"Jill Atkinson's office," a woman said.

"Is Jill there?" Darren said more evenly than he felt.

"She's out of the office today. Is there a mess—"

Darren hung up before she could finish speaking. Next he called Jill's cell phone and the voice mail picked up immediately. Darren slammed the phone down, cracking the hard plastic of the receiver.

He was afraid to go to her house because he didn't know how he would react to seeing her. Would his love for her take over his anger or would his anger boil over, causing him to say the most caustic things to her?

Even though he was hurt, he didn't want to go out of his way to make her feel his pain. Despite his anger, Darren still cared about her and he couldn't make himself stop. He had to see her and find out why she'd lied to him.

❧❧

Jill sat in her home, drapes drawn, the phones shut off and the lights dimmed to near darkness. It was bad enough that David had broken her heart all those years ago but now he had humiliated her for the whole city to see.

What did I ever do to deserve this? She pondered as she drew her knees into her chest. She knew Darren had seen the magazine by now and she was going to have to explain herself to him. Leaning back on the sofa, she exhaled loudly. She couldn't put it off any longer, she had to call Darren. Just as she reached for the phone, the doorman buzzed her.

"Miss Atkinson, Mr. Alexander is here."

"Send him up," she said, her voice quavering. It was time to face the music and Jill knew she wasn't going to like the song.

She opened the door and Darren stood there with a stoic look on his face.

"Hi," she managed.

He stood in the doorway and didn't make an effort to enter her place. Instead, he looked around the foyer. "All this time I wondered how you could afford all of this. I didn't ask you because it wasn't my business. Lo and behold, Jill Atkinson is the CEO of DVA, the company she works so diligently for and I'm just the flavor of the month."

"Darren, that article wasn't true it was…"

"Are you president and CEO of the company?" he asked as if he were asking her the score of the Atlanta Hawks game. "I mean, time and time again you talked about your boss, how he gave you tickets to the Falcons games and how he appreciated your work and all this time you were talking about yourself. Bravo, Jill, you made a fool of me. You even tricked my brother and it's not easy to pull the wool over his eyes."

"Darren, if you would just let me explain," she said. "I was afraid that if I told you the truth that you would look at me differently and I didn't want that."

"Save it." He turned to the door then whirled around to face her again. "I told you from the beginning that I couldn't tolerate being lied to and you did it every day. Every time we made love, every time I looked into your eyes and poured my heart out to you and said I loved you, you made a conscious effort to lie to me. And why? Did you think I wanted your money? Did you think that I would all of a sudden quit my job and expect you to take care of me? What the hell did you take me for? A gigolo?"

Tears welled up in Jill's eyes. "Darren, I'm sorry." Jill said, her voice wavering like a flag in the wind.

"Sorry for what? Lying or getting caught?"

"Please, just listen to me." She reached out and tried to grab his hand, but Darren yanked away from her.

"I don't know who you are," he said, "and I don't think I want to." Darren turned on his heel, ignoring Jill's desperate pleas for him to listen to her. She ran after him as he approached the elevator.

"Darren, I love you."

Pressing the down button on the elevator, he didn't reply nor did he turn around and look at her.

"Did you hear me?" she probed. "I love you and we can work this out."

He stepped on the elevator, faced her and shook his head. "How do I know you're not lying right now?"

The doors closed before she could say anything else. What more could she say? She'd known this day was coming. Had she been smart, she would have told Darren herself. As much as she wanted to blame David, she couldn't. Hearing Darren say all of those things to her had driven home the point that she had lied to him over and over again. Knowing how difficult it was for him to trust women, she'd still lied. How many times had Shari urged her to tell him the truth? How many times had she come close to telling him the truth?

She walked into her penthouse with her head down and tears streaming down her cheeks, knowing she had just lost the best thing that had ever happened to her.

CHAPTER TWENTY-FOUR

Two Months Later

Jill secluded herself in her penthouse until the hubbub about the *Atlanta Scene* magazine article died down. She didn't even bother with a libel suit against David because it would have only made the story stay around longer.

If she were truly honest with herself, she couldn't blame David for the end of the relationship. It was all her fault. She had made one excuse after the other for not telling Darren the truth about being the CEO of DVA. In the end, it was her lies that had pushed him away.

I was such a fool, she thought. *The moment I met Darren I knew he was different, I should've been honest with him from the beginning.*

Jill took solace in the fact that David's business venture was falling apart. After the second issue the magazine was quickly losing steam and advertisers were starting to pull their ads. The word on the street was that David was seconds away from having to discontinue the magazine.

Darren wouldn't return her phone calls and on the off chance that he picked up the phone when she called, he slammed it down immediately. Conventional wisdom told her to give up and move on with her life. But how could she just walk away when she loved Darren more than she loved anything.

Every time the phone rang she prayed it was him, but her prayers were in vain. He didn't stop by nor did he e-mail. Jill knew she needed help to win his heart back and the only person who could assist her was probably the last person who would talk to her— Cleveland Alexander.

Just as Jill was about to walk out the door, the phone rang. She rushed to grab it, hopeful that it was Darren.

"Hello."

"Jill, it's Shari."

"Hi," she said, disappointment peppering her tone.

"Wow, don't be so happy to hear from me."

"It's not that, I was just hoping that you were—"

"Darren?"

"Yeah, he still isn't talking to me. I don't know what more I can do to make him understand how sorry I am about what happened and for lying to him."

"You're going to have to go to him. As much as you two love each other, I'm sure you can work it out. But you were wrong, Jill."

"I know. What if he can't forgive me? Look at how long it took you and me to get right."

"That was different," Shari said. "You told my husband I was pregnant before I could and I was a little salty about it, but I got over it. When you care about somebody, friend or otherwise, you forgive them."

"I knew how Darren felt about honesty."

"And anyone could see how Darren felt about you. That man was crazy for you, and those feelings don't just disappear."

"It's been two months. What if they have disappeared?"

"Do you know how long I held a torch for Tyrell? I still care for him and he's dead and gone and I'm married and carrying another man's child. Two months is not enough time for that man to stop loving you."

"What am I supposed to do to get him to listen to me? Do you know how many voice mails and e-mails I've sent him? He has yet to respond to any of them."

"Then go see him," Shari said as if she were telling her what kind of toothpaste was on sale at Kroger this week.

"I'm afraid."

"Jill, in love, just like business, you have to take risks," Shari said.

Sighing into the phone, Jill repeated her mantra, "The bigger the risk, the bigger the return, right? I know what I have to do. Shari, I'll call you back." Jill hung up the phone and headed out the door. She knew Cleveland wasn't going to be happy to see her, but he'd get over it. With Cleveland's help, she was going to throw herself on Darren's mercy and pray that he would be forgiving.

After driving around Cleveland's neighborhood for about an hour, she finally pulled into the driveway. She squeezed the steering wheel, said a silent prayer and then got out the car. As she approached the door, her heart thudded like a flat tire, sweat beaded up on her lips and her hands felt slippery. With each step she was more and more nervous. What if Cleveland slammed the door in her face?

Stop it, she told herself. *He's not going to bite you. He's a man, not a monster.*

Jill pressed the doorbell, hoping that Cleveland would be home alone. The last thing she needed was to interrupt a romantic evening between Cleveland and his woman. When the porch light shone on her, Jill shielded her eyes.

Cleveland snatched the door opened, frowning at Jill. "You have some nerve coming here."

"I know and I really don't want to cause any trouble, but I have to talk to you about Darren."

"Haven't you caused my brother enough pain?"

"Please, let me in, so that I can explain myself," Jill pleaded.

Cleveland moved to close the door, but Jill wouldn't be denied. She pushed the door to hold it open.

"Please," she said. "I love him."

"Yeah, you love him so much that you lied to him. Lady, get off my doorstep."

"I'm not going to leave until you talk to me. I know Darren still cares about me and if he'll hear me out, then I know we can get back on track."

"Then why are you here? Why not head over to Darren's house and talk to him. Don't put me in the middle of your mess."

"You have every right not to want to talk to me or help me. But I have to know. How is Darren? Is he okay?"

Cleveland seemed to ponder the question. "He's getting there. And he doesn't need you."

"But I need him to understand that I wasn't trying to hurt him or embarrass him. Please, help me. I know you don't have a reason in the world to help me, but I love your brother and I know he loves me."

"If you loved him so much, then what was the big secret about, Jill?"

"You don't know what it's been like with men trying to use me. At first I was just trying to protect myself."

Cleveland folded his arms across his chest and glared at her. "What, you thought Darren was one of those men that wanted something from you? My brother doesn't roll like that. When he cares about a woman it's because of who she is, not what she has."

"I know that, but this wasn't about Darren. It was about me and my insecurities."

"Save it with the shoulda, woulda, couldas. Darren is doing fine without you, and I don't know what you thought coming here would accomplish. Do you expect me to call my brother up and say, 'Jill came by, she wants you back, give her a chance?' Give me a break."

"Yeah. That's what I want you to do."

"Lady, you need to leave. I'm not letting you hurt my brother again. You've had your chance."

Jill turned to walk away, but stopped at the last step. "Cleveland, you thought I was good for Darren. What's different? I know not telling him that I was CEO of DVA was wrong, but I didn't set out to hurt him and the other stuff in that paper wasn't true."

"What?"

"That paper is published by the man who tried to steal my company. When I bought the company he worked for and fired him, he wanted to get back at me and this was how he did it. I know I was wrong for not trusting Darren enough to be honest. As much as I want to blame David and his tabloid, I brought this on myself. Your brother is the kindest and most gentle man that I've ever known, and I can't just let him go without trying to make things right." Tears threatened to spill from her eyes. "I just wish I could talk to Darren and let him hear my side of the story. If he doesn't forgive me, okay, but he has to know that I didn't set out to hurt him."

Cleveland bounded down the steps as Jill began to cry. "Look, Jill, I'll try to talk to him, but I can't guarantee you anything."

Jill wrapped her arms around his neck, sobbing and hugging him tightly. "Thank you."

As Jill drove home, she felt hopeful for the first time in weeks.

∽✑∽

Darren woke up reaching for Jill's supple body. That was her he'd danced with at Red last night, wasn't it? He grabbed a handful of pillow and sat up in the bed. His throbbing head reminded him that he'd had a little too much to drink last night. The fuzzy memories were starting to come back to him.

He'd gone to Red, hoping that he'd catch a glimpse of Jill out with some business associates or her friend Shari. Darren had planned to talk to her if he indeed did see her. The last two months without Jill had been pure hell. Despite his bruised ego, Darren still loved her and he knew he hadn't been fair to her. He hadn't listened to what she had to say about the article or her reasons for hiding the truth from him. In short, he'd overreacted.

So, last night, he'd sat at the bar, downing shot after shot of tequila. Then a woman had slid onto the stool next to him. In the red glow of the bar and through his alcohol hazed eyes, she looked like Jill.

"Hi there," she'd said.

"How are you, beautiful?"

She'd smiled at him and Darren had turned to face her. Yep, that was Jill. "What are you drinking tonight?" he'd asked.

"Sex on the beach."

Darren had banged on the bar and ordered the mystery woman her drink.

"Baby, I'm sorry that we've come to this," he'd told her, reaching for her hand.

"What?"

"I know that article didn't mean anything. I love you."

"You're crazy and drunk. I don't know you."

"Jill, please, don't treat me like this."

"Jill? Who's Jill?"

Swinging his legs over the side of the bed, Darren realized what a fool he'd made of himself last night.

Why did she think I would give a damn about her money? She should have known that I was in love with her, not what she had to offer. And how much of that article was true?

According to the magazine, she was a player. He'd read that article more times than he cared to admit over the past two months. If Jill was a playgirl, she had fooled him into thinking otherwise.

Rising from the bed, Darren tried to fight the image of Jill in the arms of another man. Or maybe she was lounging at the spa with some of her girl-friends, just laughing about how she'd played him. As much as he wanted to believe that Jill was cold and evil, it went against everything he knew about her.

I can't keep worrying about Jill, he thought. *I don't need her.* The lie burned in his brain. He did need Jill, even if he wouldn't say it out loud. The only thing that actually stood between him and Jill was his foolish pride. He wanted to call her and say all was forgiven, but how could he when he still hurt? The room felt as if it were spinning when Darren walked into the bathroom. He'd lost count of the number of drinks he'd had the night before. Luckily, the bartender planted him in a cab so that he would make it home safely.

He turned on the shower. Standing underneath the steady stream of water, the lick of the water against his skin reminded him of Jill's gentle touch. Closing his eyes, he remembered making love to her, feeling her lips against his, plunging deep into her. Her scent still lingered in his mind.

What he felt couldn't have been a lie. What she'd said to him couldn't have been a lie. As the water ran cold, Darren stepped out of the shower, wrapped a towel around his waist and sprawled out across the bed. Staring up at the ceiling, his mind wandered back to Jill and the future they'd planned. The telephone rang, breaking into his thoughts.

"Yeah," he growled into the phone.

"Darren, it's me," Cleveland said. "What do you say we go and have breakfast?"

"Not in the mood."

"You need to stop hiding in your house. The only time I see you is when you come into the station."

"Maybe that's the only time you need to see me."

"Darren, I'm your brother and I know what you're going through. You need to let someone be there for you."

"You act like she died or something. We broke up because she's a liar."

"Have you talked to her?"

"Nope."

"Maybe you should."

Those words prompted Darren to sit up. "What?"

"Jill came to see me and she's all torn up about what happened between the two of you."

"So what?"

"You know that took a lot for her to come to my place to talk to me. It's kind of obvious that she still cares about you. All she wants is for you to hear her out. You don't have to take her back, but maybe you need some closure to deal with this situation."

Darren snorted, pretending that he wasn't the least bit interested in what Cleveland was saying. But he was still compelled to ask, "So what did she say?"

"You need to talk to her. A lot of the things she said made a lot of sense."

"I'm not calling her," Darren said, trying to convince himself more than Cleveland.

"And I'm going to sprout wings and fly. Darren, you need to call her, talk to her, hell, get back together with her and maybe then you'll stop being such a jackass."

"Excuse me?"

Cleveland sighed loudly into the phone. "These last few weeks, you haven't been easy to get along with at work, at home or anywhere."

"Meaning?" But Cleveland didn't have to answer because Darren knew just what his brother was talking about. At work, Darren seemed to have a *Caution: Contents under Pressure* tattoo on his forehead.

He yelled at people for no reason, snapped at someone for just saying hello and jumped down anyone's throat who had the audacity to ask him a question.

"People are starting to complain. Maybe you need a vacation."

"So you know what I need now?" Darren snapped.

"I know you need to calm down. You still love her, don't you?"

"I'm through with her."

"You can't even say her name."

"Don't be ridiculous."

Cleveland snorted. "You haven't said it since we've been on the phone."

"Jill," he spat. "Happy?"

"Nope. You need some fresh air on your face. Let's go shoot some hoops since you don't want to eat."

"Fine. When and where?" Darren asked.

"Our usual spot, let's say in two hours?"

Darren hung up without saying goodbye, and then dressed in a pair of shorts and an old jersey. The exercise would do him good. He could work off some frustration and tension. Better yet, it would take his mind off Jill.

CHAPTER TWENTY-FIVE

Jill held her breath as she waited in the dark gym. What if Cleveland couldn't convince Darren to meet him? Suppose Darren walked in, saw her standing there and ran away? And what if he'd truly moved on with his life and didn't want anything to do with her?

This is the dumbest idea I've ever come up with, she thought as she paced back and forth. The door to the gym opened.

"Yo, Cleveland, what's up with the lights?" Darren called out.

Frozen in place, Jill watched as Darren flipped the light switch. Then she walked out of the shadows.

"Darren."

"What are you doing here?"

"I-I needed to see you," she said. "You won't return my calls. It's been two months."

"I know how long it's been."

"Darren, I never meant to hurt you."

"No? You lied to me over and over again. Since the article, I guess it's kind of hard for you to play the 'I'm just a DVA employee role' now," he snapped.

Jill closed the space between them. "Darren, I wasn't trying to play any kind of role. It's just that when I first met you, I wanted you to see me for me. I was wrong because once I got to know you; I knew that my job wouldn't matter. I'm sorry, I'm so sorry, Darren."

"I know you're sorry. You knew how important honesty is to me, but you lied to me over and over, one lie after another," Darren snapped.

"I didn't lie to hurt you. Darren, have you ever met someone who just wanted to use you to further their career? Met someone who claimed to love you so that they could gain enough information about you just to take over your company?"

He turned his back to her. "You know the only thing I wanted from you was your love."

"And I gave that to you and…"

Darren held his hand up, cutting her off. "I think you got to know me well enough to know that it didn't matter if you were the queen of England. I fell in love with you, not what you had or what I thought you could do for me. Did I ever ask you for anything?"

"No, but this wasn't about you."

"What the hell was it about then? You felt like you couldn't trust me, like you had to hide something and lie. Why do you want to be with someone you can't trust, Jill? Do you just want a warm body in your bed?"

"No, I want you; I want what we had in Charleston."

Darren laughed sardonically. "Everything we had was a damned lie."

Jill tentatively placed her hand on his shoulder. "No, it wasn't, it isn't a lie. I love you and that's the truth. If you would hear me out and try to understand what I…"

"Understand? What I understand is that I was totally open with you. I laid everything on the table and you held your cards close to your chest, punishing me for what some other man did. I spent years after my divorce believing that I would never trust another woman. Then you came into my life and I thought you were a woman I could trust, the woman I was going to spend the rest of my life with. Then I find my face plastered all over the street with this sleazy tale about this horny CEO who seduces men for her own carnal needs."

"And you believe what was written about me?" Jill snapped. "That was written by a man who wanted to humiliate me because I fired him."

"Jill, what am I supposed to believe? You didn't tell me you were CEO of DVA. What else did you lie to me about? Did you even love me?"

"I love you," Jill said. "I wouldn't have said it if I didn't mean it."

He removed her hand from his shoulder. "I'm going to go," he said. "We don't have anything else to talk about."

"Darren, please don't walk out of my life. Whatever it takes to regain your trust, I'll do it."

He took a few steps back from her. Jill took just as many steps toward him.

"Do you remember what you said to me when we first met?" she asked. "You said that I didn't know how to let someone take care of me and that was the truth. When you came into my life, I was able to let go, relax and let you take care of me."

"I don't want to hear this right now," he said. "Jill, I told you that I wouldn't forgive a lie. There was no good reason for you to lie to me. Not once did I give you any reason to believe that I wanted anything from you. Hell, I knew you had money. You own a penthouse and you wear more labels than a rap star. That never mattered to me, I saw past all of that and I thought I was getting to know you."

"You were," she exclaimed. "Darren, David..."

"David, the man that you said broke your heart and the man that you said you could handle, seems to know more about you than I do."

"He doesn't. I didn't agree to that interview. He made that stuff up because he failed to steal my business from me and I bought the company he worked for and then fired him. He'd been trying to get back at me for years."

"This is too much to take in," he said. "I don't know who you are anymore."

"I haven't changed. I made a mistake, a huge mistake."

Darren glared at her. "Let me get this straight. Because this David person hurt you, you didn't trust me enough to be honest with me. You allowed him to humiliate me in his drive for revenge."

Placing her hands on her hips, she stood flat-footed in front of Darren, forcing their eyes to meet. "So, Darren, is this about your ego? Just how in the hell do you think I feel? Coming here was a mistake. I don't know how many more ways I can say I'm sorry." Jill turned on her heel to walk out the door. With each step she took, her heart crumbled. She was praying that Darren would stop her.

"Jill," he called as she grabbed the door handle.

Turning and facing him, she raised her eyebrow as if to say, "What?"

"My ego was bruised, but what really got me was the fact that you didn't trust me enough to be honest with me, to tell me that you owned the company. I had to read it in a magazine. What does that say about how you feel about me?"

"What do you mean?"

"You lumped me in the same category as all of those other men that you said used you and wanted to further their careers and causes through you. That's never been me."

"I came to understand that," Jill said as she walked toward him. "But at first, I was trying to protect myself. Darren, you made me feel like a woman, not a businesswoman, but someone who was desired and needed because you loved me and cared about me."

"I still do," he replied in a voice barely above a whisper.

"What?"

"I'm not going to lie and say I don't still love you. Hell, Jill, I wanted to marry you."

Tears blurred her vision. "Marry me?"

"Yeah. I was going to propose the day the magazine came out. But after seeing that, finding out that you'd been lying to me all this time, I needed some time to myself."

"Why couldn't you talk to me?"

"Maybe the same reason you couldn't tell me the truth."

"So where do we go from here?"

Darren shrugged his shoulders. "Do you want to go grab something to eat?"

She released a sigh of relief inwardly. "Yes."

"Hopefully we won't end up on the front of another paper," Darren said as he pushed the door open.

As Darren followed Jill to a small bistro in College Park, he thought about what she'd said about his ego. Did she have a point? It wasn't as if he'd stopped loving her.

But he'd tried. No matter how much he'd wanted to turn his feelings off for her, he hadn't been able to. At night when he went to sleep, he dreamed of her. First thing in the morning, he longed to kiss her and yearned to feel her body against his. But he couldn't tell her that, or more aptly put, he wasn't going to tell her that.

Darren understood why Jill needed to protect herself from male gigolos who would try to take her for every cent she had. But hadn't he proved that he wasn't that kind of guy? Anger began to burn inside him all over again. What it all boiled down to was that Jill didn't trust him. How could she not trust that he loved her?

Though he was tempted to drive past the restaurant, Darren pulled in behind Jill. As he watched her get out of the car, his anger began to subside. She looked even more beautiful than when he saw her standing in the gym. With her hair pulled back in a ponytail, she didn't look like a CEO and she definitely didn't look like a maneater.

"Darren," she said, "is this place all right?"

"This is fine."

They walked into the restaurant in silence. Darren didn't know if he should say something or let Jill do all the talking. Then again, getting something to eat had been his idea.

Since the restaurant wasn't full, Darren and Jill sat themselves, choosing a secluded table in the rear of the bistro.

After a few minutes of uncomfortable silence, Jill looked deep into Darren's eyes.

"Thank you," she said. "I know you really don't want to be here."

"Well, I know we need to hash things out between us," he said.

"Whatever it takes," she said.

Darren placed his hands on the table. "Maybe we just need some closure. It's obvious that our relationship was flawed to begin with." The words burned in his mouth. He didn't want to end his relationship with Jill forever. What he should have been saying was that he loved her still and just didn't understand why she didn't trust him.

"What are you saying?" she asked, her lips quivering. "Is there no chance for us?"

"How can there be, Jill? You obviously thought I was after something from you or else you would've been honest with me about DVA and all of that."

"I was afraid things would change."

Darren folded his arms across his chest. "Why would you think something like that?"

She turned her head away from him. "Let me ask you something. If you had known the night you met me that I was DVA's CEO, would you have still asked me out?"

"Yes," Darren said.

She tilted her head to the side and looked at him. "Darren."

"You know what; I think you like thinking that all men want to use you. It gives you an excuse to play these little games. Maybe you're the one with the problem."

"Excuse me?"

"I don't think I was stuttering. Jill, the man who truly loves you doesn't give a damn if you're CEO or a damn mail clerk."

"Are you still that man?" she asked.

It was Darren's turn to look away. Should he tell her the truth? Tell her how these past two months had been pure hell for him and that all he'd been able to think about was having her in his arms again.

"I don't know," he finally said.

"What do you mean, *you don't know*? You just said that all of this about me being CEO didn't matter. We can't keep going back and forth like this. Either you're going to forgive me or we need to say goodbye."

"Is that what you want?" he asked, though the answer was plain to see. Neither of them wanted to say goodbye. Neither of them wanted to let go of what they'd shared. Darren still loved her and if he could get past his disappointment and mistrust, then he could let Jill back into his heart.

But would this always be an issue for them? And what about the things that had been written about her? How much of that article was true? What if she…Darren shut his mind off. He'd been a fool for too long. He'd known that none of that stuff written about Jill was true. She loved hard and no "playgirl" could do that.

Still, he had his pride and walking back into her arms would make him look like a fool to his men at the station, to his brother and anybody else who saw that magazine.

But those people didn't really mean anything in the long run. Let them think whatever they wanted.

"Darren?" Jill said.

"I love you. I really love you. When we got back from Charleston, I wanted to take you out to dinner and ask you to be my wife. Then I got blindsided by all this. You made a good point; I did let my ego get in the way. I was embarrassed that my woman didn't trust me enough to be honest, embarrassed that my face was plastered all over town with this woman who was some kind of maneater. What can I say? Men are egocentric. I'd like to believe that I'm the only man you've ever loved or made love to, but I know that isn't true. However, to have the whole city knowing every little detail about my woman was disheartening."

"How many times do I have to tell you that article was a lie," she replied with annoyance in her voice.

"I know what you've said," Darren stated. He placed his hands on top of Jill's. "And I believe you. Maybe I took too long to say it."

"But you've said it."

Before they could say anything else, a waitress walked over to take their order. Darren watched Jill as she asked the woman about the specials. Why had he been so stupid to spend these last months without her?

"Jill," he said when the waitress walked away. "Why don't we take our lunch to go?"

She eyed him, seemingly reading the desire in his eyes. "Oh my," she said, and then waved for the waitress.

CHAPTER TWENTY-SIX

Jill stretched·her body as she woke from the most blissful dream. Darren had taken her into his arms, kissed her tearstained cheeks and made love to her until she melted. Rolling over on her side, she reached for her pillow. Instead she encountered something hard.

Opening her eyes, she realized that it was no dream. Darren was right there beside her and she was in his bed. He opened his eyes and reached for her hand.

"Are you all right?" he asked.

"I'm better than I've been in a while," she replied. "I thought I was dreaming."

"So did I, until you clocked me in the head."

Jill blushed and wrapped her arms around his waist. "Darren, I'm truly sorry about what happened and not being honest with you."

"Shh, if we're starting over right now, then nothing else matters," he said, stroking her hair. "Unless you have some other secret you need to tell me."

"There are no more secrets." She locked her fingers with his. "So many times I wanted to tell you and I felt as if I could tell you, but something always got in the way."

Darren held her face in his hands. "What got in the way?"

"Mostly my insecurities. I thought telling you the truth would mean that I was going to be alone."

"Why, Jill? Was there some kind of vibe that you got from me that made you think I was going to run? I love you, Jill, rich, poor or whatever."

"I know that now."

"But I have to know that you trust me," Darren said.

"I do."

"And that means that there are no more secrets, no more taking on the Davids of the world without me. I could have stopped him from running that article, you know."

Jill smiled as she imagined him punching David out and standing over him telling him that the lies he'd written about her were never going to see the light of day.

"Darren," Jill began. "I'm sorry."

"You don't have to apologize again. As a matter of fact, I owe you an apology. I should have never walked away from you without hearing you out."

"You won't get any argument from me," she said.

Darren smiled at her. "What I'm trying to say is that we both made mistakes. I can't let you sit here and think that everything that went wrong between us was your fault alone. I can imagine that I made it hard for you to open up to me about your CEO status with the way I talked about you working too much and everything. I wasn't trying to be difficult, but I guess I made things that way."

Jill brushed her lips against his. "Where do we go from here?"

Darren reached into his nightstand drawer and retrieved a black velvet box. Flipping it open, he said, "To the altar, if you'll have me."

"Oh my God, Darren, are you sure about this?" Tears of joy sprang to her eyes.

"I've never been more sure about anything in my life. I love you, woman."

"But your family and everyone who read that article…"

Darren placed his finger to Jill's lips. "I don't give a damn what anyone else thinks. Worrying about other people is why I almost lost you."

She held her left hand out and let Darren slip the diamond ring on. "Baby," she said, "I love it."

"And I love you." He leaned in, gently pecking her lips.

Jill greedily captured his lips, savoring the taste of his kiss as his hands roamed the curves of her body. She felt his arousal pressing against her thighs and she parted her legs, allowing him entry into her awaiting body. Darren pressed into her as she wrapped her legs around his waist. She'd never desired a man the way she longed for Darren. Making love to him was like flying up to the sun and kissing it. He was a tender lover, a compassionate man who wanted to make Jill feel good. He touched her soul as well as gave her physical release. This was what she'd missed when they were apart, his gentle way with her.

Jill gripped his shoulders as they flipped over so that she was on top. They interlocked fingers as she rode his throbbing manhood, moaning in delight. Darren took her hardened nipples into his mouth, alternating between them, sucking and licking her until she quivered in delight. Her legs began to shake as the orgasm began to rattle her senses. "Oh, Darren," she moaned, and then collapsed on his chest. Together, they exploded in ecstasy.

For the rest of the afternoon, Jill and Darren stayed in his bed, making up for lost time and celebrating their engagement.

By the time they'd pried themselves from each other's arms, stars were twinkling in the sky. Wrapped in a white sheet, Jill opened the patio doors and looked up at the sky and said a silent prayer of thanks to God for bringing Darren into her life and for him forgiving her.

"What are you doing out here?" Darren asked as he encircled her waist.

"Thinking, praying, breathing."

"Hungry?"

"Starved."

He snuggled closer to her, kissing her neck as they stared at the same star.

"That's ours," he said. "That's our star."

She turned and faced him, her eyes glistening with happy tears. "I've never had a man give me stars before."

He lifted her into his arms. "Whatever you want, I'm going to give it to you."

"All I want is for you to love me," she whispered. "Just love me."

❧ ❧

Darren watched Jill sleep, taking note of the way her chest rose and fell with each breath she took. She was going to be his wife, finally. Now how was he going to explain that to his mother? Ever since Margaret had seen the magazine article, she hadn't had two nice words to say about Jill.

"That lying hussy," she had said. "Who does she think she is, lying like that? I don't understand these young women."

Darren had just sat silently while his mother ranted and raved. At that moment, he'd wanted to hear someone curse Jill; he'd wanted to hear her being torn down. Now he was going to have to go to his mother and make her understand that Jill was the woman he loved and planned to marry. He might have had a better chance of brokering a peace deal in the Middle East. Darren stroked her cheek gently, running his index finger down her jawline. She stirred slightly underneath his touch but didn't wake up. He continued exploring her body, slipping his hand underneath the thin sheet that covered her naked body. She was his, totally and completely.

CHAPTER TWENTY-SEVEN

Darren squeezed Jill's hand as they walked up the steps to his mother's house. When he'd called Margaret and told her that he was coming over for Sunday dinner, he didn't tell her Jill was coming with him. He'd just said, "Set an extra place."

Knowing his mother the way he did, Darren knew she thought he was bringing Cleveland.

"Are you sure your mother is going to be okay with me being here?" Jill asked as Darren turned the door-knob.

"Everything is going to be fine," he said, mostly to convince himself. "Mom?"

Margaret walked into the living room with a smile on her face, but the moment she saw Jill, her smile turned into a scowl.

"What's she doing here?" she demanded.

"Ma," Darren said, "I invited Jill because I have to tell you something."

Margaret folded her arms across her chest as Jill shifted her weight from one foot to the other.

"Mrs. Alexander, I'm sorry about…"

"Jill, I really don't want to hear anything you have to say. Just where in the hell do you get off treating my son like a piece of meat? If the shoe was on the other foot, you'd be hollering and screaming that he did you wrong."

"You have every right to be angry with me, but at least hear me out."

Margaret rolled her eyes. "Since I have prepared dinner, we might as well sit down and talk like civilized adults."

Darren placed his hand on Jill's back and led her to the dining room. Margaret had a bounty of southern foods on the table, baked chicken, steamed cabbage, macaroni and cheese, cornbread, fried green tomatoes and green beans. Darren's mouth watered at the sight.

"Ma, you outdid yourself today."

"I thought both of my sons were going to be eating with me," she said.

The trio sat down and fell into an uncomfortable silence. Darren held Jill's hand underneath the table.

"So, what kind of spell did you cast on my son to make him take you back?" Margaret asked.

"Ma, be nice," Darren said. "I love Jill."

"And?"

"Mrs. Alexander, I messed up because I didn't tell Darren that I was the CEO of DVA, but that other stuff in that magazine wasn't true," Jill said.

"Did you think he was after your money? Darren can and has been taking care of himself for a number of years." Anger peppered her tone. "My husband and

I raised our children not to take anything from anybody."

"I never thought Darren would try to take anything from me. I was afraid to tell him because I was holding on to baggage from my past. And that same past came back to haunt me with that article."

Margaret held up her hand. "I thought you said this article was a lie? If that's the case, how did your past play into that article?"

Jill sighed and Darren squeezed her hand tighter. "The publisher of the magazine was once my boyfriend. Well, he pretended to be. His goal was to come into my life and steal my company away from me. And that's why I had my guard up when it came to opening up to Darren. That was wrong on my part."

Margaret leaned in as Jill spoke. Darren knew what she was doing. His mother was trying to read Jill and see if she was actually telling the truth. He'd seen her do this plenty of times when he or Cleveland tried to explain something to her.

"So what did you do to that man so he'd print these kinds of stories about you?" Margaret asked.

"I fired him. Instead of allowing him to steal my company, I took over the one he worked for and fired everybody."

Darren knew his mother was impressed. That sounded like something she would have done had she been in that situation. One thing Jill and his mom had in common was their spunk. Though he was still going to marry Jill whether Margaret accepted her or not, he wanted the two most important women in his life to get along.

"I guess he would be miffed enough to write something like that," Margaret said. "Don't hurt my son again, Jill. I mean it."

"Ma, come on," Darren said, "we're past that. Jill and I have worked out our differences and we're back on track."

Margaret nodded as she filled their glasses with iced tea. "All right," she said.

"And," Darren continued, "We're getting married."

Margaret slammed the pitcher down on the table. "No. It's too soon. You know what happened the last time you rushed into a marriage. I hope you didn't come here expecting me to cosign you making another mistake with a woman."

Jill rose to her feet. "With all due respect, Mrs. Alexander, I've owned up to the mistake I made and Darren and I have worked through that. We're getting married and putting the past behind us."

Darren stood beside Jill. "Ma, we want you to share in our future. If I can forgive Jill, why can't you?"

"Why don't y'all just sit down and let's eat," Margaret said.

Darren nodded toward Jill. He sat down and she followed his lead.

"All right," Margaret said. "Darren, you're a grown man and I can't pretend that I know what goes on behind closed doors with the two of you. But, Jill, how are you going to be a good wife and a CEO?"

That was a question Darren also wanted to hear the answer to.

"Anything worth having is worth working for and Darren is worth having. I love him and I love my work, but I finally have my priorities straight. Since I own the company, I can balance my time between my family and work easily."

Margaret took a sip of her tea. "Then all I can say is welcome to the family."

∽✌∾

The next few weeks were a blur for Jill as she and Darren planned for their wedding. One day Shari went with her to a bridal shop.

"I can't believe you're getting married," Shari said, resting her hands on her swelling belly. "My editors at *Essence* want me to interview you about the scandal with David and your upcoming wedding."

"I'm done with the press. No offense, but Atlanta and the rest of the world have read enough about my life. Darren and I want this to be as low key as possible. I'll confess, though, that a part of me wants to send David an invitation just so he can see that his plan didn't work."

"You haven't heard the latest, huh?"

Jill shook her head.

"*Atlanta Scene* folded and David is currently being sued by someone else he did a hatchet job on. I think it was the guy who used to run Concurrent. Anyway, he said this man was gay and having an affair with some high-ranking city official."

"He's such an asshole," Jill muttered. "But you know what, no more talk about David and his rag. I just want to get the right dress, marry the man I love and ride off into the sunset."

"I'm so happy for you. You deserve this happiness and so much more. I'm glad you and Darren found each other."

Happiness was too weak a word to describe what Jill felt. Deliriously overjoyed was more like it.

Finally, she had it all, a great business and an even greater love.

EPILOGUE

The clock read eleven-thirty P.M., and Jill couldn't have been happier. Just thirty minutes until the New Year rolled in. She rubbed her forearm and looked behind her. Where was her husband?

Shari walked over to Jill with her cell phone stuck to her ear. "Yes, well, I just wanted to make sure MJ got to bed all right. Did he eat? All right, thank you for indulging me. I love you too, Mom," she said, then snapped her phone shut.

Jill smiled at her, admiring how her body had snapped back into shape after the birth of Malik Jr. "This is the first time you left him alone, huh?" she asked.

Shari nodded. "Does it show?"

Eleven-forty. Jill searched the crowd for Darren again and found him bounding toward her with Cleveland and Margaret in tow.

"Hello, beautiful," Darren said, then leaned in to kiss her. "These two got lost."

Cleveland shrugged his shoulders. "I thought you said the Marriott. My bad, Sis."

He hugged Jill tightly. Since the wedding, Cleveland had accepted Jill into the family. He admired how she loved his brother and even though he wouldn't admit it, he wanted a love like that. Darren and Jill were the real thing.

Margaret hugged her daughter-in-law. "I knew something was wrong when the desk clerk didn't know who you were and what party I was talking about."

Jill smiled at her mother-in-law. Though they still had their moments, they'd been getting along better. Margaret knew her son's heart was in good hands, although she wished those hands were at home more often. But Margaret knew that times had changed and the days of the happy homemaker were no more. That didn't keep her from longing for at least one grandchild.

"They should be coming around with the champagne soon," Jill said as she took Darren's hand.

"Excuse us," Darren said as he and Jill dashed behind the stage. He pulled his wife into his arms and kissed her until her knees buckled.

Jill placed her hand on his chest. "It's not midnight yet," she said, glancing at her watch. "We have ten minutes."

"So, I have to wait a year to kiss my wife?" He stroked her cheek. "What did the doctor say?"

Her eyes stretched to the size of silver dollars. "Congratulations, you're going to be a father."

Darren lifted her off her feet and spun her around. "God, I must be the happiest man in Atlanta right now."

The band began to play George Benson's "On Broadway" as the clock ticked closer to midnight. Darren put his hand on his wife's slender tummy, ready for the day when it would be filled with their son or daughter.

"You know," she said, "I've been waiting for a night like this for a long time."

"Really? Why is that?"

"It isn't every day that I hand the reins over."

"What?" Darren asked incredulously.

"I want to spend my pregnancy without worrying about the day-to-day operations of DVA."

"Are you sure this is what you want? I don't want you to feel like you have to do this for me."

She stroked his cheek lovingly. "Don't you know by now that I don't do anything that I don't want to do?"

"Yeah, baby, I know. But I support your right to work and this company has been your baby for years."

"One minute until midnight," the bandleader announced.

Jill grabbed Darren's hand and pulled him out of the shadows. Tonight, she was going to welcome the new year with her lips glued to her husband's.

"Ten," the crowd exclaimed. Jill turned to Darren and licked her lips.

"Nine." Darren wrapped his arms around her waist and pulled her closer to him.

"Eight." Jill slipped her hands underneath his suit jacket, looping her fingers through the belt loops on his pants.

"Seven, six, five, four, three, two, one! Happy New Year!"

Darren captured Jill's lips, kissing her as if they were the only two in the room. Lost in the kiss, Jill nearly forgot that she had to deliver her annual speech.

Finally, she had her New Year's kiss, a loving husband and soon a child of her own. She might be leaving the computer business, but she was more than happy to trade it for the business of love.

2010 Mass Market Titles

January

Show Me the Sun
Miriam Shumba
ISBN: 978-158571-405-6
$6.99

Promises of Forever
Celya Bowers
ISBN: 978-1-58571-380-6
$6.99

February

Love Out of Order
Nicole Green
ISBN: 978-1-58571-381-3
$6.99

Unclear and Present Danger
Michele Cameron
ISBN: 978-158571-408-7
$6.99

March

Stolen Jewels
Michele Sudler
ISBN: 978-158571-409-4
$6.99

Not Quite Right
Tammy Williams
ISBN: 978-158571-410-0
$6.99

April

Oak Bluffs
Joan Early
ISBN: 978-1-58571-379-0
$6.99

Crossing the Line
Bernice Layton
ISBN: 978-158571-412-4
$6.99

How to Kill Your Husband
Keith Walker
ISBN: 978-158571-421-6
$6.99

May

The Business of Love
Cheris F. Hodges
ISBN: 978-158571-373-8
$6.99

Wayward Dreams
Gail McFarland
ISBN: 978-158571-422-3
$6.99

June

The Doctor's Wife
Mildred Riley
ISBN: 978-158571-424-7
$6.99

Mixed Reality
Chamein Canton
ISBN: 978-158571-423-0
$6.99

North Branch Library
220 North St.
North Weymouth, MA.
02191
781-340-5036
www.weymouth.ma.
us/library

Title: Too hot for TV
Item ID: 39999070145998
Date due: 2/4/2020,23:59

Title: The business of love
Item ID: 39999060199237
Date due: 2/4/2020,23:59

2010 Mass Market Titles (continued)

July

Blue Interlude
Keisha Mennefee
ISBN: 978-158571-378-3
$6.99

Always You
Crystal Hubbard
ISBN: 978-158571-371-4
$6.99

Unbeweavable
Katrina Spencer
ISBN: 978-158571-426-1
$6.99

August

Small Sensations
Crystal V. Rhodes
ISBN: 978-158571-376-9
$6.99

Let's Get It On
Dyanne Davis
ISBN: 978-158571-416-2
$6.99

September

Unconditional
A.C. Arthur
ISBN: 978-158571-413-1
$6.99

Swan
Africa Fine
ISBN: 978-158571-377-6
$6.99

October

Friends in Need
Joan Early
ISBN:978-1-58571-428-5
$6.99

Against the Wind
Gwynne Forster
ISBN:978-158571-429-2
$6.99

That Which Has Horns
Miriam Shumba
ISBN:978-1-58571-430-8
$6.99

November

A Good Dude
Keith Walker
ISBN:978-1-58571-431-5
$6.99

Reye's Gold
Ruthie Robinson
ISBN:978-1-58571-432-2
$6.99

December

Still Waters...
Crystal V. Rhodes
ISBN:978-1-58571-433-9
$6.99

Burn
Crystal Hubbard
ISBN: 978-1-58571-406-3
$6.99

Other Genesis Press, Inc. Titles

2 Good	Celya Bowers	$6.99
A Dangerous Deception	J.M. Jeffries	$8.95
A Dangerous Love	J.M. Jeffries	$8.95
A Dangerous Obsession	J.M. Jeffries	$8.95
A Drummer's Beat to Mend	Kei Swanson	$9.95
A Happy Life	Charlotte Harris	$9.95
A Heart's Awakening	Veronica Parker	$9.95
A Lark on the Wing	Phyliss Hamilton	$9.95
A Love of Her Own	Cheris F. Hodges	$9.95
A Love to Cherish	Beverly Clark	$8.95
A Place Like Home	Alicia Wiggins	$6.99
A Risk of Rain	Dar Tomlinson	$8.95
A Taste of Temptation	Reneé Alexis	$9.95
A Twist of Fate	Beverly Clark	$8.95
A Voice Behind Thunder	Carrie Elizabeth Greene	$6.99
A Will to Love	Angie Daniels	$9.95
Acquisitions	Kimberley White	$8.95
Across	Carol Payne	$12.95
After the Vows	Leslie Esdaile	$10.95
(Summer Anthology)	T.T. Henderson	
	Jacqueline Thomas	
Again, My Love	Kayla Perrin	$10.95
Against the Wind	Gwynne Forster	$8.95
All I Ask	Barbara Keaton	$8.95
All I'll Ever Need	Mildred Riley	$6.99
Always You	Crystal Hubbard	$6.99
Ambrosia	T.T. Henderson	$8.95
An Unfinished Love Affair	Barbara Keaton	$8.95
And Then Came You	Dorothy Elizabeth Love	$8.95
Angel's Paradise	Janice Angelique	$9.95
Another Memory	Pamela Ridley	$6.99
Anything But Love	Celya Bowers	$6.99
At Last	Lisa G. Riley	$8.95
Best Foot Forward	Michele Sudler	$6.99
Best of Friends	Natalie Dunbar	$8.95
Best of Luck Elsewhere	Trisha Haddad	$6.99
Beyond the Rapture	Beverly Clark	$9.95
Blame It on Paradise	Crystal Hubbard	$6.99
Blaze	Barbara Keaton	$9.95
Blindsided	Tammy Williams	$6.99
Bliss, Inc.	Chamein Canton	$6.99
Blood Lust	J.M.Jeffries	$9.95

Other Genesis Press, Inc. Titles (continued)

Other Genesis Press, Inc. Titles (continued)

Other Genesis Press, Inc. Titles (continued)

Indigo After Dark Vol. IV	Cassandra Colt/	$14.95
Indigo After Dark Vol. V	Delilah Dawson	$14.95
Indiscretions	Donna Hill	$8.95
Intentional Mistakes	Michele Sudler	$9.95
Interlude	Donna Hill	$8.95
Intimate Intentions	Angie Daniels	$8.95
It's in the Rhythm	Sammie Ward	$6.99
It's Not Over Yet	J.J. Michael	$9.95
Jolie's Surrender	Edwina Martin-Arnold	$8.95
Kiss or Keep	Debra Phillips	$8.95
Lace	Giselle Carmichael	$9.95
Lady Preacher	K.T. Richey	$6.99
Last Train to Memphis	Elsa Cook	$12.95
Lasting Valor	Ken Olsen	$24.95
Let Us Prey	Hunter Lundy	$25.95
Lies Too Long	Pamela Ridley	$13.95
Life Is Never As It Seems	J.J. Michael	$12.95
Lighter Shade of Brown	Vicki Andrews	$8.95
Look Both Ways	Joan Early	$6.99
Looking for Lily	Africa Fine	$6.99
Love Always	Mildred E. Riley	$10.95
Love Doesn't Come Easy	Charlyne Dickerson	$8.95
Love Unveiled	Gloria Greene	$10.95
Love's Deception	Charlene Berry	$10.95
Love's Destiny	M. Loui Quezada	$8.95
Love's Secrets	Yolanda McVey	$6.99
Mae's Promise	Melody Walcott	$8.95
Magnolia Sunset	Giselle Carmichael	$8.95
Many Shades of Gray	Dyanne Davis	$6.99
Matters of Life and Death	Lesego Malepe, Ph.D.	$15.95
Meant to Be	Jeanne Sumerix	$8.95
Midnight Clear	Leslie Esdaile	$10.95
(Anthology)	Gwynne Forster	
	Carmen Green	
	Monica Jackson	
Midnight Magic	Gwynne Forster	$8.95
Midnight Peril	Vicki Andrews	$10.95
Misconceptions	Pamela Leigh Starr	$9.95
Moments of Clarity	Michele Cameron	$6.99
Montgomery's Children	Richard Perry	$14.95
Mr. Fix-It	Crystal Hubbard	$6.99
My Buffalo Soldier	Barbara B.K. Reeves	$8.95

Other Genesis Press, Inc. Titles (continued)

Naked Soul	Gwynne Forster	$8.95
Never Say Never	Michele Cameron	$6.99
Next to Last Chance	Louisa Dixon	$24.95
No Apologies	Seressia Glass	$8.95
No Commitment Required	Seressia Glass	$8.95
No Regrets	Mildred E. Riley	$8.95
Not His Type	Chamein Canton	$6.99
Nowhere to Run	Gay G. Gunn	$10.95
O Bed! O Breakfast!	Rob Kuehnle	$14.95
Object of His Desire	A.C. Arthur	$8.95
Office Policy	A.C. Arthur	$9.95
Once in a Blue Moon	Dorianne Cole	$9.95
One Day at a Time	Bella McFarland	$8.95
One of These Days	Michele Sudler	$9.95
Outside Chance	Louisa Dixon	$24.95
Passion	T.T. Henderson	$10.95
Passion's Blood	Cherif Fortin	$22.95
Passion's Furies	AlTonya Washington	$6.99
Passion's Journey	Wanda Y. Thomas	$8.95
Past Promises	Jahmel West	$8.95
Path of Fire	T.T. Henderson	$8.95
Path of Thorns	Annetta P. Lee	$9.95
Peace Be Still	Colette Haywood	$12.95
Picture Perfect	Reon Carter	$8.95
Playing for Keeps	Stephanie Salinas	$8.95
Pride & Joi	Gay G. Gunn	$8.95
Promises Made	Bernice Layton	$6.99
Promises to Keep	Alicia Wiggins	$8.95
Quiet Storm	Donna Hill	$10.95
Reckless Surrender	Rochelle Alers	$6.95
Red Polka Dot in a World Full of Plaid	Varian Johnson	$12.95
Red Sky	Renee Alexis	$6.99
Reluctant Captive	Joyce Jackson	$8.95
Rendezvous With Fate	Jeanne Sumerix	$8.95
Revelations	Cheris F. Hodges	$8.95
Rivers of the Soul	Leslie Esdaile	$8.95
Rocky Mountain Romance	Kathleen Suzanne	$8.95
Rooms of the Heart	Donna Hill	$8.95
Rough on Rats and Tough on Cats	Chris Parker	$12.95
Save Me	Africa Fine	$6.99

Other Genesis Press, Inc. Titles (continued)

Other Genesis Press, Inc. Titles (continued)

The Missing Link	Charlyne Dickerson	$8.95
The Mission	Pamela Leigh Starr	$6.99
The More Things Change	Chamein Canton	$6.99
The Perfect Frame	Beverly Clark	$9.95
The Price of Love	Sinclair LeBeau	$8.95
The Smoking Life	Ilene Barth	$29.95
The Words of the Pitcher	Kei Swanson	$8.95
Things Forbidden	Maryam Diaab	$6.99
This Life Isn't Perfect Holla	Sandra Foy	$6.99
Three Doors Down	Michele Sudler	$6.99
Three Wishes	Seressia Glass	$8.95
Ties That Bind	Kathleen Suzanne	$8.95
Tiger Woods	Libby Hughes	$5.95
Time Is of the Essence	Angie Daniels	$9.95
Timeless Devotion	Bella McFarland	$9.95
Tomorrow's Promise	Leslie Esdaile	$8.95
Truly Inseparable	Wanda Y. Thomas	$8.95
Two Sides to Every Story	Dyanne Davis	$9.95
Unbreak My Heart	Dar Tomlinson	$8.95
Uncommon Prayer	Kenneth Swanson	$9.95
Unconditional Love	Alicia Wiggins	$8.95
Unconditional	A.C. Arthur	$9.95
Undying Love	Renee Alexis	$6.99
Until Death Do Us Part	Susan Paul	$8.95
Vows of Passion	Bella McFarland	$9.95
Waiting for Mr. Darcy	Chamein Canton	$6.99
Waiting in the Shadows	Michele Sudler	$6.99
Wedding Gown	Dyanne Davis	$8.95
What's Under Benjamin's Bed	Sandra Schaffer	$8.95
When a Man Loves a Woman	LaConnie Taylor-Jones	$6.99
When Dreams Float	Dorothy Elizabeth Love	$8.95
When I'm With You	LaConnie Taylor-Jones	$6.99
When Lightning Strikes	Michele Cameron	$6.99
Where I Want to Be	Maryam Diaab	$6.99
Whispers in the Night	Dorothy Elizabeth Love	$8.95
Whispers in the Sand	LaFlorya Gauthier	$10.95
Who's That Lady?	Andrea Jackson	$9.95
Wild Ravens	AlTonya Washington	$9.95
Yesterday Is Gone	Beverly Clark	$10.95
Yesterday's Dreams, Tomorrow's Promises	Reon Laudat	$8.95
Your Precious Love	Sinclair LeBeau	$8.95